"Debut author Florian Matusek has his finger on the pulse of our times in delivering a fast-paced page-turner that leaves you wanting more! Enjoyable from start to finish, with its awesome twists and high use of suspense, the author also provides knowledgeable insight in energy crisis, climate change and glorious politics! Kudos to Florian all the way!"

Jean-Michel Désiré, author of *Fantasy Man & The Miracle Ladies*

NOWHERE TO HIDE

FLORIAN MATUSEK

First published globally in 2023 by Senpu Publishing
Copyright © Florian Matusek, 2023

Book cover designed by Samantha Vanderhyden.

ISBN
978-9916-4-1929-8

To Erik.

PROLOGUE

ONLINE
THREE MONTHS AGO

Winter had just begun, and it promised to be one of the coldest ever recorded. Even down in southern Italy, no one dared to sit outside anymore. The streets were empty while the citizens of Europe made themselves cozy in their warm homes. In online forums, however, there was more activity than ever before.

r/climateaction. Posted by u/FightForTheFuture
„Europe is on the brink of collapse. Summers are getting hotter, and winters are getting wetter. In the south, forest fires and droughts wreak havoc. Farmers do not have enough water to feed their animals. Food stock is drying out. Spain and Portugal are becoming deserts.

Northern Europe is becoming significantly rainier, with winter floods becoming more common. Animals and plants that used to thrive in the northern climate are dying out and are getting replaced by new species coming from the south.

The poorer the country, the more dramatic the situation. There has been a drastic increase in heat-related deaths in some regions and cold-related deaths in others. And the wetness of the north brings new disease vectors for water-borne illnesses.

And what do politicians do? Nothing. They are ignoring the problem because special interests and profit are more important to them than the citizens of Europe. The only way for a turnaround is decisive action. Europe must stop using fossil fuels and change to renewable energy immediately. It must reduce energy consumption dramatically. No fuzzy 30-year goals that will not be met. This must happen now. It is the only way we and our children can survive.

We, the people, need to fight back and show Brussels and all the fossil fuel industry they feed off that we will not tolerate this inaction any longer. Radical change cannot come without radical action. Sometimes you need to burn down the old before something new can rise from the ashes.

Join me in our fight for the future."

DestructionKitten

„I'm in."

TODAY

TALLINN
06:45 P.M.

Samanta's eyelids became heavy. It was 6:45 p.m., and even though she shouldn't drink any more coffee, she clung to her reusable cup while looking through the window. The Estonian capital of Tallinn was passing by as the bus made its way through the evening traffic. Now in February, jams were always an issue with icy roads, poor visibility, and thick snow falling from the sky. She watched the snowflakes dance in the air as they slowly covered the city in a white blanket. It would have been a beautiful sight if it weren't for the cars, which turned perfectly white snow into a gray, dull mass of mud.

Most living districts looked the same: Houses built in the 1950s or 1970s without any regard for aesthetics or architecture. Big blocks of concrete after bigger blocks of concrete. In some parts of town, small detached wooden houses, which escaped the construction ambitions of the Soviet Union, broke the pattern. Plus, the central part of town still retained its beautiful mediaeval look with old but renovated houses, cobblestone roads, and the occasional mediaeval restaurant where you could enjoy a bear steak. But this was not where the bus was headed and where she lived. From her flat, she saw mostly concrete walls when she looked out of her window.

Sam was on her way home from work and, like every day, had to take the bus. In fact, at the central station, she would have to switch bus lines to make her way across town. It took her a while, but sitting on the bus also allowed her to think and reflect on the day.

Right now, the latest tasks at work went through her head. Sam was working as a software developer in one of the up-and-coming Estonian start-ups. There were quite a few of those in the Silicon Valley of Europe, the birthplace of Skype. The company was developing software to let robots navigate on Mars by themselves, like a self-driving car but 140 million kilometers away. It made sense; remote-controlling a vehicle over such a distance was challenging, and the company's mission was to let robots navigate by themselves. It was challenging and exciting work, and Sam enjoyed developing software for the firm.

She could vividly remember when the recruiter contacted her just six months ago. He had reached out at the exact right time in her life. Sam was still living in Napoli and was frustrated with her life. She had just decided that she needed a change of scenery, and the new job came just in time.

The pivotal moment of her realization had stuck with her ever since. She had been sitting in a cafeteria at the beach, opposite her now ex-boyfriend, and listening to him nagging about her appearance again. She should care more about herself, cover her freckles better, dress up a bit. Otherwise, she would never advance in her career. What would her boss think if she dressed like a homeless person?

And his rant had continued about why she was hanging out with some strangers online, late into the night, playing video games. What was so interesting about them? She should muster some discipline and go jogging with him at dawn. Why didn't she change and make more of herself?

While looking at his angry face, Sam had thought: *Such a bore.* It had been such a beautiful day, and all he was thinking about was discipline. He couldn't enjoy life! *Why am I wasting my time with this idiot? I like my beautiful red hair and my freckles. And the way I dress.* Besides, she had more fun with her online friends than with this guy. *We have nothing to tell each other anymore. This is over. Maybe I should just change the environment. As a software engineer, I could get a job anywhere in the world.* And that was when the recruiter had reached out—perfect timing. So she packed her bags and moved to Estonia and did not regret it since.

Sam looked at her reflection in the bus window next to her. Her shoulder-long, red hair contrasted with her emerald-green eyes. Her freckles, which she used to cover up with make-up in the past, she wore proudly since moving to Tallinn. Together with the small wrinkles around her eyes, which she got from laughing a lot—they fit her sunny character. Yes, she was attractive. Still, she had always had bad luck with men. *Maybe I'm just too tall for them*, Sam thought.

After moving, she quickly experienced the difference in cultures between southern and northern Europe. She was used to an active social life, meeting many friends, and getting to know new people. To sit outside late in the evening and to talk a lot. But she found none of that in Tallinn. People seemed cold and distant, staying in their warm homes rather than going out. When they greeted each other, they didn't even shake hands, while Sam was used to kissing everyone she met on their cheeks.

But all was different once you were part of a group, and alcohol loosened the mood. Then they became social and started hugging each other. Often, this group of friends seemed to be even closer than she was with her friends back home. So, once you were part of a group, everything was fine, but becoming part of a group was difficult. It took time. This was why Sam was glad to have her group of online gaming friends.

She liked to play online role-playing games and stay up late at night, finishing the latest quest. She enjoyed solving puzzles and working together towards a common goal. Since her gaming friends were online, she could take them with her to her new home in Estonia. This was her social network at the moment, and she enjoyed their company while settling down in Tallinn.

Sam continued watching the snowflakes dance in the wind as the bus moved closer to her home. She dozed off from time to time so she could rest before another long night. This time not online but seeking adventure going out. Solving puzzles was fine, but from time to time, she needed an extra kick, an adventure. And tonight, that was exactly what she would get.

BRUSSELS
DAY 0
7:15 P.M.

She was late for another meeting. No matter what she did, Lina Juska never managed to be on time for these. They were rushing down a corridor of a high-rise building in Rue Demot in Brussels, the seat of the Energy Directorate of the European Commission. Located in a side street, the gray, concrete building didn't look like much, and most people wouldn't expect that some of the most important decisions for Europe's energy future were made there. On paper, the European Parliament voted on new legislation, however, in practice, the actual decisions were made in small meeting rooms in buildings like these.

It felt like Lina spent her time either sitting in such meeting rooms or rushing from one to the next. Her staff briefed her on the most important notes of the past hour as Lina tried to make a ponytail out of her long blonde hair, which didn't look as fresh as it did in the morning. *Short hair would be more practical,* she thought. *And it would make me look more serious in meetings.*

She had already replaced her entire wardrobe because her stylist told her she needed to look more business-like, more conservative. *I already switched to only wearing dark blue pant suits. Might as well cut the hair, too.* No matter what women's magazines suggested, it was impossible to look perfect after a twelve-hour workday. Yet somehow, it seemed to be the unspoken expectation of society that women always needed to look like they just woke up from a good night's sleep, fully styled and makeup-ed. If this would apply to her male politician colleagues, none of them would have gotten very far in life.

This time, she had to attend a coordination meeting with a working group on new policies regarding the safety of offshore wind parks. They were an important pillar of Europe's renewable energy strategy, and she wanted to push for more of them. Offshore wind parks were efficient and promising, but maintenance cost was a problem. They were built a few miles offshore, often in waters that were not easy to navigate, especially close to the posts, which meant that operators had to send helicopters every time something needed to be fixed, and that drove maintenance costs much higher than traditional wind parks on land.

This led some operators to cut costs by sending crews via boat, even though it was not safe, or using old helicopters to send them. Even though the European Commission wanted to support more offshore wind parks, it was understood that they could not compromise on safety. As Energy Commissioner, it was Lina's responsibility to take care of it. And this was how she ended up in this meeting she was so late to again. She could just as well make her way to the next one already.

Just as she was contemplating if she should skip it, her phone rang—unknown number. She handed it to her assistant John to take it. Lina didn't have time for unknown numbers. Her assistant picked it up and covered the microphone, whispering to her: „It's Farkas."

She got annoyed right away. „Him again? Tell him I'm late for a meeting and will call him back when I can."

But he didn't give in so easily. „He is asking if you had time to look at the latest amendment proposals," her assistant relayed what Farkas was saying. „Tell him 'not yet', and I really do not have time right now. And then hang up before he can steal any more of our time. Thanks."

Lina wasn't new to the Brussels circus. At 44, she was one of the younger commissioners in the European Commission but was already working in the European Parliament for a few years when she was asked to change to the executive branch of the European Union. There were a lot of aspects she loved about this job, such as actually making a difference in people's lives.

The EU was often criticized for being run by a bunch of bureaucrats who were getting fat on big salaries paid for by the citizens of Europe. While quite a chunk of bureaucratic overhead was there for sure, everywhere she looked, she found people with ideals and the will to make Europe a better place. She was the same and liked to think that the other commissioners were, too. Lina was happy to work late nights and to sit in long and boring coordination meetings if it meant that she had the chance to change something. It gave her a purpose in life.

Besides, working long hours made Lina think less about her recent divorce. A long-distance relationship with this kind of job just didn't work, with her in Brussels and her husband back in Lithuania. But the distance was not the only problem. Her husband was a defense lawyer, and his job was to win cases for his clients. He didn't care what *was* right; he only cared about *being* right. For him, the truth was not absolute—it could be massaged and changed as one wished. It was just important to win. But Lina was different. To her, things were either right or wrong; there was nothing in between. She needed to be sure to stand on the right side of history and would fight for what she believed in.

This was why they regularly got into a fight. Her husband could not relate to the things she believed in. He told her to think more strategically and align with important people and lobbying groups to get ahead in her career. But she didn't agree. In the end, they both had to concede that the divide between them had grown too large, and they filed for divorce. Thank god they didn't have kids. That would have complicated things.

Nevertheless, the divorce hurt. Every time she was sitting at her desk, she saw the fountain pen he had given her. She liked it very much and didn't want to give it away, but it brought back the hurtful emotions of the divorce. To help her forget, she poured all her energy into her new job. Finally, she could make a difference in this world, and the high-energy work didn't leave any time to think about her personal life, which would have depressed her. In a way, this job was all she had at the moment.

Pal Farkas, on the other hand, was an example of what she did not like about her job. He was a lobbyist, one of many. This was another misconception about work in the EU. It was often thought that European politicians were in the pockets of lobbyists and that Europe was being run by big corporations.

Sure, commissioners did get invited here and there to dinner or a vacation, thinly disguised as a conference. But these were easy to handle. You could just refuse. The main and much more powerful tool of lobbyists was to be just so damn annoying.

They were contacting you repeatedly until you broke and just gave in. It took a certain breed of human being for this: overly friendly while annoying as hell. Lina promised herself that she would concentrate on her wind parks for now and ignore that Farkas called her today, again.

DAY ONE

OBERBERG
02:35 A.M.

Ding, ding, there was another one. He quickly clicked it away. Karl Herzog, the security guard on duty in the security operation center, was staring at a large wall of video screens in front of him. The four screens were illuminating his tired face. No other light source except the screens was present in the room. And it was Karl's job to stare at these screens for hours on end.

They were showing video feeds of the numerous video surveillance cameras spread around the facility. Most of them were mounted around the perimeter and some within its walls in case someone was breaking in. From the outside, it looked like a perfect security system, like in a high-security prison out of a movie. The reality was that all these cameras led to a small room with a single person in it, the tired security guard, Karl Herzog. Besides the large screens, there were two smaller ones on his desk. But they were switched off since they were only used to investigate incidents and look at recordings from the past.

The security of the whole facility hinged on Karl Herzog being concentrated enough to look at every single alarm coming in. He was used to it, but that didn't mean it was an easy task. The system was a technical masterpiece, it could do much more than it was used for, but Karl was never trained to use it. And he did not care to learn. So he continued looking at all the alarms coming in.

And alarms were commonplace. A fox wandering about, leaves on trees dancing in the wind, and many more inconspicuous events could trigger them. Unsurprisingly, there were days with few and some with many of them. Karl Herzog passed the time between the alarms by looking at his phone, checking his emails, and reading sports news—a player of his favorite soccer team received another yellow card!—scrolling through his social media feeds, and giving out likes and smiles. Sometimes he wrote about his slow life on the night shift at 02:00 a.m., and once he even posted a picture of the video screens, all of them black. He immediately received the expected responses from his friends: „Wow, I wish I had such an easy job", „More relaxting than vacation in the Bahamas!". *They have no idea what they are talking about,* he thought.

There were constant updates and changes to the system. Recently, Karl was attending a training where he was told that after an extensive study by NASA, they had found that people cannot concentrate for longer than 20 minutes at a time. *Well, they don't need NASA for that. They should have just asked Karl Herzog,* he had thought, but he hadn't said anything.

The result of this insight was that they had switched the operations to so-called Black Screen Monitoring. The idea was that as long as nothing happened, there was no point looking at video screens, which just made you tired and miss events. So Karl was now staring at black screens instead of green meadows. Only if something of interest happened, the relevant video feed would show up on the screen, and Karl needed to verify if it was a true or a false alarm.

There was an incident once. The facility was a central distribution hub, which transported gas from Russia through Ukraine and Slovakia towards here, Oberberg in Eastern Austria, where it was distributed further to Italy, Germany, Hungary, Slovenia, and Austria itself. And a few years ago, an explosion next to a pipeline had triggered a small crisis. For security reasons, the pipes needed to be sealed and gas transport was halted. This caused a cascading effect and eventually a state of emergency in Italy as they ran out of gas.

This pipeline was the lifeline of the country—its main gas supply. If gas stopped flowing, Italy would be in serious trouble. This incident made everyone painfully aware of how important this facility was for the European energy infrastructure, and that a high-security standard was paramount. Consequently, the whole security system was overhauled and brought to the latest standards.

Karl Herzog could vividly remember the day when the new system was presented. The chief security officer had been guiding a group of EU experts through the facility, explaining proudly and in great detail how modern the system was, the latest state-of-the-art. How well it secured the facility and how reliably it operated. He had been pointing here and there, walking around the perimeter, and finally ending the tour in the small security operation center, where Karl had been sitting.

He had pointed at the video screens and highlighted the thermal cameras, which used artificial intelligence. „There is no need for manual surveillance anymore. These thermal cameras detect the difference in temperature between the environment and humans with an accuracy of 0.2 degrees centigrade, even in complete darkness. And the artificial intelligence automatically detects intruders on the video. No one goes undetected. We also have laser fences in the immediate vicinity and radar to check the wider perimeter. There is no way someone could break in undetected. This system is fool-proof!" the chief security officer had explained.

But what he had failed to mention was that no single sensor worked perfectly. He was aware of that but had no good solution for it. So they had just installed more sensors to compensate for the inaccuracies. But each of them had its quirks. For example, whenever there was heavy wind, the artificial intelligence system triggered false alarms because everything in the image, trees, bushes, and the cameras themselves, was moving, and the system thought these movements were people.

On the other hand, during a snowstorm, the laser fence triggered false alarms because the laser light was reflecting on the snowflakes, assuming that each snowflake close to the sensor was, again, a person. The system just did not know if it was a tiny snowflake close to the sensor or a large human far away. The result was just a lot of false alarms.

Karl Herzog, the person who should know because he used the system every day, could have told many stories about it. For example, he knew everything about the wildlife that came out of the woods at night. He had a pretty good idea of how many deer, rabbits, and foxes there were. One time, the systems detected frogs, even though they were very small and should not trigger any sensor. But to his surprise, they did.

Who would have thought that frogs would jump towards the fence as a group—or was it a flock?—and trigger alarms just like a larger animal. The group was just large enough to trigger the sensors. Karl also had the feeling that the system was getting worse since they installed it. He wouldn't have been surprised because they didn't take the maintenance package, and the systems were just left as they were installed, slowly deteriorating. Karl sighed. „But nobody is asking me. All they want to know, they get from marketing brochures from security manufacturers. They are probably not even looking at how many false alarms I must deal with every day."

Nobody was ever interested in helping Karl stay concentrated. So he devised his own strategies to stay awake and pass the time as best as he could. What helped was his smartphone, an automotive magazine, a thermos with coffee, and a box of cigarettes. He wasn't supposed to smoke in here, but who would really care when he sat here alone all night? Not even his colleagues who were patrolling outside ever came in. Besides, there was nothing else to do.

Karl was bored, as he was every night. He had checked all the emails—nothing interesting happened here or in the outside world. Yes, of course, there had just been several false alarms. No wonder, there was this snowstorm outside, and the laser fence did not stop triggering false alarms.

Sometimes Karl liked to imagine that he could compete with the sensors, click an alarm away before the next one came in. It was almost like a computer game. Could the sensors trigger so many false alarms that he could not click them away fast enough? If so, his black screens wouldn't remain black but would be filled with alarms all the time.

He had to think about this NASA stuff again. It's all nice and good to know that a security guard cannot see anything happening on video screens after 20 minutes. But has anyone looked at what happens after looking at false alarms for 20 minutes without a break?

What gave him comfort was thinking about the girl he had met a few weeks ago. He started talking to her at a poker game and was immediately enticed. His friends had said, „Karli has found his match," referring both to his quite decent poker skills and his not-so-decent personal life. Poker was really the only thing he enjoyed. He thought that he was not a great player but good enough to be better than his friends, which was what mattered.

Unfortunately, it was not the best place to get to know new people, not girls, anyway. If any girls came there, they were usually the girlfriends of one of his friends. But not this one. She came alone and was not a bad player at all. He liked her boyish look, not holding back, and looking for adventure. They fell for each other head over heels and met every day since. She hadn't moved in yet, but it almost felt like it. Karl dreamed of taking her out on a road trip with the red cabriolet he had found in his magazine.

How long would it take until he could afford it? Maybe he should look out for a better-paid job. Then they could settle down with a nicer house, a bigger garden, and a dog... He dreamed how beautiful life would be with this woman. And she seemed to care about him too; tonight, she even brewed him his coffee for the night shift and gave him the thermos he used to stay awake. And right now he desperately needed it as his eyelids were getting heavy. He couldn't remember going to bed so late, he was usually better at staying alert during the night shift, but now his mind drifted off, and his whole body was screaming to take a nap, just a quick one. Karl Herzog took another sip of coffee.

Another *ding, ding* brought him back from his daydream. He quickly clicked the pop-up of the false alarm away. The new system was now in operation for a year, but Karl was not sure it had achieved what it had promised. His job was just as boring as before they had all those fancy systems. The only thing that changed was that now he had even more systems he didn't quite understand.

Suddenly, the buzzer of the door to the security operation center rang. Karl was startled and immediately felt adrenaline rush into his veins. This never happened. He was supposed to be alone in here. There were just a few guards patrolling outside, but they never came into the operation center. Karl was not expecting any of his colleagues to check in.

He got up and went to the security lock, an entrance made up of two doors for security reasons. Essentially, one had to be let into the first door, then wait until it closed and the second one opened. This added an extra layer of security and prevented people from sneaking in behind another person when they went inside. He checked the security camera of the door to see who it was. He couldn't believe his eyes, immediately opened both locks and said, „You?"

He couldn't hear the response to his question as the world became a dark veil of nothingness, and Karl Herzog collapsed on the floor.

Brrr, brrr. Brrr, brrr. In his dreams, Karl Herzog thought, *Not another false alarm*, but then he woke up and realized it was his phone vibrating in his pocket. He was surprised to lie on the floor of the security operation center, not remembering what had happened. He felt dizzy, and it was hard to concentrate. He had a hard time focusing on anything, his left and right eye looking in different directions. He rubbed his face and tried to focus on finding the strength to talk. Karl pulled his phone out of his pocket to find that it was his supervisor calling.

„What the hell is happening down there?" A polite greeting was apparently not required.

„What do you mean?" was all Karl could respond, still dizzy.

„The control panels that regulate the compressor are completely destroyed. Someone must have entered the facility to mess with them. I don't have to tell you that this means we had to turn off the gas. There is nothing coming through the pipes anymore. This is a shit show. I have everyone from our CEO to the ministry of infrastructure and the chief of police on my back. All of them got woken up in the middle of the night. Now tell me how this could have happened. How could anyone have broken into this facility without you noticing?"

Karl briefly considered telling his supervisor about the NASA study but immediately discarded the idea as not helpful in the current situation. He told him all he knew, which was not much. The last thing he could remember was drinking his coffee in front of the black screens. The next thing he knew was being woken up on the floor by the buzzing of his phone. Karl sighed as he understood that this would be a long night. And not a boring one at that.

THE HAGUE
DAY 1
07:00 A.M.

Arnaud Navarro's alarm rang at 07:00 a.m. sharp. His eye sockets felt like someone had punched him in both eyes at the same time. Slowly, he turned a few times in bed to gather the strength to get up and open the window shades, which he achieved after pushing the snooze button on his alarm clock three times.

After he had sat up in his bed, he looked at the new fitness tracker on his wrist, which informed him how he slept. He got a sleep score of 51 out of 100, which his tracker considered „Very bad". He didn't need this fancy device to tell him that. His brother had given it to him last Christmas because he thought it would magically improve Arnaud's fitness. It hadn't. But it did inform him that his level of fitness was not great, that he slept badly, and that he needed to move more. He knew all that before. Another nonsense gadget.

He couldn't understand why nowadays people got more and more technology to do things for them while all these devices did was create the illusion that life got easier. It didn't. They only made us depend more on technology, and we lost the ability to trust our gut feeling. And right now, his gut told him he needed a coffee and a croissant.

Getting a decent breakfast was the hardest part about living in The Hague. As a true Parisian, Arnaud didn't ask for much for breakfast—a simple espresso and a croissant would do. Both wasn't easy to get a hold of here, though. Luckily, he had one of these new hip coffee places right around the corner where they served drinkable espresso, but he would have to get his croissant from somewhere else.

He slipped into his tracksuit that he once bought in a sudden touch of ambition to start jogging and went down to the coffee place. He was living in Casuariestraat, close to the main railway station and a big park. It was a small flat in a two-story, old building, very typical for the Netherlands. It didn't have an elevator, which probably was a good thing for his fitness.

The park around the corner would have been perfect for jogging, if he were the jogging type, and if it wouldn't just be so hard to gather the energy for it. He was also living right next to the old town, and, in general, it was a nice place to walk around in the small streets and parks all around.

Some tourists were already on the streets at this early hour, but he observed business types, who were stiffly walking in a brisk stride, working at one of the numerous international organizations in town, probably for the International Court of Justice or the International Criminal Court. Surprisingly, those were two completely different institutions, the former being a UN organization to settle disputes between nations and the latter being an independent court to try crimes against humanity.

Arnaud went around the corner to Bleijenburg street, closer to the old town, where he found the coffee house he was looking for. The hipster bartender with a long beard handed him his espresso with an overly friendly smile. He must have remembered Arnaud by now. With his medium-long black, wavy hair and unshaven look, Arnaud stuck out in the Netherlands.

Arnaud would compare his own looks to Antonio Banderas, but others would rather think of Javier Bardem instead: A 50-year-old born in Paris to Spanish parents. With his coffee in hand, he went to a mini-mart right next door and bought one of those shrink-wrapped croissants that had as much to do with the real thing as an Americano with a Ristretto. It was the best he could do right now.

With his two most prized possessions, he quickly made his way home again, because he already felt the cold creeping in under his tracksuit. It must have been well below zero degrees this February morning. He looked at his fitness tracker, but it wouldn't tell him how cold it was. That would have been a useful feature.

Everybody was talking about global warming, but now he couldn't feel any of it. It was the coldest day he could remember since moving here, so he was careful not to slip on the icy road as he tried not to spill the coffee. Finally in his warm home, he drank it and ate the croissant. He was still eating these terrible artificial shrink-wrapped things because they reminded him of home.

Arnaud's parents had moved to Paris from northern Spain before he was born, and if you asked them today, they would probably still say they are Spanish. But he couldn't feel more French. It was his home, and he was proud of it. So when he relocated to The Hague for his ex-wife, it was not an easy move for him, leaving everything behind: the exhilarating thrill of

Paris, the passionate and, yes, a little arrogant but lovely Parisians, and all his friends he grew up with.

Now he was living in a city with a quarter of the population of Paris, and while it was a nice town, „exhilarating" was not the word he would use to describe The Hague. If he had known that they would divorce a year after, he probably wouldn't have moved. But now it was not only him living here but his five-year-old daughter too, and he wouldn't want to miss seeing her for the world, even if it meant just on the weekends.

Besides, Arnaud had a job at Europol now. Europol was another one of those international organizations headquartered in The Hague. Founded in 1998, the lesser-known cousin of Interpol was of similar size with similar tasks. As the law enforcement agency of the European Union, it was tasked to investigate organized crime and terrorism by working together with EU member states. Europol didn't have any executive power but was somewhat the central point of contact for any serious cross-border crime in Europe.

When something happened, they were the ones getting the heat of the European Commission and the Council of Europe to get it sorted out. Arnaud had found a job as an inspector in one of the operations departments, the European Special Operations Centre, or ESOC. And he thought he was quite good at his job, at least when they didn't force one of their latest high-tech toys that blew their budget on him.

This reminded him to get ready for work. He was supposed to be in training for a new system they were introducing. While he would have nothing against accidentally being late and skipping it, he would probably get in trouble for doing so again. He finished his coffee, jumped into the shower, and got ready.

Arnaud was walking to work, as it was just around the corner. And he was planning to use the time to talk to his daughter. He powered up his phone to dial the number of his ex-wife but was immediately bombarded with missed calls and text messages by his boss Gusta. It wasn't very surprising to him. She panicked quite quickly, though the number of messages was more than usual. He ignored them and called his ex-wife, who picked up after some rings.

„Hey!"

„Hi."

„I was hoping to talk to Zoé quickly?"

„Oh, how nice of you to think of her! How about instead of calling, you pick her up from kindergarten once? Or spend the weekend with her? You are her father too, you know."

„Yes, yes. But you know that I have a busy work schedule. I want to see her, but there is just so little time."

„You know what? The problem is not time; the problem is priorities. If you wanted to see her so badly, you would just make time. You need to prioritize your family life, Arnaud."

„Yes, darling. May I speak to her now?"

„Sure, I'll hand her the phone."

„Allo?" came a soft voice from the other side of the line.

„Zoé, mon chérie! Are you getting ready for kindergarten?"

„Oui, Papa. Today, we will make carnival costumes! I want to be a dragon!"

„Wow, I cannot wait to see that! You will be a great dragon, darling," Arnaud said.

„Papa?"

„Yes?"

„When will I see you again?"

„Soon, very soon!"

„When?"

„Uhm..." Arnaud was about to talk about the importance of work again but realized how ridiculous it was to tell that to a five-year-old. Hearing the soft voice of his daughter on the other end made him rethink.

„Uhm... how about I pick you up from kindergarten today, and we go play in the park?"

„Oh yes, oh yes, thank you, Papa!"

„I love you. See you later today. Bisous."

„Bisous."

Arnaud quickly talked to his ex-wife to let her know that he listened to her and would pick up Zoé today. He was making his daughter a priority and would spend time with her today. He felt proud of himself, like the grown-up man that he was.

When Arnaud arrived at Europol headquarters in central The Hague, he went straight for the elevators but quickly realized that he didn't know where he was supposed to go. He looked at his phone to find out where the training took place.

„Catapulting law enforcement to the 21st century with automatic facial recognition. Meeting room: B1M44. 09:00—17:00.„

He released a long sigh as he read the meeting invite. Arnaud knew there was no way around this and headed towards the elevator to make his way to meeting room B1M44, just when Gusta intercepted him furiously.

„Damn it! Why can't I reach you again?"

„Uhm—"

„That was a rhetorical question! You should be reachable, for god's sake! All hell is breaking loose here since 05:00 a.m.! I need you to jump on an urgent case right away."

She seemed even more enraged than usual, the color of her face resembling a strawberry rather than a healthy peach. This had to be serious. Arnaud couldn't have been happier for the distraction but didn't want to seem too eager to get out of the meeting. „I'm supposed to be in training for the new facial recognition system—"

„Forget it. This is important! Walk with me," she insisted as she led him to the elevator and took him to the fourth floor, where her office was located.

Gusta Jansen was the head of the ESOC and the point of contact for other agencies and outside stakeholders. It was mainly a political job, but he was lucky to report directly to her, so he got important information first and, most importantly, the most interesting assignments. On the flip side, he had to deal with her temper tantrums. They exited the elevator and walked down rows of workplaces where investigators were looking at their screens.

„So what is this about?" Arnaud asked.

„How nice of you to ask. A gas distribution facility in Austria had a major incident. And this is not just any facility. It's a central hub to distribute natural gas coming from Russia to a third of the European continent. I cannot overstate the importance of this. For the past five hours, no gas has been flowing, and I assume you can imagine what this means during the coldest February we have seen in years."

„People freezing, riots, energy shortages, production standstill, economic disaster. All in all, pretty bad press," Arnaud said.

„Exactly. I just got off the phone with Italy's minister of the interior. They are considering announcing a state of emergency if it continues during the day. I will have similar conversations with representatives from the other affected countries. Plus, I have the Energy Commissioner texting me every 15 minutes to find out what happened." Gusta was talking fast while walking faster, and a big vein on her forehead Arnaud had never seen before was becoming visible. He could almost smell the adrenaline that was powering this woman right now.

„All signs point towards an act of terrorism, even though we do not have any details yet. I want you on the next flight to Austria and meet with our local colleagues, get a closer look."

„The next flight? Are we sure this cannot be done over the phone?"

„I assume I do not need to explain that this incident is very time sensitive and even more political. Everybody is looking at us now. Solving it quickly is our number one priority at the moment. And if you want to keep your job, you better solve it."

Arnaud sighed. „Yes, madam."

„Get moving right away and turn your frickin phone on!" she yelled as he was already out the door making his way to the airport. No time to pack.

On the way to the airport, the impact of what had just happened sunk in. He wouldn't be able to pick up his daughter. He hadn't made her a priority as he had promised. *Shit.* But there was no choice; stopping a terrorist was important. Zoé would understand. *No, she won't. Shit.* He texted his ex-wife about the change of plans and promised to make it up to both of them. This was bad. If they weren't divorced already, it would happen now. He felt bad but quickly focused on his new case as he arrived at the airport to take the next plane to Austria.

BRUSSELS
DAY 1
09:11 A.M.

Lina Juska was sitting at her desk, staring at her laptop screen. Her office was sparsely decorated and located on the seventh floor of the Energy Directorate. It wasn't a small office, but one might expect a more luxurious workplace for a commissioner.

Photos she put up when she moved in hung on the walls, as well as a whiteboard with notes scribbled on it. One small houseplant and a cupboard were in the corner. Her desk was a mess. Sheets of paper lying here and there, printouts, and numerous notes with her handwriting on them. One large cup of coffee. And a photo frame, which showed her as a child with her father.

Lina lifted the frame to take a closer look at him. He was a good man. He grew up in a poor family, with his father barely feeding the family as a shoemaker, but, by working hard, he managed to provide his two children with the opportunities he never had. Lina owed him all that she was today.

From him, she learned the value of knowledge and integrity. There was almost nothing as valuable in life as knowledge, but it was equally important how you used it. Do not lie, do not cheat, and be honest. This is what he taught her, and this is what she tried to live by. In stressful situations like this, she liked to be reminded of him and of what he stood for. May he rest in peace.

When Lina came in the morning, she already had a hunch that this would not be her day. Yesterday's coordination meeting on offshore wind parks went on long into the night, so she got to bed late, only to be woken up by the news of an attack on a gas distribution facility. As Energy Commissioner, this fell right into her area of responsibility. Her main job was to ensure that energy supplies were not disrupted, which they just were.

Lina had been up since 05:00 a.m. and was rushing around, assuring everyone that everything was done to solve the issue while regularly calling Europol and the Austrian gas distribution operator for an update, neither of which brought any new information. Her phone was constantly ringing, but she didn't have any answers, only many questions, just like everybody else.

There was nothing she could do to speed up the repairs or the investigation, so she was focused on making sure all emergency protocols were being followed, and backup plans to ensure Europe's gas supply would kick in. For now, it looked like a wider-ranging crisis could be averted. If the broken parts in the facility could be fixed within the day, shortages should stay minimal. It would be an unfortunate incident, but the impact would largely concern criminal investigators. If the facility could not be fixed within the day though...

Her train of thought was disrupted when someone knocked at her door. It was her assistant, John, who brought coffee and breakfast. Lina was thankful for the distraction and had to admit that she could use something to eat. Dinner had been cancelled the day before, and the stress had made her forget to get something into her stomach.

Slowly, she began sipping her hot coffee and tried to calm down, to fade out all the noise and panic around her. She switched her phone to silent and leaned back to stare at the white ceiling. Lina began to ponder the wider political implications of this disruption. As much as she was fighting to push renewable energy, the fact was that Europe was still relying heavily on natural gas, regardless of whether Lina liked it or not. It was needed to cover spikes in energy needs, such as now, during cold times. Even though wind power and photovoltaics were built at an unprecedented rate, these technologies were heavily dependent on environmental factors that were out of human control.

If you took the so-called energy profile of a typical user, how much they used during different times of the day on different days during the year and overlaid them with the energy profile of wind production and photovoltaic, they did not match at all. In winter and at night, when you needed the most energy, the sun was down and didn't produce any, and the wind was following a random pattern that was as unpredictable as the weather itself.

So, renewable energy could not be produced at the same time users needed it. This meant that energy needed to be stored to fill consumers' needs, and to meet ambitious CO_2 emission goals, coal-based power plants had been reduced dramatically. That left a gap that was mainly filled with natural gas, along with nuclear power.

One of the topics on her desk right now, represented by a thick ring binder, was a new gas pipeline project planned to increase gas supply to Europe. The Trans Carpathian Pipeline Consortium wanted to build a pipeline from the Black Sea through Romania into Poland, delivering 55 billion m3 of natural gas annually from Turkmenistan to central Europe.

This would significantly increase the amount of natural gas flowing into Europe and had geo-political importance as it would make Europe less dependent on Russia and the United States, who wanted to deliver more liquefied natural gas to Europe. The Consortium wanted the Commission to support the project financially and politically to secure Europe's energy needs. Energy was a highly politicized topic since it represented a large portion of the budget of the member states, billions and billions of Euros every year. Of course, a lot of interests collided in this space, and Lina's job was to manage them.

She was a member of the European Green Party, and reducing CO_2 emissions was the reason she had been elected as the Energy Commissioner. She was determined to live up to this calling, and while she knew how much they still needed natural gas, she would make sure they would rely on it as little as possible.

So, Lina had always been against this new pipeline. It was the same as with cars: you do not solve traffic jams by building bigger roads. It just motivates people to drive more. And just as with traffic, the solution to gas shortage was not more pipelines but more alternatives.

So far, Lina had blocked any attempts to bring a proposal to build this new pipeline to the agenda. Which was why Pal Farkas had been bugging her so much; he was their lobbyist. The attack on the gas distribution facility was bad news indeed, both for the current situation of the citizens of Europe and her political ambitions. She would need to handle the situation carefully and fast and hope for the best—that gas would flow again very soon.

TALLINN
DAY 1
09:15 A.M.

The ice crushed beneath her shoes as Samanta Di Vincenzo made her way to the bus station to get to work. It was minus 21 degrees Celsius, and it was the first time she had experienced such temperatures. Ever. She knew how cold temperatures felt from her family's skiing trips back in Italy. But there was normal cold, and then there was northern cold, which was a different story altogether.

The light was just changing from dark blue to shimmering purple as the first rays of light pushed out the night, creating this magical moment between night and day when time seemed to stand still. Dark high-rise apartment buildings rose against a purple backdrop. It looked like being in a fairy tale. Sam loved it. This easily made up for the cold.

It wasn't very early at the moment, but darkness was the default state in winter in the North. When Sam had moved to Tallinn, it had been the exact opposite. In fact, during summer, it was almost constantly light. She remembered when midsummer was being celebrated in June. It had been hard to go to sleep; there was always some light left, even at midnight. It was her first winter there, and the darkness caught her by surprise. Of course, she knew how the northern hemisphere was tilted towards the sun in summer and away from the sun in winter, which resulted in extreme differences between the seasons in the north versus the south. But experiencing it in real life was completely different. Now, in winter, you were lucky to get some rays of light between 09:00 a.m. and 03:00 p.m. *Better take some drops of vitamin D*, she thought.

Sam's phone rang—Nonna. Her grandmother called from time to time without warning, whenever she had something to say. When Sam had moved away, she bought her one of these old-people mobile phones with the big buttons and big screen so they could stay in touch. Ever since, her Nonna used every chance to call her. It was unpredictable when this would occur, but Sam was happy talking to her family to get some social interaction and feel the pulse of events back home.

„Nonna, good to hear you!" she started.

„Nipotina, it is so good to hear your voice! How is life?" her grandmother asked. Her voice sounded weak and worried, as always. Phone calls with her tended to take an hour or longer. She wanted to know all the details of Sam's life, but Sam would try to keep it short this time. She had to get to work, after all.

„All good, all good. Before you ask: Yes, I am eating properly, don't worry. I just had a big breakfast." That was a bit of a white lie since she actually started skipping breakfasts to lose some weight, which she had gained in her late-night gaming sessions. But she didn't want her grandmother to worry.

„That is good to hear. I needed to hear a calm voice. You would not believe what is happening here. All the gas was cut off!" she said.

„What do you mean, cut off? Did Babbo forget to pay the bills again?" It was not unusual for Sam's father to not pay the bills. Not because of any financial reasons, he was just very unorganized and constantly forgot things he didn't like to do.

„No, no, there is no gas anywhere. Not in our house, not at the neighbors', nowhere. In the news, they said that almost all of Italy is without gas! I woke up freezing cold and found our heater was not working, the stove wasn't working, nothing was working! We cannot take warm showers. This is the beginning of the end! I told your brother he shouldn't go to the horse track. Greed is a deadly sin, and now God is punishing us for it."

Nonna always complained about Sam's older brother. Sam was the good girl, and he was the bad boy in the mind of their grandmother. Granted, he wasn't very successful in life in the traditional sense, still living at home at age 35, with no job but a constant need for money, which he spent instead of saving it up. He used to get a lot of slack for his behavior, but at one point it was just too much, even for their understanding Nonna.

But he had a good heart and always looked out for his younger sister. Sam considered him a close friend and tried to defend him whenever her grandmother complained. Besides, she felt like she needed to calm her grandmother down. „Don't worry. I'm sure gas will be back very soon. And I don't think God would go through so much trouble just to punish my brother. God has better things to do, you know."

„Don't tell me what God wants, Nipotina! He moves in mysterious ways."

„Sorry, Nonna. How are you keeping warm now?" Sam grew worried about the lack of heating. Even though they were living in southern Italy, winters could still get chilly, which did not agree with the frail elderly.

„Your father is making a fire in the old fireplace. He will try to make some warm water too. God help us, the apocalypse is near." She always had a sense of drama.

„Nonna, I'm sure everything will be back to normal soon. We will talk in the afternoon, and everything will be fine. I have to run to work now."

„From your lips to God's ears. A dopo, Nipotina."

„Baci e abbracci, Nonna. And kisses to everyone else too!"

Sam hung up and got on the bus. As much as Sam loved talking to her grandmother, she wasn't in the mood right now and hated being on the phone while riding the bus. She had a feeling that others were listening in, even though they likely didn't speak Italian. Plus, she didn't want it to be so obvious she was a foreigner.

In her experience, people tended to find Italians exotic and interesting, but the feeling of being a stranger was not pleasant. Sam felt like unwittingly intruding into other people's lives as they lived in their own country. She knew that this was not the case and that living abroad was very common now, but she couldn't shake the feeling of being a foreign body in the organism called Estonia.

Her grandmother always worried. Today it was gas being cut off. Last week it was that the garbage truck didn't come again. Gas would be back soon, for sure. It was winter after all, and the gas company will get it back as soon as possible. Sam would call her in the afternoon, and everything would be fine again.

VIENNA
DAY 1
12:15 P.M.

Arnaud landed at Vienna international airport shortly after noon. He had taken the earliest flight from Schiphol he could get. His flight had been smooth and getting out of the plane and through the airport had been fast, without any passport control within the Schengen area. Once in the main arrival hall, he went to one of the many rental car companies to get a car to drive up to Oberberg.

The facility was located on the capital's east side, well outside any other town. Arnaud figured that using a rental would be more flexible than waiting for a taxi in the periphery. The airport was a bit outside the city, and he needed to drive in the other direction, which meant he would be avoiding heavy traffic close to the city. It would be a smooth drive.

On the way to Amsterdam, he had called the local criminal police investigating the case. The responsible inspector, Manfred Huber, was already on site for several hours; they would meet there. But Arnaud had gotten the first details on the phone. It sounded like they secured quite a bit of video footage, and the case seemed clear-cut. But Arnaud would take a look by himself. In his experience, the most obvious cases were anything but.

After a 45-minute drive, Arnaud arrived at the gas distribution facility. It was located between fields and a forest, which would be the border to Slovakia if you went through it. Now, everything looked dreary in winter, but in summer, it also wouldn't exactly be a vacation hotspot. No mountains, no variety, just fields and fields, which were snow-covered and lay bare in winter. Not the typical landscape you would expect when thinking of Austria.

The facility itself was like any other industrial site. A large concrete wall surrounded the whole compound, only interrupted by the few entrances where employees and vehicles could go in and out. Arnaud also noticed the cameras around the facility, mounted throughout the concrete wall, about every 50 meters. They were pointed alongside the wall and seemed to cover the perimeter of the location quite seamlessly, recording any person wanting to break in. A good basis for an investigation. He parked his car right outside in the facility's parking lot and got out.

Manfred Huber greeted him at one of the entrances. „Nice to meet you. As I mentioned on the phone, I am the inspector assigned to the case." They shook hands and exchanged pleasantries.

„So, I understand you have been on site for some time? What is the situation?" Arnaud asked.

„It's best if I just show you once we are in. We will need to pass through security, and there is a safety briefing waiting for you," Huber said. Arnaud wasn't thrilled about getting a safety briefing, but a quick rundown on how to keep yourself safe in a gas facility was probably a good idea. They first passed through the security lock, where their belongings and IDs were checked, essentially the same drill as at an airport.

In addition, all visits were logged to keep track of who went in and out of the facility. This was usual. But to Arnaud's surprise, the safety briefing was anything but brief, considering a 20-minute video he had to watch. „Is this really necessary? I'm here on official Europol business," Arnaud said.

„Safety first. Everyone has to get trained on how to act in case of an emergency." The security officer at the entrance was not the flexible type.

The pace of the video was painfully slow, and it looked like it was filmed in the 1990s. It reminded visitors to wear their personal protection equipment at all times and stick to the assigned routes. And smoking was strictly forbidden. *Okay, that makes sense in a gas facility*, Arnaud thought.

Once he was done watching the video, they were handed yellow safety helmets and vests, just as Arnaud had just learned. He was spared the safety boots, which otherwise would be mandatory as well.

Manfred Huber and Arnaud were greeted by the site manager on duty, who guided them to the place where the attack happened. On the way, he gave a summary of the facility's operations.

„The way gas distribution works is quite simple on a high level. On one end, natural gas comes in from Russia, and on the other, it is distributed to five different pipelines, going to Italy, Slovenia, Hungary, Slovakia, Germany and, of course, Austria itself, as it is the main gas supply for the country. Now, natural gas does not flow by itself. In order to make it move through the pipes, it needs to be regulated by a compressor station, such as we have here in Oberberg. By increasing the pressure of the gas, the energy is provided to move it along."

„How many of these compressor stations do you need?" Arnaud asked.

„This has to be done every 60 to 160 kilometers as the pressure decreases with time. You can think of compressors as pumps that pump gas through the pipeline. Here in Oberberg, we use an electric centrifugal compressor driven by a high-voltage electric motor. We compress gas before it goes into the different pipes for distribution, so the compressor is a critical point in our infrastructure. If this fails, gas stops flowing in all the pipes. And this is what was attacked. Come, I'll show you."

Arnaud and Manfred Huber were led between small huts and large pipes to a central point that Arnaud suspected would house the motor to pump gas. Even from far away, it was obvious something was going on as a dozen workers were busy working around a small building.

The site manager was nodding to them as they walked by, and Manfred Huber and Arnaud mumbled an informal greeting. Inside the building, more people worked on a metal box on the ground, close to the pipes that went through the building. Only the box didn't look like it should. It had irregular holes and almost looked like an animal bit a piece off. The metal housing was not silver anymore but black. The workers were just lifting the housing, revealing more destruction underneath.

„The control unit for the motor is completely broken. By the looks of it, I would say someone poured some kind of acid over it that completely destroyed its inner workings. Moreover, they destroyed all wiring and the connections to the motor, making it hard to replace. My people have been working on it since it was discovered in the early morning, but it will take several hours to get all the broken parts out and clean it. Then we need to replace them," the site manager said.

„When do you think gas could be flowing again?" Arnaud knew this would be the first question Gusta would ask him.

„Hard to say. If we are lucky, at midnight tonight, but it could take until tomorrow. All men were asked to stay and work on repairs 24/7. We organized a catering company to feed them while they are working on it. This is 100% our priority right now, and everybody is doing their best. But the problem is not the work we put in. These are parts we do not have a replacement for here. Even if we can clean everything up fast, we need to wait until the replacement part arrives from the manufacturer."

This did not sound like a small incident to Arnaud. He was sure this would get political. That was why it was even more important to get some answers fast.

„What do we know so far? How could someone enter the facility and do this without being stopped?" Arnaud wanted to get on with the case as fast as possible.

„What we know so far is that the intruder climbed over the walls there." Manfred Huber pointed to a section of the wall not far from them. The concrete wall was easily three meters high and not easy to climb from the outside. „The intruder had prepared a foldable ladder before and used it to climb the walls. Easy to transport, easy to hide. This triggered several silent alarms by the perimeter protection systems, and the incident was recorded on video, so we have a pretty good idea of how they got in.

"The intruder then proceeded to the security operation center, where we will go next, and knocked out the security guard, presumably to be sure no alarm would be raised early. Finally, the compressor over here was destroyed, and the intruder escaped over the wall. The whole incident was only detected when the gas stopped flowing, which the next compressor station noticed. The intruder was gone by then." Huber seemed to already have a pretty good idea of what had happened. But Arnaud would need to see the evidence himself.

The site manager was taking them to the security operation center next. It was in a small house closer to the entrance, with a few rooms: a small kitchen, a wardrobe, a meeting room, and the control room itself. All were equipped with video surveillance cameras. Even inside, there was no way to get in without being recorded. Access to the control room was only possible with a key card, and one had to pass through a security lock, so sneaking in behind someone else was out of the question. Either you had a key card to get in, or someone opened the security lock for you.

The site manager led them through the lock. It was a typical control room: some screens on the wall, some on the desk. On the wall hung a large map of the facility, with the location and number of the cameras marked. Arnaud looked at the map. It gave him a pretty good idea of how the break-in had happened and how the intruder must have moved throughout the facility.

Arnaud noticed the building with the security operation center, where they were now, was far away from the compressor station, which was sabotaged. It must have been important to go to the security operation center before sabotaging the compressor station and knocking out the security guard. The intruder climbed over a section of the wall to enter right next to the security operation center as well, not the compressor station. It was not a spontaneous decision to go there—this had been carefully planned.

Next to the map on the wall, there was an old calendar of Playboy. The desk was filled with papers, a keyboard and mouse, and an ashtray. *So much for not smoking on the premises*, Arnaud thought.

„Let me show you the recording. We have almost the whole incident on video," Huber offered and opened an application on the PC. The video took some time to load, and once it did, Manfred Huber explained what they were seeing. „Here you see where the intruder climbs over the wall." He pointed to a surveillance video playing on the screen where a person went to the wall with a foldable ladder, unfolded it, and started to climb. The video had a high resolution, but everything was in black and white, and the person was about 40 meters away from the camera. On top of that, it was snowing that night, which made it especially difficult to make out anything.

„Don't we have a recording in color?" Arnaud asked.

„Unfortunately, no. The break-in happened at 2:35 a.m., and with no visible light sources, the cameras switch to infrared mode with built-in IR spots. Since infrared light is not in the visible light spectrum, we do not get color images at night," the site manager explained. Arnaud was surprised about his level of technical know-how but didn't really care about the details. Even without color, you could make out a slender body shape dressed in dark clothes with a dark backpack.

„Next, we see the person running to the control room where we are now. Look closely."

The video showed how the intruder moved towards the building with careful, deliberate moves and entered the first door. Inside, another camera caught them. Unfortunately, the face couldn't be made out since a mask covered it. Then, the intruder went to the security lock, where a close-up camera caught everyone entering the room in high resolution. Suddenly, they lifted the mask, and, in high resolution and color, the face of a young woman, maybe in her early 30s, was clearly visible. Shoulder-long red hair, light skin, around 165cm. She rang the bell of the control room. The door was opened, and she went in. That's where the video stopped.

„Do we have a recording from inside the control room?" Arnaud asked.

„No, we do not have any cameras in here. This is considered to be a secure area where cameras are not required," the site manager explained.

„However, we do have a recording of when she went out again." Huber showed a video that saw her leave the building, again masked, and run over to the location of the compressor. Apparently, there was no camera recording of the actual sabotage, but it was clear from afar that she had taken something from her backpack. She then ran towards the wall and used an enclosure, presumably housing electrical equipment, to jump over the wall. It was not uncommon that inside such walls were plenty of opportunities to climb over. It was hard to get into those facilities, but easy to get out. The camera outside caught her again and showed how she folded the ladder and ran towards the woods.

That was all there was of the recording. Arnaud stared at the freeze frame of the woman climbing over the wall. That's when he noticed the timestamp: 4:40 a.m.

„Is this time correct? She leaves two hours after she has entered the facility?"

„We noticed that too. It looks like she spent almost two hours inside the control room. We are not sure why. Our working theory is that she got cold feet and took some time to muster the courage to finish it," Huber said.

„Seems like too simple of an explanation for such unusual behavior," Arnaud found. „Do you have an explanation for why the security guard opened the door?"

„Not yet. He woke up on the floor and doesn't remember a thing. Looking at the footage, he said that he doesn't know the woman. We think that she might have used some sort of spray to incapacitate him. We took samples from his skin and blood for testing."

„Where is he? I would like to speak to him," Arnaud demanded.

„We sent him home. There was nothing he could contribute here," Huber had to admit.

Amateurs, Arnaud thought. There was a lot more he wanted to know, so he tried once more: „Did you take samples of the coffee?"

„Which coffee?"

„Don't you see the coffee stains on the table? I assume this room is being cleaned regularly, so these stains are new. Ask the security guard if he drank coffee and what he did with it. We need to test it for any residues that could explain his blackout." *Amateurs indeed.*

53

„Send the video recordings to my office. Here is my card. I assume this could be done by tonight?" Arnaud wanted a copy right away.

„The only way we can get video recordings out of the system is by burning it on a DVD, which takes a while. But we can airship the DVD for you."

„Never mind. After you burn it, send someone to the airport for me to pick up. I will take it when I leave." For once, Arnaud thought that new technology might have helped here. He was hoping they could send it over the Internet to his colleagues, but he would take whatever he could get.

„Can you at least send a picture of the face of the woman to my colleague to start a search warrant?"

„I already provided one for our local search. I'll send it to you as well," Huber said.

Before leaving the facility, Arnaud would call his colleagues in The Hague and instruct them to issue a Europe-wide search warrant for the woman in the picture. He didn't intend to lose any more time and wanted to make sure the search was started while he was still traveling.

„Also, I need the private address of the security guard. I will drop by before I leave for The Hague." He got the address, thanked them, and left. He needed to talk to the security guard as soon as possible. He was the key to what happened here.

TALLINN
DAY 1
03:41 P.M.

Sam got up from her workstation in the open space and went to the kitchen for coffee. The office looked like all the offices of well-funded startups: high ceilings, large windows, large rooms with rows of computer screens, and many perks. They had a corner with a billiard table, a game console, and free beer. Next to it was a freezer with a never-ending supply of ice cream. In the middle of the room was a sauna that employees could use any time they wanted. Whoever was using the sauna could watch their colleagues sit at their desks through a small window while relaxing inside.

The first and second floors of the office were connected via a slide, giving the impression of being on a playground rather than a place of work. Nobody used it, it was too much of a hassle in the every day, but people were proud to say that they worked at a place with a slide. All of this was designed to make the experience in the office as pleasant as possible and keep employees in the office as long as possible. In the end, all these perks were there to attract the best talent and keep it. And Sam was part of this exclusive group of people.

Most of the office was designed as an open space, with large numbers of software developers sitting next to each other. The prime maxim of the company's CEO was radical transparency, and the open-office design reflected that. And Sam had to admit that it was followed most of the time. Except for one part of the floor, which was closed off, and no one really knew what was behind it. Only very few employees had access rights to this section. Sam was just passing the door to it and thought, *I wonder what they are doing in there. I guess transparency only goes so far.*

The kitchen was located right next to it, and Sam got herself a short espresso and sat down on the couch next to the billiard table to call her Nonna, as she had promised earlier. Her grandmother picked up right away.

„Nipotina, I'm so happy to hear your voice! What a tragic day." She sounded agitated.

„Nonna, what happened? Did you get your heating back?"

„Nothing, nothing works. Niente. No gas. Everyone was sitting in front of the fireplace all day. Your father made a bit of warm water there. But we are running out of firewood, and there is none available in any shop. We will have to find more wood to burn so we don't freeze to death," her grandmother said.

„Don't worry, you won't be freezing to death, Nonna."

„How do you know? This is the apocalypse!"

„What happened to our electric heater? Didn't we have an old one lying around?"

„As soon as your father plugged it in, all lights went out, short circuit. But on the news they said that we might have to conserve power, anyway. If this continues, they might cut it off during certain times of the day. Even if the heater would work, we couldn't use it. Oh, mio dio!"

Sam grew worried, more so than she was before. A whole day without gas was no joke. She was used to the government being chaotic but providing basic means of life had never been an issue. After all, heating, the ability to cook, and warm water were basic necessities everyone needed.

„What about emergency services, the police, the fire brigade? Isn't there anyone helping you?"

„No one is. It is the same all over the country. They are just not prepared for such an emergency. They created shelters for people with no place to live, but that's it. Everyone else is left on their own. Neighbors help each other. Our upstairs neighbor brought us some firewood, and we handed out food. But I'm telling you, Nipotina, God is punishing us. I pray for Him to show us mercy."

No wonder the authorities are not prepared, Sam thought. Napoli was a warm place. Even in February, it didn't get much colder than 15 degrees in normal years. But this wasn't a normal year; it was much colder than usual. And in combination with the gas crisis, this was the perfect storm that would guarantee absolute chaos. It would be up to the citizens to make sure they were warm. Sam was glad that her grandmother had the rest of the family there to take care of her as much as they could. All Sam could do now was comfort her Nonna and help her calm down. And pray that this crisis would be resolved soon.

„Nonna, I send all my prayers to you and the family. Don't worry, it will get better. You will get everything back soon, I'm sure."

„Grazie, Nipotina. Pray for us, and may He listen to you."

„Many kisses to Babbo and Mamma, and to my brother, too."

„Of course, Samanta. A dopo."

„Please call me as soon as there is any news. And I promise to call you tomorrow morning! Baci e abbracci, Nonna."

Sam was wondering how she could help her family. Sending money wouldn't help bring back gas. Should she return home to support them? She wouldn't be able to change the situation, but emotional support would help. On the other hand, everything would likely be resolved soon, before she could even get on a plane. Sam decided to wait and see how the situation developed during the day and decide the next morning what to do next. If everything was back to normal, the whole situation would just be a scare and an interesting story they would talk about next Christmas.

She finished her espresso and returned to her place in the open space. Sam still had a project to finish today and would probably have to work late in the evening to meet her deadline. The situation with her family back home was a distraction, which didn't help her make any progress. She must have looked worried since her colleagues were asking if everything was okay. Sam wasn't in the mood to tell the whole story and was assuring them that everything was fine. She wanted to get out of these conversations as soon as possible. Best concentrate on work at the moment. She put her large noise-canceling headphones on to listen to heavy metal bands from the 1980s and started to code.

STRASSHOF
DAY 1
4:35 P.M.

The town where Karl Herzog, the security operator, lived was only a 20-minute drive away. The landscape reminded Arnaud of The Netherlands, with its absolute flatness and never-ending fields. Instead of old windmills, he saw oil pumps in the middle of the field or next to the road. Some were moving, some just standing there, a reminder of the industrial age coming to an end. Behind the oil pumps were large wind parks, some operational, some being constructed. *What a representation of the day and age we live in*, Arnaud thought. The new age of renewable energy was coming, but it wasn't fully there yet. Both fossil fuels and renewable energy were needed to power the civilization, which was why a small disruption in the gas network could create such chaos.

Arnaud drove up to the house of Karl Herzog. It was a detached house like any other: two floors, a garage, painted light yellow. The ground in front of the house was all concrete, and in the back, a small garden. He rang the bell, and a man in his 30s opened the door.

„Hello, are you Karl Herzog?" Arnaud asked.

„Yes."

„I'm inspector Arnaud Navarro of Europol, and I would like to ask you a few questions about tonight's incident."

„Yes, of course, come on in," Herzog responded.

Arnaud was let inside and brought to the living room, where he sat down and gladly accepted an offer for coffee. He was sitting on a new but cheap-looking couch with a small coffee table. Picture frames were lying on a small table next to the couch, all turned upside down. He was wondering what that meant. A recent divorce?

„I understand you were the operator on duty last night?"

Herzog scratched his arm and fiddled with a pen, clearly nervous, either because of the incident or being interviewed by a police officer. Or both. „Yes."

„Tell me what happened before the incident."

Herzog took a deep breath before answering, repeating a story he probably had told multiple times by now. „It was a night like any other. I was sitting at the desk watching the security alarms coming in. Looking back, I must have missed the one when the intruder broke in, but we get so many false alarms all the time! I watch foxes, deer, and even frogs trigger alarms constantly. How can you blame me for missing one real one? How can this be my fault?" Herzog was close to tears, visibly shaken by what had happened. The man was still in shock.

„You just get tired of watching and miss stuff, you know? It was snowing, so we got even more alarms than usual. Next thing I know, I wake up lying on the floor, and my boss calls me, screaming."

Arnaud was sipping his cup of bad filter coffee while pondering the implication of this. Did the intruder know about the bad state of the security operations? Did she expect the security guard to miss the break-in alarm? Did she have inside information?

„So you have no memory of opening the door or why you might have done that?"

„No, nothing." Arnaud was studying the expressions on Herzog's face. He looked nervous, but not like he was hiding something. He told the truth. He really didn't know what had happened.

„There are drugs that induce short-term memory loss. Maybe that is what happened. Did you take any medication or other kind of substance?"

„Uhm, nothing."

„Can you identify the woman on the surveillance video?"

„No, I have never seen her before in my life. No idea why I would open the door for her." This was not helping at all. He wrote down the little information he got on his notepad.

„Uhm, okay. Do you have any idea what the intruder might have done for two hours inside the control room?"

„There is not a lot to do there. Of course, she could have looked at the surveillance video while I was logged in. But there is nothing special to see there. And as a regular security operator, I do not have access to any sensitive information. There is only so much I can do on my PC."

„How long do you record video?"

„We record for 96 hours. After that time, it is automatically deleted."

„96 hours? Isn't that much longer than GDPR allows?" GDPR was the General Data Protection Regulation in the EU, regulating how privacy-relevant data like the video had to be handled.

„No idea, but I once heard my boss say that nobody checks for that anyway." *That's what's wrong with Europe*, Arnaud thought. *If there are good initiatives like GDPR, they are not enforced.*

„Could she have made copies of the videos?"

„I guess so, but copying all video recordings would take much longer than two hours. And no idea why someone would want to do that anyway."

Arnaud had heard enough. Karl Herzog could not help finding out what happened there. Arnaud asked for his phone number, left his own card, and said goodbye.

He went to his rental, sat down, and checked his watch. It was shortly after 05:00 p.m., and he would be at the airport before 06:00 p.m. to catch the 07:00 p.m. plane back to Amsterdam. Arnaud made his way back to the airport, and during the drive, he recapped what he knew. There was an attack on the gas distribution network. A woman had climbed over the wall, went to the security operation room, and was let in by the security guard. Then she left, sabotaged the gas pump, and left again over the wall.

There were recordings of almost the whole incident, and there was no doubt about what had happened. They even had a clear image of the face of the woman. And still, nothing made sense. Why would the security operator let her in if he didn't know her? How was he incapacitated? And what did she do in the operation room for two hours before sabotaging? This case was so clear-cut and didn't make sense at the same time. On the surface, it seemed clear what had happened, but his gut told him that something was wrong. It would require a thorough investigation to get to the bottom of it. Besides, Arnaud needed to find the perpetrator anyway.

He arrived at the airport, bought a ticket at the ticket counter, and went to Check-In. A police officer was waiting there whom Arnaud recognized—he had been with Manfred Huber at the gas distribution facility. The officer handed Arnaud a DVD with the video recordings. Arnaud would make sure to take it to his colleague in forensics right after returning to The Hague. It would be a long night, but anything beat sitting in training on the latest new tech toy Europol played around with.

BRUSSELS
DAY 1
05:15 P.M.

Lina Juska was in full crisis mode. She had been on the phone and in meetings all day. In the morning, it had sounded like the problem could be fixed within an hour, but that turned into a couple of hours, which turned into a whole day. Now, she just got word that they are unsure they could make it within the day. What a catastrophe.

By now, Italy had declared a state of emergency, just like in 2017, when there was an accident in Oberberg. Authorities had learned nothing from the incident, neither in Austria nor Italy. Each country had backup plans for this situation, gas tanks large enough to supply citizens for weeks. But this year was different. Due to high gas prices, the government of Italy gambled and was hoping for lower prices to fill up the silos, which never happened, and now the emergency supplies were depleted.

In Italy, most households relied on gas for heating, cooking, and warm water, and were now completely cut off from any gas supply. People were freezing. The military had to step in to provide electric heaters to homes and offer basic services in temporary locations where people could warm up and take a shower. Austria was considering announcing a state of emergency as well. There were similar situations in Slovenia, Hungary, and southern Germany.

But being unable to warm up, shower, and cook was only part of the problem. Gas was also one of the main sources of power production in Europe. In fact, natural gas was by far the most important source for conventional power plants in Europe, with twice as much energy output as the one in second place, which was still coal. Lina was trying to change that energy mix, but it would take time. A sudden drop in gas supply meant that these power stations were not producing energy anymore, causing a sharp drop in the electrical grid of Europe.

The grid was a very delicate thing. It had to run at a frequency of 50 Hertz, with a maximum allowed deviation of 0.5 Hertz. If the frequency increased or decreased more than that, the complete network would break down, causing a blackout. What caused the frequency to change was a sudden overproduction or underproduction of energy. Like now, when 20% of Europe's natural gas power plants stopped producing energy. It was a carefully managed balance. If one part failed significantly, everything would fail.

Of course, there were contingencies in place for such a situation. The frequency of the grid was monitored constantly, and emergency generators would kick in seconds after it dropped. These short-term emergency generators could provide energy for up to 30 minutes, during which larger power providers, which took longer to start but could last for days, were powered up. These energy storage facilities were charged during times of overproduction and used up in times of underproduction. This worked so far but could not last forever.

To top off the list of issues caused by a stop in gas supply, many industries relied on it to power their production. And it was not only heavy industry, such as steel production, but also the production of simple things we use in everyday life, such as milk. Gas was an important component of the production process, where it was used to pasteurize milk and sterilize bottles. If the gas supply stopped, milk production facilities would stand still. No gas, no milk.

This meant that Lina had to ensure the gas supply was being re-established. She spent the first half of the day negotiating with different nations to reroute part of their gas to the affected regions, which helped, but it could not make up for the loss of one of the main gas lines in Europe. If this took longer, she would have to organize LNG shipments, liquefied natural gas, from other countries, such as the United States. But luckily, it seemed like this would not be necessary this time. If the pipeline could be fixed in the next few hours, they could establish normal operations very soon.

She needed an update on how the criminal investigation was going and decided to call the head of the ESOC at Europol again. She took out her phone, and before she could dial a number, she saw the numerous messages of this lobbyist Farkas again. He had been texting her all day. This attack on the pipeline was an additional tailwind for him. Lina would have to talk to him eventually, but not now. She dialed the number of Gusta Jansen.

„Gusta, it's Lina Juska."

„Hello, Lina. What can I do for you?"

„You know exactly why I'm calling. What's new?"

„Lina, as I told you before, I assigned one of my best inspectors to this case. He is in Austria as we speak. We can say for certain that this was a planned terror act, and we do have a video recording of the perpetrator, a woman. We put out a Europe-wide search warrant for her."

„That's nothing new. You told me the same an hour ago!" Lina couldn't believe there was no update. She needed to inform her colleagues in the Commission and had nothing to go on.

„Lina, you need to let us do our work. Such an investigation cannot be done in such a short time frame. We are already working on high-speed. This is of the highest priority."

„And that is what I expect."

„Sorry, that's all we have so far. A criminal investigation takes time, unfortunately. Rest assured, we are working as fast as we can."

***

Gusta Jansen hung up. She would never admit it, but she felt the same way as Lina Juska. Arnaud did not update her and was not reachable on his phone, again. She texted him, asking with the strongest language she could muster to give her an update on what was going on.

PRIVATE GROUP CHAT
DAY 1
08:40 P.M.

FightForTheFuture entered the room

FightForTheFuture: „Well done. Post the manifesto.“

DestructionKitten: „Roger.“

FightForTheFuture left the room

THE HAGUE
DAY 1
10:05 P.M.

Arnaud had just landed in Amsterdam and drove down to The Hague. It was already past 10:00 p.m., but he wanted to get the video material analyzed as soon as possible. He checked his phone and saw multiple messages from Gusta. He called her to say that there was nothing new except more open questions that needed answers. She was already home but picked up her phone, anyway. You could call her in the middle of the night, and she would pick up. As expected, she was not excited about the lack of progress, but at least Arnaud had updated her.

He arrived at the ESOC at 11:00 p.m. His colleague Henrick in video forensics would be there. He took the night shift tonight. Video forensics specialized in analyzing any kind of video material. He went to see Henrick right away.

„Henrick, I have some videos to be analyzed." He handed him the DVD.

„Is this a DVD? Where did you get this, a time machine?" Henrick asked.

„Don't ask me. It was the only thing the security people were able to give me. It is from the pipeline case, so we are in a bit of a rush."

„Okay, what do you need?"

„I want to review the video again tomorrow morning. Also, see if you find anything out of the ordinary or a trace that could lead us to the perpetrator. I don't know what, but something is off about this whole case." Arnaud would need to get some sleep before starting with this fresh in the morning. At least something would happen overnight while he got some rest.

„Alright, will do Arnaud. Good night," Henrick said.

„Night."

As he turned around to walk home, a young sergeant stopped him. „There you are sir. I was hoping to catch you."

„What do you want? I'm on my way out."

„A manifesto was just posted online. It is about the pipeline case. And I think you will want to read it. Here it is." She handed him a piece of paper.

„Thanks, I will read it at home."

Arnaud was exhausted when he arrived home. He placed his thick coat on the chair next to the entrance and placed the candy he picked up at Vienna airport for his daughter Zoé on the desk nearby: *Mozartkugeln*, chocolate balls filled with marzipan. He would bring it over to her as soon as he had some time. She would love it. Arnaud did want to see her more often, he really did, but sometimes work came in the way of life. That's how it was.

The last time he saw her, they had gone to Sea Life, an ocean animal zoo right next to the beach of The Hague. They had met on a Saturday morning, her mother had dropped her off at Arnaud's place, and together they had gone to the zoo. Zoé had been overjoyed seeing all the different animals. Her favorites were sea turtles, and she had every kind of turtle toy imaginable:

stuffed animals in droves, stickers, T-shirts, pencils, you name it. This time, she had brought her favorite turtle stuffed animal with her, and once they had been inside, she headed straight to the water tanks. It had been one of the best times of her life, and Arnaud had to admit he felt the same way.

After they were done at the zoo, he had bought her cotton candy, and they had walked down the promenade next to the sea. It just had felt perfect. It must have been last summer... no, the summer before! One and a half years! Arnaud could not believe that he hadn't seen his daughter for one and a half years. Time was flying, and she was growing up while he wasted his time with some case files. He promised himself that he would see her next weekend and bring her the Austrian candy.

Arnaud considered if he should muster his strength and go jogging still. He had to start at one point. But he decided that today was not the day, surely not at night after such a trip. Instead, he poured himself a glass of red wine, a Bordeaux from Château Margaux he brought home from his last visit to Paris. He chose a big red wine glass to enjoy this special drop, something he couldn't afford to enjoy every day. He missed the wine collection that he used to maintain back in Paris, and now, in The Hague, he only had a few special ones in stock. Arnaud sat down in his armchair next to the window to read the print-out the sergeant had given him.

This is a manifesto for the citizens of Europe. Wake up! You are being ruled by puppet governments, controlled by an elite you didn't elect who serve only special interests. Every day, decisions are being made in your name, but not your interests. The rich are getting richer, and the poor remain poor. The EU presents itself to the world as a role-model in *protecting the environment while doing nothing. Europe depends on non-renewable natural gas more than ever, producing more and more CO_2 emissions. The only thing being done is buying CO_2 certificates from poorer nations. This is nothing more than utilizing our incredible wealth to avoid any relevant action. We are doing nothing to switch to renewable energy, just shifting the problem.*

The European Union is doomed to fail, paralyzed by bureaucracy and self-interest by its representatives.

Today's attack on the European gas network should be a wake-up call to our politicians. It showed how vulnerable we all are with our reliance on gas for our energy needs. But this was just the beginning. If the following demands are not met within 72 hours, more attacks on the gas infrastructure will follow. And make no mistake, these attacks will be devastating.

We demand:

- *A formal decision by the European Parliament and Council to abandon all use of fossil fuels within six months.*
- *Immediately halting CO_2 emission trading and a commitment to reach net zero greenhouse gas emissions within two years.*
- *A formal decision by the European Parliament and Council to dissolve the current European Commission with re-elections in a new regime where the people of Europe can vote for the Commission directly.*

The European Parliament should not take this lightly. They have 72 hours.

Arnaud looked at the time the manifesto was sent: 11:00 p.m. That meant they had a little under three days to stop the terrorists. He led out a long sigh. He wasn't expecting this. It was very common to receive demands following a terrorist attack, but often they were not public and usually somewhat fulfillable, such as asking for a sum of money. The stance of „we do not negotiate with terrorists" was just the official line not to encourage more people to extort money. Ransom fees were being paid; some situations made that necessary to avoid further damage. Of course, it could never be admitted to the public.

But this was different. These demands were impossible to meet. In such a short timeframe, nothing would move in the political arena. Money was easy, but getting politicians to agree on something was not. Either the person who wrote this had no idea how politics worked, or the demands were designed to be unfulfillable.

Arnaud picked up the phone and called the ESOC to check if the search warrant had turned up anything. Disheartened, he found out that it hadn't. The picture of the perpetrator was sent out to local police all over Europe, but none had an idea who she was. He decided to check on Henrick, just in case. He called his number, and Henrick picked up right away.

„Did you find anything yet?"

„No, nothing, still copying the videos. But I hear you have an image of the person you are searching for. Why are you not sending it through the new system?" Henrick asked.

„Which new system?"

„Did you miss the training today? We have a new facial recognition system for these kinds of purposes."

„I have more important things to do than sit through training. If I send you the photo, can you run a search for me?"

„Okay, will do. I'll call you when I get something."
The manifesto changed the stakes of the whole case. If they didn't find the perpetrator, more attacks could follow. And they only had 72 hours to stop them.

DAY TWO

THE HAGUE
06:04 A.M.

The sound of a phone ringing woke Arnaud up in the middle of a dream. He was dizzy, his eyelids so heavy he could hardly open them. He groped purblind between the sheets and then on his bedside table to find his mobile. A coffee mug and a newspaper fell to the floor before he finally took hold of it and looked at the display. He saw that Henrick was calling, so he picked up reluctantly.

„Yes?"

„Finally I've reached you! I found her. Come on over, and I'll show you."

Arnaud had not expected Henrick to mean it literally when he had said he would call when he got something. But one had to respect his dedication. Arnaud took a quick shower and got dressed to go to work. He would pick up his double espresso on the way and skip the croissant this time.

The ESOC was still quite empty in these early hours. They did have 24-hour operations, because crime never slept, but it was less critical than for his colleagues at Interpol, who had to cover all time zones globally. Europol relied on a skeleton crew who took the night shift just in case something of interest happened.

Arnaud took the elevator to the third floor of the forensics department. Forensics was important for the ESOC and was made up of around 40 experts with different fields of expertise. While Henrick specialized in video forensics, there were others for audio forensics or traditional forensics not related to IT. The floor was one big room, which was used as an open office divided by small cubicles. He found Henrick at a desk in the middle of the room.

„Morning, Henrick. So what do you have to show me that is more important than my beauty sleep?"

„You slept? Such luxury! I ran the photo you gave me through the new system. It took me a while to set it up, and I needed to get more photos from the video, but in the end, I made it work. Since you missed the training, here is how it works. Europol purchased a new facial recognition system called Hawksight, which automatically matches a person's face with all faces available in the database. It's like when you are unlocking your smartphone—"

„My what? I don't think that this old thing deserves the name smartphone. It can make calls and has a calendar, but that's it." Arnaud thought about his brother's brand-new fitness tracker, but that probably wasn't the same thing.

„Oh my. Well, if you had a modern phone, you would be able to unlock it automatically by just looking at it. Phones use facial recognition too. But our system is more advanced than that. While the phone just confirms that you are the one looking at it, our system can search for your face in a database of millions, if not billions, of faces. But here is the kicker: the database is not a regular police database, as you would expect. To build it, the system searches all over the Internet and captures all faces it can find online. Every time a photo is uploaded to the Internet, and can be accessed publicly, the system will find it. All accessible social media profiles of everyone in the world are automatically scanned. And I mean everyone.

"If you didn't post any photo of yourself online, someone else might have. If you were at a birthday party and someone posts a photo of you in the background, it will find it. So the system will find you, even if you have never been in any police database. And it will collect all information relating to the picture: name, address, phone numbers, email addresses, friends, relatives, everything available," Henrick explained.

„That sounds dystopian. How can this be legal?"

„Basically, all data protection regulations in Europe have exemptions for police use, so there are no restrictions there. What's more, while the European Artificial Intelligence Act explicitly regulates the use of facial recognition, police use is again excluded."

„So, again, something useful was turned toothless by special interests. Great."

„Well, it still limits the use by private firms, but yes, police use is not. Lucky for us. Anyway, let me show you." Henrick pulled up an application on his PC.

„So here I'm loading the face of our perpetrator, the woman with the red hair." Arnaud saw how the face was added; it looked similar to a social media profile.

„And next, we let the system match this face against the database. This actually takes a while, and contrary to how it is depicted in movies, it will not show you how it is actually matching all the faces. So instead of looking at a loading bar for fifteen minutes, I'll just skip to the results. Here you go."

On the screen was the picture Henrick uploaded to the left. And on the right were four other pictures of the same person, but in different situations. One seemed to be a regular social media profile image of the woman with red hair smiling into the camera. There was another photo of her at a party with many other people, one where she was apparently at dinner with her family, and one where she was on a hiking trip. She was wearing shorts, a blue checkered shirt, and a backpack. It looked like she was hiking in the Alps somewhere. In every picture, the woman looked straight at the camera, and it was clear it was the same person as in the video recording. Henrick had really found the perpetrator. And below all the pictures, Arnaud saw a name flashing in big letters: Samanta Di Vincenzo.

TALLINN
DAY 2
08:25 A.M.

Samanta was riding the bus to work again, but today she would be on time. Even though she had stayed late at work yesterday, she was happy she made it out of the house early. Her project finished at night, and Sam was glad she could get that out of her head. But she did worry about her grandmother back home. Their conversation yesterday did not sound like it would get better soon.

Luckily, there were no shortages in food and water, but freezing and not being able to take a warm shower wears people down, especially 83-year-old grandmothers. Sam had read the news in the morning and could not get any new information. If anything, the situation all over Italy seemed to be the same as the day before. She would call her grandmother as soon as she got to work.

Sam was looking outside as she was used to, watching the city pass by. It had started snowing, and there was a bit of a snowstorm, reducing visibility for her and the bus driver. The bus slowly made its way through morning traffic, which was worse than usual, with snowy roads making it harder for everyone to navigate.

Finally, the bus arrived at the main bus station, where she had to change. There was some kind of commotion: four police vehicles, all with their blue lights on. Three police sedans and one van, with the blue and yellow stripes so typical for Tallinn police and interested onlookers standing around them. Sam was wondering what was going on.

As she was about to step out of the bus, five police officers rushed towards the entrance, guns raised, and blocked her from going out. They screamed something in Estonian that she did not understand. When she didn't react, they took both her arms, twisted them, folded them behind her back, and put her in handcuffs. She was pushed around to make her go in the direction the police officers wanted her to go, which was the van. Everything happened so quickly.

Inside, there were no windows and just one glass panel with bars in front of it, looking towards the driver waiting in front. She was pushed inside, the doors were closed, and the van rushed away much faster than allowed. Sam was wondering how they could safely drive so fast in these weather conditions, and the answer was they were not. The police siren howled outside, making way for them.

Sam felt sick in her stomach, her head turned. *What is happening?* she thought. She did not understand the world anymore. Sam had seen police arrests in movies and computer games, but she never expected it to actually be like that. In fact, it was much more unpleasant than it looked in the movies. It was profoundly humiliating.

Since there were no windows, she couldn't really make out where they took her. After around 15 minutes, the vehicle stopped, and she was pushed outside. She realized they were at the airport, directly on the tarmac. They took her to a plane waiting nearby, a commercial one. Inside, there were regular tourists and businesspeople waiting to lift off. The first few rows, mainly first and business class, were cleared, and they seated her there. She felt the stares of all the other passengers on her, silently judging. She had no idea what she was doing here.

Sam was seated in the window seat with police officers all around: next to her, in front of her, and behind her. They didn't wear any uniforms; they were in civilian clothes. When Sam asked them questions or otherwise tried to communicate with them, no one spoke. After another 15 minutes of waiting, the plane took off. The police officers did not seem to have a problem sitting there motionless for the whole flight.

Since her travel companions did not talk, all that was left was reading the onboard magazine and listening to the crew's announcements. It wasn't too hard to figure out that the flight was headed towards Schiphol airport, Amsterdam, which gave her a rough idea that they would be flying between two and two and a half hours. These would be long hours to pass. A lot of time to think about what was happening to her, but no answers whatsoever.

Sam tried to distract herself by reading the magazine but got bored right away. She tried to sleep to make the time pass but quickly found out there was no way she could fall asleep under these circumstances. So she ended up reading the same articles in the magazine repeatedly until, after two and a half hours, they landed at Schiphol. During the approach, she had recognized Amsterdam immediately; she had taken a trip there once with friends, and Amsterdam had a distinct look from above.

Before the doors opened, a police van approached and waited for them to get off the plane. She was, silently again, transferred from the plane to the van and handed over to different police officers, this time in Dutch uniforms. Apparently, a different team took over, and the Estonian team left. The van had no windows, and Sam tried to guess how long they were driving. What felt like an eternity must have been 30 to 40 minutes until they finally arrived at their destination. It was a city, but she was pretty sure it was not Amsterdam.

They were driving through several streets when they stopped, and somebody said something. She heard the creaky sound of a gate opening, and the van started moving again. They must have arrived at their destination. The doors opened and Sam was brought, still handcuffed, into a large concrete building with glass facades. There were strict security protocols at the front entrance, and men with guns patted her down. Once inside, they went through a long hallway, took two turns, and locked her into a cell.

Suddenly, everything was silent around her. She looked around her jail cell. A small room, concrete walls, concrete floor, a small window high up that she couldn't reach, and a metal door with a small slit to look through. Her bed was small, but as uncomfortable as she would have imagined. There was a toilet behind a small niche. All in all, not a place she liked to be in.

Sam sat down on the bed and tried to reflect on what had just happened in the last—was it four?—hours. What did she do to warrant an arrest? Why would they take her like that without even telling her why? Did they make a mistake and wanted someone else? And if not, how did they know she would be on that bus? Didn't she have a right to get information in a language she understood? And what would her Nonna think if she didn't get the promised call today?

THE HAGUE
DAY 2
01:14 P.M.

Arnaud was impressed by how fast everything went. Once Henrick had shown him the name of their suspect, they had tried to locate her as fast as possible. She was an Italian citizen, which was good since Italy was one of the few countries which used electronic resident registration with a record of everyone living in Italy.

Unfortunately, the register stated that Samanta Di Vincenzo had moved away from her address in Naples six months ago. Not really a surprise. If one planned such a sophisticated attack on European energy infrastructure, they likely would not be stupid enough to be found so easily. Arnaud would still send some local police to Naples to interrogate her relatives, but they would likely not find her there. And she did not pop up on any other resident registration in another country, but that did not mean much since only around 30% of European countries maintained such a register.

In other countries, resident information would be recorded by banks, telecom operators, insurance companies and utilities, but since these were private enterprises, there was no central point of contact you could go to. You had to at least know in which country you were searching for someone before contacting a private enterprise. And then it was still questionable if Arnaud would get the information without a local warrant. He could try to track her mobile phone, but that required a warrant too, which took time they didn't have. And if she was not in Italy anymore, they had to first find out in which roaming network she was logged in and then get a warrant for the operator in whatever country she was now, and by that time, she could have moved on. All of that made it complicated and time-consuming to track someone by phone across Europe.

So they had to find another way to find the red-haired woman. This was when Henrick had introduced Arnaud to another functionality of Hawksight. It turned out that the same software was provided to local police forces all over Europe. And most of them used it not only to search through the face database but to connect it live to video surveillance cameras in the cities. Those included not only those surveillance cameras, which were already operated by police, but also included cameras from public transportation and sometimes even private enterprises such as shopping malls.

With this, you could get an alert whenever a face you were searching for was found on any of these cameras all over Europe. A constant search engine in the real world, looking for people without them ever knowing. No wonder the purchase of this system was not publicly discussed. If European citizens knew about it, there would have been public outrage.

They had input the face of Samanta Di Vincenzo into the search engine of Hawksight. Now they had to wait. It would alert them when her face was found on any public camera in Europe, but it had been still early in the day, and it was no surprise that nothing had popped up right away. In fact, it could even take days, or they could find nothing at all if they were unlucky. Many countries did not have a lot of cameras in public, and you could avoid them finding you by just covering your face. Even a simple cap was enough to hide.

But after two hours—Arnaud had time to get his croissant by now—they had gotten an alert in Tallinn/Estonia as she was entering a bus. It was clear by looking at the image that it was her. This was the person from the database and the one that broke into Oberberg. They had informed the local police and had asked them to apprehend her right away to fly her to Amsterdam. Europol didn't have any authority over local police, so it was asking a favor, but the local police had been happy to help. At Amsterdam airport, colleagues of Europol had taken over and had driven her to Europol headquarters in The Hague. And now, just four hours after they first found her, she was sitting in a cell right next door, waiting to be interrogated.

Arnaud asked her to be taken to an interview room. The interview rooms with two-way mirrors that everyone knew from the movies did exist but 20 years ago. Nowadays, police relied on modern technology to look at interviewees without them knowing. Interviews were regular rooms, without two-way mirrors but with cameras in each corner of the room. Each of them had sensitive microphones built-in, and an additional microphone on the table for the best audio quality.

Samanta was seated at a plain desk in the middle of the room, her hands chained to the desk. They left her there alone for a few minutes and observed how she behaved. She looked scared. She looked around the room, but there was nothing of interest there. Then she started to yell and ask what was going on. If she acted, she did it well.

Arnaud entered the room and sat down opposite her. „Samanta Di Vincenzo, 31 years old, Italian citizen, software developer. No criminal record. Yet." He paused for a moment and looked her in the eyes. No reaction. „I suppose you did not expect us to find you so soon?"

„What am I doing here?" Sam asked.

„Interesting question. After committing the worst terrorist act in Europe in years, I would have expected you to at least have an idea why you might get arrested. To be honest, I was a little bit disappointed. I thought that someone who could carry out such an attack would be smart enough to avoid cameras."

„I did what? I am a simple software dev, not a terrorist. This is a mistake!"

„What did you do two nights ago?" Arnaud asked.

„Uhm, I went to a bar in Tallinn, alone. I wanted to meet some new people but in the end didn't. I had one drink and went back home."

„Can anyone attest to that?"

„No." Sam had a bad feeling about where this was going.

„What is the name of the bar?"

„Valli," Sam said.

„Okay, we will check your story."

„Have you ever been to Austria?"

„No."

„Sure? Is this you in this picture?" Arnaud opened a folder and presented the photo they took from the surveillance video.

„It—it looks like me, but I have no idea where this was taken. Where did you get this?"

„Just answer the questions, please. I even have a full video of you." He opened his laptop and showed her the video from the entrance of the control room in Oberberg. She could be seen clearly in high resolution as she looked at the camera. „Any comments?"

„I have no idea what this is, please believe me!" Sam said.

„Let me show you something else." Arnaud took the printout of the manifesto that was posted online. He laid it in front of her. „Do you recognize this?"

„No, what is it?"

„How come then that in the metadata of the document, we found your name?" Forensics had just discovered it an hour before. The case seemed to be ironclad now.

***

Sam felt her situation was becoming more hopeless by the minute. „I have no idea," she said.

„So let me summarize: You say this is you in the video, but you have never been to Austria, where this was taken. You have also never seen the manifesto before, even though we found your name in it. How do you explain all of this?"

„No idea, maybe someone dressed up like me? Or just looked similar to me? Metadata in documents can be easily faked, too!"

„Come on, are you kidding me? This is the real world; it doesn't work like that. It is obviously you in the photo. You can even see your freckles on it! So, stop pretending you have no idea what is going on. You broke into a gas distribution facility in Austria and caused the greatest European energy crisis in years!"

Sam was shaken as she realized what she was being accused of. This man was saying it was her who caused her family in Italy to freeze? It was unimaginable that she ever did something like that. She wouldn't even know how. She was abducted, flown across half of Europe, chained against a desk in a windowless room, and was accused of something she had never done. How could something like that ever happen? She had to admit that it was her in the photo, but she had no recollection of ever being there, let alone committing such an act. Tears started to fill her eyes. She had nothing to bring forward to improve her situation. They would lock her up, and she might not see her family ever again. It will break her Nonna's heart. Her situation was hopeless.

„Your crying game does not work on me. Tell me why you broke into Oberberg and sabotaged the compressor station."

Sam could not speak anymore. Her throat swelled up like she had swallowed a balloon. Her stomach felt sick, and everything was twisted. Suddenly, she felt the breakfast in her stomach starting to move and vomited on the floor next to her.

Arnaud sighed. He gestured to the camera to let the guard come in. „Take her to the bathroom to clean up. Bring her back right after."

THE HAGUE
DAY 2
02:17 P.M.

The guard unlocked Sam from the interrogation table and handcuffed her hands before leading her outside. They were walking down the same hallway they had come from. The guard stopped at the women's bathroom and took the handcuffs off. „Five minutes," he said and waited outside.

Sam went into the plain facilities. Three stalls, one sink, and a small mirror. She watched herself in the mirror and decided that she looked terrible. Red eyes in hollow eye sockets beneath a messy hairdo. She could confidently say she had the worst morning of her entire life. Sam was glad that she had a few minutes to process everything.

They had compelling evidence against her, and she had no alibi. Even if they asked around in Valli bar, she was sure no one would remember her. She hadn't spent a lot of time there and was not a regular. And there was no one else who could attest to her whereabouts on the evening in question. Europol was convinced of her guilt, and they had the evidence to prove it. All cards were stacked against Sam. No judge in the world would believe her, faced with this evidence.

How could she even get into this kind of situation? How could she be apprehended without explanation, flown across

Europe, and interrogated without access to a lawyer? Didn't she have basic civil rights? She was being mistreated. Her desperation changed into anger. Sam decided she would not accept this treatment without a fight and felt new-found strength arise. Her only chance was to get out of there, hide, and prove her innocence, even if difficult.

It was like her brain had switched from panic to gaming mode, and she looked around the bathroom for escape routes. There was always a way out. She checked the windows. They had thick metal bars in front of them, of course. There was no way she could escape through those. She checked the ceiling, hoping to find a ventilation shaft or a double ceiling she could climb in to get out. There was none.

Figures, she thought. It was naive to believe that they wouldn't think about all of that when they constructed a jail. There was no other exit from than the door she came through. No way to escape. In a video game she was playing once, she had to hide in the bathroom to make her attackers believe she escaped, only to run away once they started searching for her elsewhere.

Sam was searching for places to hide when she heard a mobile phone ringing outside. Someone picked up. Shortly afterwards she heard a man yelling. Maybe she could use this distraction? Sam carefully opened the door to peek outside. It was the guard who brought her there, arguing on the phone: „Ik zet het vuilnis elke dag buiten! Neem je me in de maling?"

It was probably Dutch, she couldn't understand, but it sounded like trouble at home. He was standing a few meters away from the bathroom and his back was turned against her. No way! She couldn't believe her luck. As carefully as she could, she slowly stepped outside and closed the door without a sound. She was now in the hallway, the guard facing away from her, still yelling into his phone. Without making a sound, she slowly walked in the other direction until the corridor made a corner and she was passing into the next one. She leaned against the wall of the hallway that opened up. Sam's heart was pumping like it never had before, sweat started to run down her face. Every cell in her body was yelling: *Run. Run. Run!*

But she knew that running was the worst idea. The only way to get out was to walk confidently, pretending that she belonged here. It wasn't far to the exit, she had remembered the way. But her first big obstacle was already in front of her: a glass door that would only open if you had an access card, which, of course, she didn't. She was waiting some meters away, thinking what to do, when she saw someone on the other side approach the door.

Sam walked towards it, carefully pacing her steps so that she would arrive at the door shortly after the woman on the other side. As Sam hoped, the woman used her card to open the door and even held it open with a smile. Sam thanked her and smiled back, not believing her luck. She walked towards the exit where the men with guns were guarding the entrance. They were currently checking a visitor; everyone was focused on the people going in. All their efforts seemed to be directed towards making sure no unauthorized persons entered the building, not exited. In fact, exiting didn't even require a key card, probably because it was a guarded door. She walked out and stood on the street.

It felt unreal. Cautiously, she turned to take a look at the entrance again, when she noticed a plaque that read „European

Union Agency for Law Enforcement Cooperation / Europol".
Did she just escape Europol? The same Europol she knew from
cheap TV series? This place was real? *It must be a dream,* she
thought. Suddenly, she was reminded that this was indeed a
hard reality when she heard an alarm sound inside. Sam knew
that if she didn't do something right now, she would end up in
a cell again. She had to resist the strong urge to just run, but
instead, she briskly started walking down the street towards the
next corner, where another street with rows of parked cars
started. As soon as she turned, she started running down the
street as fast as she could, past pedestrians, which turned in
wonder when she passed. Hastily, she ran like that for a few
minutes when she saw a park ahead of her. This seemed like a
good opportunity to hide. Sam entered it, and just after the
entrance, she jumped behind a bush. Exhausted, she broke
down behind it and lay down on the grass, panting.

THE HAGUE
DAY 2
02:38 P.M.

Samanta Di Vincenzo was lying on the ground behind a bush, between scattered coffee cups and some Kleenex, suggesting the place was used as a hiding place for the homeless and as a natural garbage can for the people eating their hamburgers during lunch break. The penetrating smell made her sick. Her stomach was still revolting, and her head was spinning. *This can't be true. I am in a nightmare. I will wake up and everything will be back to normal.*

In the back of her head, a senseless hope remained that the last hours did not happen, and everything would be as before. No police, no running, just her boring, regular life. But she knew this was not a dream. It was all real, and she had to concentrate now. She had to keep moving, otherwise they would catch her. *Get up, Sam, get up!*

She thought that having left the building when the alarm sounded, by now every policeman and policewoman would be out to find her. She was in a foreign city, she did not even know which one, and had no idea where to go.

First, she needed to get further away from her prison. Then she could make a more thorough plan. She continued in the park, which was more like a forest within the city. The road went to one side and towards the other there were endless rows of trees and bushes, thick and impenetrable, with small pathways in between. A good place to hide, but she did not want to become a sitting duck either, waiting to be found. She decided to run at the edge of the park, parallel to the road.

Sam had been jogging like that for about 15 minutes when the park ended, and she stood at an intersection. Was this far enough from the prison to risk asking a pedestrian for directions? Probably yes. An old woman was walking across the street and Sam walked over to her. She asked for directions to the nearest train station in English, but the woman did not understand her. And Sam didn't speak Dutch, so this was a dead end. She smiled and searched for someone else to ask and found a young man in his 20s on a skateboard. The right demographic to speak English to. This time it worked, and he pointed her to a train station, which was just a three-minute walk. From there, trains went to Den Haag Centraal, the main railway station. At least she knew in which city she was now.

When she arrived at the train station she realized she would need to buy a ticket, but she had no way to pay for it. They had taken her wallet and her phone. Then Sam realized they had forgotten the smart watch she was wearing. Probably they thought it was a regular old-school watch and didn't think it was a threat. But it had a payment function that allowed her to pay wirelessly, just like a bank card. Sam knew well enough that it was not a good idea to pay by card when you were on the run, but she didn't have a choice. Instead of paying for her ticket with her watch, she would rather use an ATM to get as much cash as possible. The police already knew that she was in the city, so information where she took cash was not a great giveaway. But at least they could not track her further movement. She found an ATM at the entrance to the train station and withdrew as much money as it would give her, which turned out to be €400. It would be enough for now.

Before she went to the train, she entered the only shop in the station—a drug store. She bought scissors, hair dye spray and a tourist cap, one of these orange ones you could find all over the Netherlands. She remembered the inspector talk about cameras they had used to find her, and she didn't want to take any chances. For now, Sam wore the cap and tried to hide as much of her hair under it as possible. As soon as she would have some time, she would try to change her hair too. Luckily, the train arrived just as she came to the station, and she took the ten-minute ride to Den Haag Centraal.

Den Haag Centraal was a large railway station with trains going to many different places. Before going further, she needed a bathroom to cut and dye her hair. She hadn't bought regular hair dye because there was no time for proper coloring, so she chose black hairspray that was used to dress up for carnival. Now in February, everything was full of costumes, and these kinds of sprays were exactly what she needed. After she cut and dyed her hair black, she looked at herself in the mirror and was satisfied by her accomplishment. It wasn't perfect, but her short black hairdo looked surprisingly well.

Sam went outside the bathroom in search of the board which listed departing trains. She kept her head low. There were cameras everywhere. Who knew which technology they had to find her? On the board, three trains were listed that would leave within the next ten minutes. One to Amsterdam, one to

Utrecht, and one to Rotterdam. Rotterdam it is, she thought. From there she would try to take a train to Brussels. She used her cash to buy a ticket and entered the waiting train. Sam sat down in a window seat. It would take half an hour until they arrived in Rotterdam, so she tried to get some rest and think while there was nothing to do. What could she do to get out of this? Where could she hide? And even if she managed to hide from the police, she could not do that forever, she had to prove her innocence. But how?

THE HAGUE
DAY 2
02:38 P.M.

Arnaud was sitting in the interrogation room, nervously tapping on the table with his fingers. He looked at his fitness tracker: it had already been ten minutes since he sent a guard with Samanta Di Vincenzo to the bathroom to clean herself up, and they had not returned. Arnaud decided to check and got up to search for them. He found the police officer on the phone in front of the women's bathroom. When he saw Arnaud, the officer hung up and straightened his posture.

„What are you doing? Why is this taking so long? Is she still inside?" Arnaud asked.

„I'm sorry, sir, I must have forgotten about the time. She did not leave the bathroom yet." the police officer said, dutifully.

„Okay, that's it. I have lost all patience for the day. We go in." Arnaud opened the door to the bathroom and looked around. He couldn't see Di Vincenzo anywhere. They checked all the stalls, nothing. There were no windows and no other means to hide. The suspect was nowhere to be found. She must have sneaked out while this idiot was on the phone.

„Shit! You imbecile!" Arnaud screamed furiously. Somehow, they had managed to lose their prime suspect in the most important terror investigation in years. And he was responsible that they let her escape. But he would also make sure that Gusta would know who exactly lost her and how. This officer will have to pay. But for now Arnaud had to focus on getting his suspect back. Di Vincenzo couldn't have gotten far. After all, this was a secure building where prisoners were not supposed to just waltz out.

„Sound the alarm. We need to get her back right now. And make sure everyone has a description of her. She must still be in the building; we will find her. And if you want to make up for the huge mess you just created, you better find her yourself, fast." Arnaud said.

„Yes, sir!" the police officer said, his voice clearly shaken.

Arnaud ran down the hallway in the direction of the exit. The glass door in the middle of the hallway had access control on it. She would have to pass through there to get out. Without an access card, the doors wouldn't open for her. Just to be sure, he rushed to the main entrance. His colleagues could take care of sweeping the building. Arnaud asked the guards at the entrance if they saw someone matching Di Vincenzo's description. And indeed they confirmed that a woman exited the building, just a few minutes ago. They hadn't thought much of it, as she looked like any other employee. Did they check if she had an employee badge? No, they hadn't. *Shit, shit, shit!*

They would need the help of The Hague local police department. Arnaud instructed the guard who lost her to ask the local police for assistance in the apprehension of a high value suspect and provide her description. They also needed to check the cameras that were lining the building of Europol and were looking towards the square in front. They would see on the recordings where she went after she exited. But this would cost valuable time. Arnaud wanted to catch her right now, before she got far.

He ran towards the street and looked left and right. No sign of her. Go left or right? The best place to hide would be Van Stolkpark. So to the right. He ran towards the park, which was about hundred and fifty meters away, but quickly had to admit he was out of shape. He hadn't even reached the park yet and was already out of breath. Oh, what would his brother say right now? He would mock Arnaud, most likely.

Arnaud continued as fast as he could, more walking than running, until he reached Van Stolkpark. It was a large park, resembling rather a forest than anything else and finding someone in it would require a big team. And time, which Arnaud did not have. Multiple paths crossed the park, easily ten separate ways, with many intersections and smaller trails wandering off the main tracks. If she ran in there, she could hide behind the many bushes or even climb a tree. Any team would have a hard time finding her, but it was useless for Arnaud alone to go into it now. His time would be more valuable somewhere else. Reluctantly, he had to admit that they had lost Samanta Di Vincenzo, for now. But that didn't mean they couldn't get her back. He made his way back to Europol and took his phone out to call Henrick on the way.

„Salut. We lost our suspect. Please don't ask me how. I need you to activate Hawksight again; we need to find her right away. She is still in The Hague, but who knows for how long. Can you start a search for her right now?" Arnaud was still out of breath as he was asking Henrick for help.

„When you talk about a suspect, you mean Samanta Di Vincenzo? I just found her for you!"

„Yes, Di Vincenzo, and I know. I need you to find her again," Arnaud said.

„Sure, Arnaud, no problem. And yeah, no further comment."

There was daylight for another two hours and they would use this time to comb through the city. But Arnaud had little hope. Maybe this time, technology really was superior to classical police work. Hawksight found her the first time around. Maybe it could find her again. He had a lot of questions left for the woman. Why did she do it? Were there any others? Where did she get the skills for such an attack? And what did she do in the two hours between entering the control room and destroying the compressor?

THE HAGUE
DAY 2
03:10 P.M.

Arnaud was back at Europol. There was nothing he could do now to help get his suspect back, except wait. He decided to grab a sandwich and go for a walk. He could gather his thoughts and avoid running into Gusta, who would be furious. He had informed her of the events by text and then switched off his phone. Listening to her yell at him did not help the case right now.

The air was chilly and the sky clear and sunny. The smell reminded Arnaud of skiing holidays of the past. When you were standing on a mountain on a sunny day, ready to go downhill, that was what it smelled like. Cold, but full of adventure. He took a deep breath. Arnaud had to admit that he missed this excitement, and while losing the suspect was very, very bad, not least because it offended his ego, it also brought a much-needed change in his life.

They had a decent bistro right around the corner where he grabbed a ham and cheese sandwich to go. He went to Van Stolkpark park again, trying to get into the head of Samanta Di Vincenzo. There was something that bothered him about her; she did not fit the profile. Why would a software developer commit such an attack? Where is the motivation? Why would she return to the place where she lived in Estonia right after instead of hiding or returning to Italy, which was much closer? And during the interrogation, she seemed very convincing, which could be an act but, if so, a good one.

But the video evidence, together with the manifesto, was irrefutable. There could be no doubt that she did it. Sometimes, people did stupid things you would not expect from them. And sometimes, such attacks were made by one-time criminals. There was no evidence supporting his doubts, so likely, deep in his mind, he just did not want it to be her, with her sassy red hair and freckles. Were the circumstances any different, he would have been attracted to Samanta Di Vincenzo.

Since he could not help with the chase right now, he decided to investigate further. Having finished his sandwich, Arnaud returned to his office at Europol, where he would make some calls. First, he would call Manfred Huber from the local Austrian police. Arnaud needed to track Samanta's movements from and to Austria, and he needed flight logs to do that. After sitting down at his desk, he picked up the phone and called the number of Huber.

„Hello, this is Arnaud of Europol. I need your help again."
„Sure, what is it?"

„We identified the woman in the video, an Italian citizen living in Estonia. We already apprehended her in Tallinn." Huber didn't need to know the rest of the story yet.

„Since she was back in Estonia already the next day, she must have taken a flight from Vienna to Tallinn. Can you check the flight logs of the airlines if a Samanta Di Vincenzo flew that day? Don't just check direct flights only but any flight out of Vienna that could be used to eventually reach Estonia."

„Will do. I wouldn't get my hopes up, though. If she is smart, she wouldn't use her real name to fly. And as long as she is staying in the Schengen area, no one would check her ID anyway," Huber said.

„I agree. This is why I would like you to also run her face through Hawksight and see if she pops up on any video recordings on that day at the airport."

„I see, good idea. We haven't used the system yet. Not sure if we can access the cameras at the airport, but I'll see what I can do."

„Thanks. Let me know if you find anything." Arnaud hung up. It was a long shot. But if they found something in the flight data, it might help to reconstruct what happened before and after the terror attack.

Next, Arnaud needed to get a better idea of the background of his suspect. He would ask the Italian police if they could dig anything up. A first search hadn't revealed any criminal record, but sometimes there was more in local archives. He called the local police in Naples and requested they take a closer look at Samanta Di Vincenzo.

Arnaud wanted to talk to the family as well. He typed into the search bar on his PC, „phone book Naples". There was a website which allowed you to search for phone numbers. He tried „Di Vincenzo". 92 results. Too many to call. He needed to know the exact names of her relatives. He asked the Italian police for their names, but apparently, they could not find them right away and promised to send them as soon as possible. Arnaud didn't want to wait, so he decided to ask Henrick for help.

„Henrick, is there a way to find the names of the family of our suspect online?"

„Well, in most countries, health insurances or the ministry of finance hold this kind of information, but if you want it fast, we could just see if we find anything on the public Internet," Henrick said.

„Okay, do it. I would like the names of the parents and siblings of Samanta Di Vincenzo."

Five minutes later, Henrick called back: „That was actually not difficult at all. She has a profile on one of the largest social media networks. I just looked through her ‚friends' there and searched for Di Vincenzo. Based on their age, it's pretty easy to guess who they are. I found a mother, father, and brother. I'll send over the names now."

Arnaud was satisfied with how fast that went. Sometimes, in order to get ahead with an investigation, going through official channels just took too long and you could find the same information by just searching on the Internet. Well, not Arnaud himself, but he could ask someone who could.

He typed in the names in the Naples phone book and found a landline number of Samanta's parents. He dialed it.

„Pronto?" Arnaud heard the voice of an older woman.

„Hello, this is Inspector Arnaud Navarro."

„Pronto? Nun ve capisc." Arnaud realized that the woman on the other end did not speak English and thus could not understand him. His Italian was not great, but he could understand when people talked, and using a mix of his basic Italian and native Spanish, he managed to communicate.

„Sono l'inspettore Arnaud Navarro. Voglio parlare con Samanta Di Vincenzo. Sei su madre?"

„Song' ,a nonna. U gesù, che è succiess'? Aveva ritto che me chiammava ogge, ma nun me responne ,a stammatin'!" Her Naples dialect was hard to understand, but he understood the basics. She was Samanta's grandmother, not her mother. The tone of her voice sounded alarmed, worried. Apparently, she was worried because Samanta did not return her calls. Of course, she didn't, Europol had taken her phone.

„Non so dove sia ora, voglio parlare con qualcuno che sa dove potrebbe essere." Arnaud did not want to alarm her more than necessary and assured her that he was trying to find Samanta. Maybe her relatives would know where she would go.

„Non si preoccupi, starà bene. C'è qualcuno con cui posso parlare in inglese?" Arnaud realized his Italian was too bad for this conversation. He had a hard time understanding this woman's heavy dialect, and it took too much effort to respond, so he asked for someone who could speak English.

„Si, chillu buon a nient' ro frate. Tutte l'autre stann' faticann'. Mo` ,o vago a chiamma`." Arnaud understood he could talk to her brother, who was just as good as her parents.

„Yes?" Her brother picked up the phone.

„Hello, I am Inspector Arnaud Navarro and have some questions about Samanta."

„What did she do? Run a red light in one of her computer games?" The response of the brother was slow, almost like he just woke up. Arnaud wondered if he was on drugs.

„There is an ongoing investigation I cannot share details about, but she ran away, and we cannot find her. Do you have any idea where she would go?"

„No idea, we don't really talk. Especially since she moved out last year. She is not a very social person, spending a lot of time online instead of meeting people. If I were you, I would start by finding out with who she plays her online games with. Maybe she went to see one of them," the brother said.

„Thanks. Do you know if she was ever interested in activism and politics? Climate change action and the like?"

„No, never. Samanta was always more interested in technology than anything else. I have never seen her show any interest in climate change or politics at all."

„Has she ever been to Austria?" Arnaud asked.

„Not that I know. For skiing trips, we always stayed in Italy. And other than with the family, she never really traveled."

„Thanks, this is useful. Do you have a mobile number I can reach you at if I have any further questions?" The brother gave him the number and said goodbye.

This conversation helped but didn't provide any answers. First, he got a tip to look at her online gaming activity, which was a good idea. Arnaud would ask Estonian police to seize her PC and take a look if they could get any information out of it. Second, nothing the brother said fit with the profile of the attack. This did not bring Arnaud further in the case but fed his skepticism. Instead of providing more evidence, the conversation brought more doubt. He would have to look deeper.

Arnaud looked at his watch. It was 04:10 p.m., just 55 hours left before more attacks would happen. They had to hurry.

BRUSSELS
DAY 2
06:32 P.M.

Sam exited the train after it arrived at Brussel-Zuid railway station. She had changed trains in Rotterdam from the local Dutch train to an international one connecting the Netherlands to Belgium. To avoid being identified, she had pulled her cap low and had tried not to look suspicious, whatever that meant, and so far, it had worked. Nobody had stopped her.

Crossing borders between the Netherlands and Belgium made her nervous: what if they introduced passport controls between European borders again? You never knew. But to her relief, no one asked for her ID or other documents, and she had no trouble taking the train to Brussels. Likely, police in the Netherlands and neighboring countries were out looking for her but had not gone so far, yet, as to check every passenger on the trains. Now, as Sam was walking through the main hall of the railway station, she had to decide where to go next.

She would need some food but was cautious not to spend too much time among people. Sam went into the first sandwich restaurant she could find and bought a Subway sandwich, a chocolate cookie, and a coke to go. She had never been to Brussels before and was surprised by the bleak sight when she went outside. Concrete office buildings, a street and a car park, nothing more and no place to sit down without being exposed.

She decided to head left to what looked like a residential and quiet part of town. After a few minutes, she sat down at the stairs of a building entrance to eat what would be her breakfast, lunch, and dinner, all in one. So far, she hadn't felt any hunger. The adrenaline in her veins had made her ignore her basic needs. When stressed, your whole body switches to survival mode and makes you ignore anything else except getting out of harm's way. But now hunger had caught up with her, and it felt good to have something in the stomach again.

How could she get out of this whole mess? It was no surprise the police assumed she committed this terrible attack; the person on the video definitely looked like her. Except that it wasn't her, it couldn't be. She could clearly remember sitting in this bar in Tallinn, far away from Austria, having a drink and not talking to anyone. And for sure she did not write any manifesto. Or did she? Was she slowly going crazy? Could she be schizophrenic, living two lives that did not know each other? Was there a Hyde to her Dr. Jekyll?

Sam became unsure of herself, unsure of what was real and what was not. Of course, like her whole generation, she was somewhat worried about climate change, but it didn't play a big role in her life. She was concentrating on her work to make robots navigate on Mars and didn't care about the gas supply of Europe. At least the Sam she knew didn't. Either she had split personalities, or someone had set her up.

Why? Sam didn't have any enemies. She didn't even know a lot of people, not in real life, anyway. And her online-gaming companions all liked her. Someone else must have done it, but

Samanta had no clue why, and why they would frame her. It was a riddle for another day. Right now, more important than finding out the truth was to find a place to hide. She needed to get as far away as possible from the police to a place she could feel safe before deciding on any next steps. If she was sitting in jail, she couldn't prove her innocence. So, she needed a place to hide, fast.

Sam could not go back to her home in Tallinn. First, police would be waiting for her there and second, taking a plane was out of the question anyway; it was way too risky to be caught by some border police. They would be looking for her. She needed to avoid any form of travel where they checked her name. To live with her family in Napoli was also no option; the police would search for her there as well. She needed to hide with someone there was no obvious connection to, someone that could not be found by looking through her contacts on her phone or interrogating her family or work colleagues.

My gaming friends, she remembered. They could help her out. There was no trace to them except through gaming chat rooms. The police would have a hard time finding out about them, and they would certainly be willing to help, even though they had never met in person. Out of the four, five candidates, Erik would make the most sense. He was living in Bonn, which was not too far away from Brussels, definitely reachable by train. Plus, he was a pretty good hacker and could help her track the manifesto to find out who was behind all this. Yes, Erik was the perfect candidate to hide at.

Sam needed to find a place to access the Internet and connect with him via their gaming chat rooms. She wasn't sure if Internet cafés still existed. The shops, which used to provide a PC and Internet for as long as you were willing to pay, felt like remnants of times long past, but maybe she was lucky. Besides providing her access to the Internet, they would allow her to surf anonymously, which was exactly what she needed. So she was walking back to the railway station, searching for an Internet café. If there was any at all, a railway station would be an obvious location for such a place.

Sam walked past the Subway restaurant and the escalators leading to the railway platforms. She passed a bakery, a clothing store, and a piercing studio, of all places. But no Internet café. Nothing she was looking for was to be found at first sight. Sam didn't give up. She needed Internet access to contact her friend. Internet cafés were niche offerings. For sure, they couldn't afford the rent at the best locations of the railway station. They would likely be located in some less prominent place.

She went far to the back, in a corner that looked a bit shady, not frequented by many people. There she finally saw a sign that read Internet café. That was it. Sam paid for a 30-minute session, in cash, of course, and navigated to a platform dedicated to online gaming. It provided access to online games and other resources, and it also allowed players to text and talk with each other. Now Erik would just have to be online for Sam to talk to him. She was relieved to see that he was indeed available.

They used their gaming handles to communicate. In the gaming world, Sam was called Enchantress and Erik was known as FeralMayhem.

Enchantress: „Hey, buddy, you there?"
FeralMayhem: „Always am! Ready for a sesh?"

Enchantress: „No time to play today... can't explain atm."

FeralMayhem: „Uhh... okaaay..."

Enchantress: „We need to meet IRL[1], asap. Can I come over?"

FeralMayhem: „Come over to my place? When? What's going on?"

Enchantress: „It's an emergency. Can we meet or not?"

FeralMayhem: „Sure. Here my address:" Erik sent her his exact address in Bonn.

Enchantress: „Thanks. OTW[2]. CYA[3] in a few hours."

FeralMayhem: „Few hours? Where the hell are you?"

FeralMayhem: „Sam? What the hell did you do?"

Sam couldn't answer. She was already gone and had left the chat room. Finally, Sam had a plan for the next few days. To stay with Erik and find out who was behind all this. She just needed to find a way to get to Bonn as fast as possible and not get caught. She was already at a railway station, so this shouldn't be too difficult. Or should it?

---

1   Meaning „In real life"
2   Meaning „On the way"
3   Meaning „See you"

BRUSSELS
DAY 2
07:10 P.M.

Lina Juska had spent the day with a newly formed special action committee to deal with the attack on Europe's gas infrastructure. Right after the attack, most experts agreed that it had been an individual, targeted incident, potentially by a rogue state actor or an individual. Something that would stay isolated. But after the manifesto was released, it became apparent that the entire European infrastructure was threatened, and decisive steps needed to be taken to protect it.

This was when a crisis team was created, the special action committee to secure gas supply, or SGS for short. Members included representatives of the ministries of the interior and infrastructure of all member states, the European Commissioner for Crisis Management, the Commissioner for Counter Terrorism, the head of the ESOC at Europol Gusta Jansen as well as Lina Juska herself. It was obvious that not much would happen in this committee, but it was all part of the political circus they had to play a part in.

They had just decided to take a short coffee break, and Gusta approached Lina at the coffee table. „Are you okay? You seem to be stressed out," she said. Gusta was an old friend, and even though Lina sometimes became impatient with her when

Europol did not deliver results fast enough, they stayed close. And in the SGS committee, they were the only female representatives, which made them stick together even more.

„I am stressed out. The whole situation comes at the wrong time. Just when I am about to push my policies on renewable energy, this attack happens, which throws everything off the rails. And honestly, that your people let our suspect get away doesn't help."

„Lina, trust me, I couldn't believe it myself when I heard. The level of stupidity one has to endure in my job is unbearable sometimes. After this is over, it will have consequences for my lead inspector on the case."

„Who is that?"

„Inspector Arnaud Navarro. Very experienced but sloppy and doesn't care about the rules. I would have gotten rid of him long ago if he weren't the best on my team. He gets cases solved. This is why I put him on this one," Gusta said.

„A name to remember, then."

„Yes. For better or for worse."

„Well, I trust you will find our suspect fast. We need to close this as soon as possible. I get enough pressure as it is, not least from your boss."

„Jean-Baptiste Moulin is not my boss, just responsible for Europol, as the Commissioner for Counter-Terrorism."

„Be that as it may, I'll be the first one to admit that I do not like this colleague of mine. He only looks after himself and doesn't care about what is best for the people but what is best for him. And that he sits on this committee with us is bad enough."

„Speak of the devil, here he comes." Moulin was just walking over to them with a paper cup of coffee in his hand. He was wearing an expensive dark blue suit with a blue tie. Classic dull understatement. His full, white hair had too much product in it and was combed back, making him look like a used car salesman. As if he wanted to project his sleaziness to the whole world, to make it painfully obvious. The wrinkles on his face suggested a life full of friendly smiles in politics, and right now, his facial expression suggested shallow friendliness with a cynical undertone.

„Ladies, it is such a pleasure to work with you on this committee. I am sure that together we will find swift solutions to our problem," Moulin said with a grand hand gesture and a fake smile.

„The pleasure is all mine," Lina said with fake friendliness, barely hiding her disgust towards her colleague.

„Ms. Jansen, do we have any news on the case?" Moulin asked, turning to Gusta.

„Not on finding our suspect, but I just got word that Oberberg managed to repair the broken compressor and gas is flowing again. It sounds like our immediate energy crisis is averted for the day. But you all read the manifesto. We are not out of the woods yet, not by a long shot. We must anticipate new attacks, even when we find our suspect. She might not be working alone," Gusta said.

„This is a glimmer of hope in grim times indeed, Gusta. We all hope that this situation will get resolved soon. Otherwise, Lina will need to revisit her priorities on where to invest in the coming years. We are too reliant on gas to be ignoring our infrastructure so badly, I'm afraid."

115

„There is nothing to revisit, Jean-Baptiste. I will get ourselves out of our dependence on gas and focus on the future, not the past," Lina said.

„I am sure you will do the right thing, Lina. This is your area of expertise, after all. Ladies, I must excuse myself and get back to work. Enjoy your coffee."

„What was that all about?" Gusta asked.

„He just wants to get on my nerves. The new Trans Carpathian gas pipeline is up for discussion on the parliament floor, and Moulin has been pushing for that for a while. It won't get approved, though. I will make sure of it. It would throw back my renewable energy plans for years. He is just poking around and wants to annoy me."

„Well, not the most likeable character, as you said. Let me know if I can help," Gusta said.

„The best way to help is to close this case as soon as possible. If there is no risk on our infrastructure anymore, any argument for new infrastructure is moot."

„You know we are doing everything we can. Arnaud is my best inspector."

„But he doesn't have much time left before the deadline of the manifesto. And he needs to get his suspect back, let alone solve the case," Lina said.

„Don't worry, he will," Gusta replied. In fact, she was not so sure herself. Yes, Arnaud was good, but the time pressure was tremendous. Not only had he had to follow multiple threads, but he needed to be in different countries across Europe at once to follow all of them. Plus, he had never had to solve such a critical and politically charged case before. All

Gusta could do was hope that he would be up for the job. If anybody could do it, it was Arnaud. And he had only 52 hours.

VIENNA
DAY 2
07:15 P.M.

„Gas pipeline repaired, Italy lifts state of emergency," she read. It was the main headline of the day. Mia Bernert lay on the couch in her small apartment and read the news on her phone. Her apartment was sparingly decorated, with just the necessities. She had a couch, a kitchen table, and a mattress on the floor. It wasn't very cozy, but it was functional. On the wall hung some posters by Greenpeace, a polar bear, and icebergs breaking away at the north pole. The most equipped part of her apartment was her desk. It had one large, curved computer screen in the center, a laptop to the left, a keyboard, a mouse, and a wireless headset. Mia spent more time in cyberspace than in the real world, or „meatspace", as it was called, and her apartment reflected that.

She didn't need a lot, as long as she had her laptop and a decent Internet connection. Besides, she would leave this place for her next mission, and she wouldn't take much more than her laptop with her. She just needed to make sure she didn't leave a trace.

That was quick, she thought. Mia didn't expect them to repair the damage to the pipeline in Oberberg so quickly. She was disappointed; Mia had hoped for more damage. Fossil fuels were destroying the world and needed to be stopped. In Vienna, 80% of households were heating with natural gas. Even her apartment was using it; she had no choice. Contrary to Italy, Austria had enough gas reserves and wasn't affected by the broken gas pipeline, but even if it were, Mia would have happily spent a few days in the cold for the cause. The more the gas supply was disrupted, the more people would realize that fossil fuels were not the answer and that we needed to switch to renewable energy right now. The only way to bring radical change was radical action.

Mia's job was breaking into IT systems. She worked for a cyber security company, looking for security vulnerabilities to improve security for her clients. She was hacking into systems not to exploit any holes in their security, but to fix them. She was what they called a white-hat hacker. However, sometimes Mia would use this knowledge to break in for other reasons that were not strictly lawful. Mia felt that her own moral compass should guide her instead of laws that corrupt politicians wrote. Because of this, some would call her a gray-hat hacker: white by day, black by night. But to her, that didn't make a difference. What was important was to do the right thing.

To get into Oberberg, she didn't even need her hacking knowledge. She had researched a bit about the facility and found that they had renewed their security system a few years ago. This had been done through a public tender process where they asked companies to submit their bids, and these tender documents could be found online if you knew where to look. They had described in detail what kind of security system they were looking to purchase: high-resolution cameras with automatic intruder detection, laser perimeter detection system, access control, software for their control center; it was all there.

Her first thought had been to just hack into the security system to switch it off before breaking in. Depending on how well they had protected this critical infrastructure, it would take between one day and a week. But then she'd had a better idea.

One thing she learned from ten years of hacking was that the biggest security holes were not backdoors or bugs in the software. They were humans. No matter how secure a system was, there was always a way to get in through unsuspecting humans. They were sloppy, irrational, emotional—the biggest vulnerability of all. And after some digging, she had found the perfect candidate: a security guard working in Oberberg who was active on social media and constantly wrote about his work.

It had been easy to learn that he spent his free time playing poker every Saturday evening, always in the same place. So that's where Mia had preyed on him. She had made sure she would be at the same poker table as him. She knew how to play but was careful not to show too much of her skill. Men needed to feel in control, and a woman who played better than them wouldn't be appealing. There was nothing more attractive to a man than a woman whom they could explain how the world, or poker, worked.

Karl Herzog was tall and muscular with black, short hair. Not really her usual type, but attractive in a way. Not a complex personality, simple-minded. Perfect for her purpose. They had gone to his place on the first night, and she had made sure they spent every day together in the coming weeks. Over time, she had learned all details of how security at Oberberg worked. That he was alone in the control room during his night shifts.

That they did not have many guards patrolling. That there were so many false alarms, he ignored all of them. Oberberg seemed to be an easy enough target: expensive security equipment but lacking security discipline.

When the time came, she had been sure to spend the evening with Karl before he started his night shift. Mia had offered to drive him to work since everything needed to be perfectly timed. She had prepared a thermos with coffee but needed to be sure he didn't drink it before he was at work. Flunitrazepam took 15 to 20 minutes to take effect. It would cause dizziness, bad concentration and, most importantly, short-term memory loss. It was important that he didn't remember anymore who visited him in his control room. And at the same time, Mia had to be there in time so he could open the door for her before he passed out.

Karl had kissed her goodbye, not knowing that it would be the last time, and had gone to work. Mia had gotten to work right after. She had prepared a bag with everything she needed: a black hoodie, a cap, a flashlight, and two bottles of acid. Nitric acid would dissolve most metal components of the compressor, and hydrofluoric acid would get to work on any electronics inside.

Mia had spent two years in the French Foreign Legion, which was part of the French army and comprised exclusively of foreigners who wanted to earn some money fighting in a war. Before she knew that she would earn her living hacking IT systems, it seemed like an adventurous way to earn money. There, she had been trained as a chemical weapons expert and had learned how to create improvised explosive devices with household chemicals. Together with her military training, it would come in handy for what she was about to do.

In the forest close to the facility, she got the ladder she had hidden there days before. It was one of those retractable ladders: easy to transport, easy to hide, yet large enough to get over the walls in Oberberg. And now the time had come to use it to climb over the wall and get inside. She knew where the control room would be and went straight there.

Mia had made sure to pull her hoodie down low so her face could not be seen by the high-resolution cameras all around, except at the control room where she had rung Karl to let her in. He had seen her on the camera and had opened the door right away, as planned. Mia had been surprised he didn't hesitate or ask her what she was doing there before opening the door. But then again, she wasn't surprised at all. Hormones and Karl's lack of discipline played their anticipated role.

After opening, there had not even been time to greet him as the Flunitrazepam kicked in just in time and he collapsed on the floor. The timing had been as perfect as it could have been. Had it kicked in just a minute before, there wouldn't have been anyone to open the door for her. *Poor guy. Cute but too gullible,* she thought. Mia now had had all the time in the world to get the job done.

Now, two days later, she was still in her apartment in Vienna and was following the news. But increasingly, she felt like it became too dangerous to be there. She had read that Europol apprehended a suspect, which was good news, but you never knew if they would somehow trace her, anyway. She would have to move out of her apartment and cover her tracks immediately. And Mia would leave a little surprise for whoever would come looking for her. Once more, she would use her knowledge of the French Foreign Legion.

BRUSSELS
DAY 2
07:32 P.M.

Sam stepped outside the Internet café, ready to take a train to meet Erik. She looked around for screens showing departure times to choose the next available option to Bonn. A little to the right of her, farther down the main hall, she saw what looked like large screens. Just as she started to move towards them, she noticed two police officers about 20 meters away. This was not good news.

One of the police officers turned around, and Sam met his eyes. For a few seconds, they stared at each other. Time slowed down around Sam. It was like she was in a time bubble as she realized the implication of being caught by the police. Surely, there was a search warrant, but did they know she was in Brussels? Was there a camera somewhere she missed, was she not careful enough with covering her face? Sam felt panic arise. If they recognized her, she needed to run, but if they didn't, running would give her away. *Do they know?* Then the other police officers started to move towards her, shouting. *They know.*

Sam turned around and raced in the opposite direction. It was the other entrance of the railway station that she had taken before, so she had to re-orient. Again, a street, busses, a tram, and high-rise office buildings in front of her. No obvious place to hide. Between the buildings was what looked like a pedestrian zone. Hopefully that would slow down any pursuit by car, she thought, and started to race across the street. While running, she looked over her shoulder. The two police officers were still roughly 20 meters away, running franticly, shouting. She had a bit of a head start but not a lot.

Sam headed down the street—mainly residential buildings, a large construction site and a small walkway for pedestrians next to it with wooden boards serving as makeshift floor. They were creaking and bending strongly as Sam ran across them. She felt they could give way under her weight and the pressure of her steps any second. But they didn't, and neither did they when the police officers ran across them, closing in fast.

She needed to get some distance between them before thinking of hiding. So she continued to run as fast as she could, straight, then the next street to the right, and another to the left. Running zig-zag through the small streets like a rabbit might make it harder to track her. She looked behind: still the two police officers, and now she heard sirens howling in the distance, coming closer. They must have called for backup. Soon, the whole city would be on the lookout for her. She needed a place to hide, to get away. But where? Brussels was an unknown city. All she could do was continue to run in the hope she would find a hiding spot.

Sam came to the end of the street she was on, which opened up towards a large square with a car park that was largely empty, just a few teenagers sitting there, smoking. Light shone through most of the windows in the buildings around the square, suggesting people enjoyed their dinner at home instead of spending their time outside on a cold night. To the right of the car park were a few trees and a large gothic church. This could be a place to hide, to take a breath and get her thoughts straight. Would they follow her in? Would they dare disrupt the peace of a church? Sam had to risk it. It was evening, but if she had any luck, the doors were still open. February was carnival time, and maybe they were open for the celebrations.

She ran to the right to what looked like the main entrance. No sign that the doors were open, but she had to try. She had never been religious, but now she prayed that the doors would be unlocked. And they were. She took one last look at the running police officers who watched her as she entered the church.

It was dimly lit inside and smelled like a mix of incense and humidity. Sam found a table right at the entrance, with flyers and Bibles on it. She moved it to the large door to block it but found it would not stop anyone. So she took the chair next to the table, lifted it on top of it, and used it to block the door buckle so no one could move it. This would hold for a bit.

She went into the main nave, the central part of the church. It looked like most catholic churches with high ceilings, ornaments on the walls, and windows, which would look colorful when the sun shone in during the day. At the moment, only a few spotlights and the occasional candle lit the large room. It was completely empty, not a soul to be seen. The utter silence was only interrupted by her panting. Sam sat down on one of the chairs and tried to calm down. Her hands were shaking, sweat ran down her red cheeks, and her heart was racing.

Suddenly Sam realized what she had done. She was trapped. Even if the police did not dare to enter. Even if she could find a side entrance to the church, in a very short time, the police would have it surrounded. They would catch her wherever she attempted to leave the church. No way out.

She couldn't believe it. Just when she had found a way forward with the help of Erik, when she finally made a plan how to hide for a longer time, the police would arrest her. She heard sirens from the outside, and blue light was shining through the glass windows of the church, filling the room with flashes in various shades of blue. She thought that she could hear the sound of a helicopter. Sam let her head sink into her hands. Her eyes filled with tears, and she felt the energy leave her body. For the first time today, she felt truly helpless, without an idea of how she could go on. She felt like giving up. Thoughts of resignation filled her mind. Being on the run and hardly eating for a day took its toll.

This was when she felt a presence. Slowly, she looked up and saw a man in a black robe standing in front of her, staring, not saying a word. He was tall with silver hair, old but ageless at the same time. He just watched her solemnly. *This must be the priest*, she thought. She stared back through her wet eyes. Sam and the priest remained like this for what couldn't have been more than ten seconds but felt like minutes. Sam didn't dare to say a word.

„Welcome to the Church of Our Blessed Lady of the Sablon, my child. I am Father Thomas," the priest said.

„Hello." Sam felt stupid for not responding with something more dignified.

„What is it, my child? Why are you upset?"

„The police want to arrest me for a crime I did not commit. If they caught me, I would be locked away for life, with no way to prove my innocence! Please help me. There is no way forward."

The priest sighed and took a long look at her. Then he closed his eyes for a few seconds and opened them again. It seemed like he was contemplating what the right thing to do was. Maybe he was seeking answers in silent prayer.

„You know, churches used to be a safe haven for people chased by police. In earlier times, no policeman would be allowed in here. But times have changed. They will come inside and arrest you."

The blue lights intensified. Then she heard someone using loudspeakers:

„Samanta Di Vincenzo, we have the church surrounded. Give up and come out with your hands raised. Otherwise, we will storm the church and take you by force. You have 60 seconds to comply."

Suddenly, there was a flicker in the priest's eyes. It seemed like he had chosen a side. „Come with me, hurry."

He led Sam along the main aisle, between the row of chairs in the middle of the church, towards the altar. Before reaching it, they took a turn towards a small door to the right, a place usually reserved for the priest. They entered through the door, which opened to a small room, his private chambers. He picked up a flashlight, which lay in a niche in the stone wall. At the other end, there was another small door, which led to a narrow spiral staircase. They hurried downwards in the spiral.

When they arrived at the end, Sam felt dizzy. It smelled musty down there, and the walls, the doors, everything looked ancient. The floor was sandy and didn't look like it was well-maintained. They rushed along a hallway towards another door opening to a larger room with small niches on the sides of the wall. In some of the niches were squares made of stone, looking like benches. In others were rows and rows of bones stapled on top of each other, even some skulls looking through their empty eye sockets at them. Now she realized where they were: the catacombs.

The priest started to explain while they were moving between the niches, which turned out to be tombs, not benches: „The history of the original chapel, on which the Church of Our Blessed Lady of the Sablon was built, goes back to the early 13th century. Back then, Henry I recognized the Noble Serment of Crossbowmen as a Guild and gave them a piece of land outside the city walls. There, they built a chapel dedicated to Our Lady. Since the chapel lay outside the city walls, it was a dangerous place for the Guild, and as trained warriors, they were very much aware.

So they decided to build a secret passage from the chapel to another place inside the city they could use should they be attacked. When they built the church on top of the chapel, they maintained the secret passage, which was used when the church was sacked by Calvinists in the 16th century. The passage was closed when the Guild fled through it, but later, in peaceful times, they opened it up again. It exists to this day, and the knowledge of it is only passed from priest to priest. This is where we are going now."

Father Thomas her into one of the niches, which didn't have a tomb. Spider webs were hanging from the wall, and it didn't look like someone had been down here for a very long time. The priest pushed the back wall, which gave way and turned out to be a door that opened to a long, dark tunnel.

„This tunnel leads to the catacombs of the Cathedral of St. Michael and St. Gudula. When our church was built, the cathedral was largely built already, even though it took 500 years in total to finish it. The Crossbowmen chose to connect to the Cathedral because it lay inside the city's walls back then," the priest explained.

„How will I find my way? Is the other end open?" Sam asked, concerned about walking down a pitch-black tunnel that hadn't been used in centuries. Who knew if the other end was closed, or the tunnel fell in. If there was no exit on the other end, she might be trapped inside.

„I know the priest of the cathedral and will inform him you are coming. He will open the door on the other end for you. I will have to close the door on this end, so the police won't find it, but don't worry, there is enough air in the tunnel, so you won't have any problems. It is only a ten-minute walk. Here, take my flashlight." This did not sound reassuring at all. But Sam was truly grateful for being given a chance to escape. It gave her a shot to prove her innocence and see her Nonna again.

„Thank you very much for your help, Father," Sam said.

„May our lord the savior bless you. One thing: do not tell anyone about this passage. We kept it secret for a very long time, and it should stay this way."

„I promise," she said and turned around to face the void.

BRUSSELS
DAY 2
07:45 P.M.

There was a creak as the door to the dark tunnel closed behind Sam. Her flashlight shone down the dark void, which seemed to go deep with no end in sight. A long passage of nothingness with no sound. The air was musty from the damp moss growing on the walls. Even though the light illuminated only her immediate surroundings, it was enough to see numerous spider webs hanging from the ceiling. Spider webs come in different forms. The fresh ones form beautiful patterns, almost like a piece of art that the spiders craft. Old ones, however, are very different. If no one cleans them away, they collapse and form long, thick, gray strings that spiders have long abandoned. Those were the ones dangling from the ceiling, and Sam was grateful she had cut her hair and worn a cap. Otherwise, they would be caught in her hair very quickly. When she looked closely, she did see a spider crawling here and there, but there were many more webs than spiders could create in a lifetime. This was the work of spider generations.

Every time she moved her flashlight, the shadows of the webs jumped around the tunnel walls, and Sam caught herself imagining that those were the shadows of ghosts who were awakened from the tombstones. *Of course they aren't,* she thought. *Or are they?* It startled her every time. Very unsettling.

Sam made her way down the tunnel. She moved slowly in the beginning, choosing her steps carefully not to slip on the moss on the floor, which overgrew some of the cobblestones. Avoiding the spider webs while watching her steps required concentration and coordination, which meant it would take her longer than the ten minutes the priest mentioned. From time to time, she found bugs and spiders climbing the walls, escaping the unusual intruder into their kingdom. After a while, she turned and looked back and couldn't see the entrance anymore. Similarly, when she shone her light into the distance ahead, she couldn't see an exit. The tunnel must make a turn without her realizing. Or she had a very long way to go.

After what felt like an eternity of cautiously stepping on moss and damp stone, Sam reached the end of the tunnel. When she looked at her watch, she realized that she had been walking for just eleven minutes. She had been going faster than it felt. The end of the tunnel looked like a wall, just like the entrance. She suspected that, similar to the entrance, there would be a way to open the hidden door, which was now closed. Had the priest forgotten to call his colleague? Maybe he didn't pick up his phone. Or was it some kind of wicked trap, and she would be stuck down here forever?

She searched the walls for an indication of how to open the door. After all, if it was an escape tunnel, it had to be possible to open it from the inside. Then again, a lot of things had changed over the centuries, and the door could just as easily have been replaced and built anew. There was nothing, no handle or sign that would indicate that the door could be opened from the inside. Likely, just like the entrance, you had to push from the outside to open it.

Sam started to panic, and the feeling of being trapped grew stronger any second she remained inside this tunnel. Her mind drifted off, flashing back to her early childhood as a five-year-old when she experienced claustrophobia for the first time. She had been on the playground with her Nonna, who was chatting with another woman on a bench. Sam had found a small hut on the playground, an abandoned shed for garden tools. Naturally, she had wanted to explore it, looking for adventure. But as soon as she had gone inside, the door had swung shut. Sam could vividly remember her panic, the fear of never escaping again. She had screamed at the top of her lungs, and after what felt like an eternity, her Nonna came to the rescue.

Probably, Sam had been trapped for not more than a minute, but the event had scarred her for life. Now, every time she had the feeling of being trapped, her claustrophobia kicked in. She knew her fear wasn't rational. She knew there was enough air in the tunnel to last for days and at one point, the priest would come searching for her. She wouldn't die down here. But claustrophobia doesn't listen to rationale. It is an irrational fear, housed deep down in one's mind. Her panic just grew. Sam started to sweat in the otherwise cold tunnel, and her heart was pounding.

Hastily, she touched every part of the exit in the hope of finding a small crack or a slight seam between the stones. Anything that she could get a hold of to pull the exit towards her. Suddenly, dust started to fall off the wall. First subtly. Then more. Then, she noticed small movements of the wall, more and more. Light shone through a crack that was forming, and the door was opening. On the other side, there was another priest waiting. „Welcome. I am Father Nicolas, and I apologize for the delay. I am never down here and couldn't find the right niche between the tombstones. Our catacombs are vast," the priest said.

„I am just very grateful to get out of this tunnel. Thank you very much for your help, Father," Sam said, relieved. She dusted herself off and shook his hand. She found herself in a similar room to where she entered—a hallway and niches with tombstones left and right. The catacombs.

The priest led her upstairs to a small room. „I am afraid I can offer only humble accommodation, but you are welcome to stay for the night. I have prepared some food for you. You are safe here. No one will find you."

Sam was glad for the offer. It was late, and she wouldn't get to Bonn tonight. The church seemed like the safest place to stay until tomorrow. She would figure out in the morning how to get to Bonn without being seen. After all the events of the day, she felt exhausted. In less than six hours, she had escaped Europol in The Hague, took the train to Brussels, ran away from the police again and went through a secret medieval passage. That was enough for one day. All she wanted to do now was rest.

„Thank you for the kind offer. I would be very grateful for a warm place to stay. How could I ever repay you for your help?" she said.

„Bless our lord, my child. Now rest. You must be exhausted," the priest said.

Sam gladly accepted. She sat on the bed and ate a few slices of bread and cheese, but before she could finish, she drifted off into a deep sleep.

STRASSHOF

DAY 2

08:45 P.M.

Arnaud was driving a rental car to Strasshof. He had decided to go back and speak to the security guard of Oberberg, Karl Herzog, again. Too many things didn't add up. Nothing in Samanta Di Vincenzo's life suggested she would have any ambition to commit an eco-terror crime. No particular passion for politics or climate change, no activism. Neither did she seem to have the capability nor the training to commit something like that. Not to forget, she vigorously denied any involvement, and Arnaud wanted to believe her. And yet all the evidence pointed to her. It was a water-tight case.

He hadn't told Gusta that he was going back to Austria. She wouldn't understand why he was spending time talking to witnesses and not focusing all his energy on getting Di Vincenzo back. But Arnaud found it the best way forward, the best way to solve this case. All of Europe was on the lookout for her, and it wouldn't make a difference if he randomly wandered the streets searching for her. His energy was of better use here. He could focus on what he did best: finding answers. And right now, the question that concerned him the most was: *are we searching for the right person?*

He was driving between the windmills again. It was dark by now, and the red warning lights on top of each windmill created an eerie look. They blinked to warn any aircraft flying to the nearby airport, and the blinking was synchronized between them, creating a carpet of red flashing dots. It looked like hundreds of red eyes watching him through the dark of the night. There was beauty in it, but the eerie feeling remained.

Arnaud pulled up at Karl Herzog's house. It felt like a long time ago that Arnaud had been there before he realized it had just been the day before. Racing against the clock stretched time. Herzog opened after the first ring of the doorbell. He was wearing sweatpants and didn't look like he had showered since the day before. Compared to last time, not much more than 24 hours ago, he looked like a broken man.

„Hello, Mr. Herzog. Thank you for receiving me at such a late hour," Arnaud said.

„Not a problem. I have nothing to do anyway." They sat in the living room, and Herzog offered a drink, which Arnaud refused.

„Nothing to do?" Arnaud asked.

„I got suspended because they deemed it too risky for me to return to work. I am not fired yet, but they will start an internal investigation into what had happened and if it was my fault. I'm expecting to lose my job over this." Karl Herzog was pale, and his voice trembled as he spoke. Dark rings beneath his red eyes made him look sick. Arnaud was wondering if he was devastated just because of the prospect of losing his job or if there was something else.

„Are you living alone here, in the house?" he asked, digging a bit.

„Yes. I used to live here with my ex-wife, but after the divorce three years ago, she moved out. Luckily, we didn't have kids; she got the dog, and I kept the house. I'm not used to being alone here, though. In recent weeks, my girlfriend spent basically every day here. But since yesterday, I cannot reach her anymore. She doesn't answer my texts, and her phone number is not reachable. I don't know what to do." When he mentioned his girlfriend, tears formed in his eyes, and he had to clean his running nose.

„How long were you together?" Arnaud asked.

„We met three weeks ago. I know, it doesn't sound like a long time, but this was different, more intense. We got to know each other in a deep, meaningful way. It didn't feel like three weeks but three years. It was true love. And now she is ignoring me!" Herzog couldn't look Arnaud in the eyes and turned his head away.

Quite the coincidence, Arnaud thought. *Better take a closer look at this woman.*

„Do you have her address?"

„No, we never went to her place. I have no idea how to find her."

„Name?"

„Martina, Martina Bauer," Herzog said.

„Can you give me a description of her?"

„She is 28, around 160cm. Silver dyed hair, cut short on the sides and medium long in the middle. Looks a bit punky, likes to wear black and smokes a lot." Herzog's voice was trembling when he described her.

„Which cigarettes?" Arnaud asked. It sounded like a random question, but he had found that cigarettes could be helpful circumstantial evidence. Smokers religiously stick with their brand. And the more obscure, the better for the case.

„Gitanes cigarettes. The ones without a filter," Herzog said.

„What about her phone? Can you give me her number?"

„Sure." Herzog let Arnaud copy the number from his phone. Arnaud saw that Herzog had called this number numerous times, just on this day. He must be desperate.

„Is there anything else that you remembered after we met last time?" Arnaud asked.

„Uhm, no, nothing. What am I going to do with my life, Inspector? Everything I had is gone. I will lose my job. My girlfriend abandoned me. Life has no meaning anymore." Herzog was close to tears.

„Look, I'm no psychiatrist." Arnaud paused, and a silent tension started to fill the room. Herzog was clearly expecting Arnaud to continue, but Arnaud had not planned to.

After some long, awkward moments, Herzog finally asked, „But?"

„But I can tell you that I have seen a lot in my career, and what you experienced is nothing compared to what others had to go through. You will be fine, trust me," Arnaud answered. *Get a grip, man*, Arnaud thought.

„Thank you for seeing me so late, and good luck. I'm sure everything will turn out fine," Arnaud said, even though he was not so sure.

He said goodbye and went to his car. In his mind, he went through the new information he had just gotten. First, the security guard, who played a vital role in the attack on the gas facility and who had screwed up, had a new girlfriend for just a few weeks. Second, he didn't know where she lived and had no way of finding her except her phone number, which she didn't pick up anymore, just one day after the attack. Very suspicious. If she was connected to all of it, the name was likely fake. And that raised the question of how to find her. He called Manfred Huber while starting to drive.

„Hello, Manfred. I need your help. Can you get me the address of someone, even if I have only a fake name?" Arnaud asked.

„Not easy. We do have a central register for everyone living in Austria, but it is not really possible to be listed there with a fake name, since you need an ID for that. I can run the name in the register, but I wouldn't get my hopes up. And if someone is using a fake name, I doubt they would register themselves there anyway. However, our energy-operating companies must all use an energy network provider with a monopoly in each state. So if the person is living in Vienna, I can ask a contact at the Viennese network provider if they have anyone listed under the name there. Send me the name, and I'll see what I can do," Huber said.

„Thanks a lot. I'm driving towards Vienna now. If you can get it in the next 30 minutes, that'd be great." Arnaud didn't have time to lose, and he didn't plan on spending the night in the city. If his new suspect lived in Vienna, he wanted to seize the opportunity and interrogate her right away.

„Relax, don't get stressed out. It is already late in the evening. I cannot promise anything. But I'll see what I can do," Huber said.

Arnaud had heard of the calm ways of doing things in Austria. It was charming when he went on skiing trips for vacation, but right now, it just annoyed him. He sent Huber a text message with the name but was not hopeful to hear back the same evening.

However, five minutes later, he received a text message with an address, which pleasantly surprised him. No Martina Bauer existed in the central register, but the utility company had someone listed under that name. This could not have gone through official channels. Network providers are not allowed to give out personal information just like that. But this did not concern Arnaud at the moment. He was glad he had a lead. He thanked Manfred Huber for the quick turnaround and drove towards the address in the city of Vienna.

VIENNA

DAY 2

09:45 P.M.

Arnaud arrived at the address of Karl Herzog's girlfriend close to ten o'clock at night. It was located in the tenth district of Vienna, a residential area, with plain concrete buildings from the 50s lining the street and no trees anywhere to be seen. A tram passed through between the car lanes in the middle of the street. On the sides were long rows of parked cars and, behind them, one restaurant after the other, their interior lid up with bright white lights. There wasn't a big variety of food offered. The restaurants switched between either Kebab or Lebanese food, with the occasional hairdresser in between. A lively area, even at night, but likely not the best part of town.

Arnaud double-parked his rental in front of another car—finding a regular parking spot seemed impossible. He wouldn't be long, anyway; the interrogation of Martina Bauer would be over quickly. The building at the address he got was a plain, gray five-story building that looked like its best days lay in the past.

He went there and noticed that the front door was locked. So he pressed every button on the intercom system to ring the residents. It was an old trick he learned when he was at the Paris police department, and they had to investigate break-ins. It was a different time back then, being young and part of a group of ambitious detectives, eager to solve crimes, hungry for success. A lot of what made him a good detective today, he learned back then. And one of the tricks he learned was pressing any button on the intercom system to get access. There was always someone who expected a delivery or a pizza and who opened the door.

Arnaud heard a cracking over the intercom. Someone answered his call. The person spoke German, so Arnaud couldn't understand, but he replied in gibberish and pretended that the intercom system didn't work. That was another trick he learned: people tend to believe it is their mistake that they could not understand someone and feel pressured to comply and open the door. Sure enough, it opened, and Arnaud got into the building.

He entered the main hallway and noticed how run-down everything was. Dust was everywhere, and the walls needed a paint job. Straight ahead, an open door led into the courtyard where the trash bins were located. Before the door, a staircase on the left led to the different floors of the building. A sign on the wall informed him that the apartment he was looking for was located on the third floor. Unfortunately, there was no elevator. *Third floor, not a problem*, Arnaud thought, *I can take the stairs*.

After climbing the first set of stairs, Arnaud looked at the sign on the wall. But instead of „first floor", as he was expecting, it said „Hochparterre". *Bizarre*, Arnaud thought. Maybe that was a special name for the first floor in German. He climbed another set of stairs and looked at the sign of the next floor. Instead of „second floor" it said „Mezzanin".

Curious, he thought, *but just one floor to go.* So he climbed another set of stairs, glad to have finally made it. But when he looked at the sign, it said „1. Stock", meaning first floor [4]. *You got to be kidding me! What is wrong with this country?* Arnaud could not believe it. He still had two floors to go—at least!—and he was already out of breath! But there was no choice but to push on.

After another floor, he looked at his fitness tracker to check his pulse: 180 beats per minute, way too much. *Moving is not healthy,* he thought. He made a short break to catch his breath before taking on the final floor. He finally arrived at the third floor, at least what they called the third floor here.

Old light bulbs barely illuminated the hallway. Like a chessboard, black and white tiles lined the floor, covered in dust. A window on the left side opened to the courtyard, allowing an icy breeze to move through the empty space. Large wooden doors on the right side of the hallway led to individual apartments. The apartment of Martina Bauer was easy to find, the fifth in a row.

Next to the door, a window protected by metal bars allowed a glimpse inside. Arnaud could not see anything. It was dark. Either she was asleep, or no one was home. Arnaud rang the bell—no reaction. He rang it again, but still nothing. He tried to listen for any movement inside, but nothing whatsoever.

---

4   Why are floors numbered differently in Vienna? The story goes that empress Maria Theresia wanted to have a good view over the city from her castle at Schönbrunn with no houses blocking the sight. So she ruled that no building was to have any floor above the fourth. So what did sly house owners do? They came up with new floors between the ground floor and the first floor so that many buildings have a „Sous parterre", „Parterre", „Hochparterre" and „Mezzanin" before the first floor.

Probably no one was home, but Arnaud didn't have time to wait until someone returned, so he decided to break in.

He looked at the window with the metal bars that he was looking in through. It opened towards the hallway. He found this unusual. Maybe it was meant to create a draft in the apartment to get air in quicker. But right now, it was a great opportunity to break in. The metal bars in front of the window prevented him from climbing in, but this was not what Arnaud had in mind. He looked left and right; he didn't need any witnesses of this. Breaking in without a warrant wasn't exactly official Europol policy.

After making sure that no one else was in the hallway, he broke the glass, reached between the bars and through the broken window, and tried to reach the door handle. If he was lucky, the door was not actually locked and could be opened from the inside. Arnaud had to stretch quite a bit but eventually reached the handle inside and pulled it down.

The door was not locked. Slowly, he opened it and looked inside. No light, no movement. Indeed, it seemed like the apartment was empty. Arnaud took out a small flashlight he used to carry around on his key chain and looked around before going in. The apartment was sparsely decorated, almost like no one lived there. He would have to sift through everything he could find, even more so since there didn't seem to be a lot. He decided to start with the living room straight ahead.

Arnaud stepped inside, noticing a red light beam in the corner of his eye. *This is weird*, he thought. It was the last thought Arnaud could form before a deafening explosion covered the apartment in smoke and fire, and everything around him went dark.

EN ROUTE
DAY 2
10:18 P.M.

Mia Bernert was about to get some sleep when she received a notification on her phone. *I knew it*, she thought. Someone had triggered the booby-trap in her apartment. Mia grinned. As much as it was bad news that they were on to her, as much it was satisfying that they paid dearly for it, and her tracks were now covered. This problem was solved. She took out the old student ID she carried with her anywhere she went. With a mixed feeling of nostalgia and pure hatred, she looked at it and thought: *Payback time. Finally.*

Mia pulled a handle to let her backrest tilt back and fell asleep with a smile as the train moved at full speed through the dark of the night.

DAY THREE

BRUSSELS
09:12 A.M.

Sam awoke as she heard murmurs in the distance. It must be her neighbors again, with their little kids. They always woke her up when they prepared them for school, way too early. She would try to ignore them and go back to sleep. But the murmur didn't go away and was met with the voices of many people in between. Did they have friends over?

Slowly, everything came back to her. Her arrest, the interrogation, how she fled from the police, the chase through Brussels. Painfully, she realized it had not been a dream, and she wasn't in her bed at home in Tallinn but on an old mattress in some church in Brussels. She glanced at her watch. It was shortly after 09:00 a.m. The voices she heard were from the morning mass held by Father Nicolas, who greeted her when she came out of the dark tunnel, fleeing from the police.

Sam was looking around the room and found a small sink with a new toothbrush and a glass. She was glad she could clean herself up a bit. But her stomach told her she needed food, too.

She dressed and walked outside the little room to find that it led through a passage to the main part of the church. It was even larger than the other one where she had sought refuge the day before, like a true cathedral. It looked catholic too, probably gothic, with additional ornaments added later during Baroque times. Thick columns lined the nave, each with a larger-than-life statue of a saint attached to it.

In front of the altar, Father Nicolas was reading a sermon in French. He was only interrupted by the occasional „Amen," which was the only part Sam understood, and which brought back childhood memories from back home in Italy. Likely, the mass had just started. Sam was pondering what to do. Certainly, she would not want to leave without thanking the priest for his help, but she also needed to keep moving not to get caught. And her growling stomach didn't help either.

Sam returned to the room to search for a piece of paper and a pen. She was in luck and found what she was looking for to leave a thank-you letter to the priest. She could not include any information that gave away where she was about to go, but she signed with her full name and address, hoping one day she would get a chance to say thank you in person. The police already knew who she was and where she lived, so disclosing this information didn't give away anything new.

Sam found the main entrance and went outside. It was a beautiful day, the bright sun reflecting on the icy floor before the church. Snow had covered the trees in the park next to it where sun rays shone through, which were moved by a light breeze. The world didn't seem so dark anymore, and it was hard to believe that just last night Sam had been running through an old dark tunnel, away from helicopters and police cars. It all felt unreal and like a bad dream now.

Sam knew that it hadn't been a dream, and she needed to keep moving. Meeting Erik in Bonn was still a good plan. Yesterday, she had told him she would be there before midnight, which obviously didn't work out. He was likely worried, but there was nothing she could do about that now. Sam just needed to get to Bonn as fast as possible and turn up at Erik's. But how to get to there? Last night, she had had to find out the hard way that the police were searching for her at railway stations, now more than ever. And she wouldn't be surprised if they found her through some cameras again. So going by train was out of the question, as was taking the plane. She could go by bus but couldn't rule out that bus stations were monitored, too. Car rental was not an option since she didn't have any ID. So the only thing left was hitchhiking.

Hitchhiking was illegal in Italy, but she had done it a few times as a teenager. It was risky, but she only had good experiences the few times she tried. Sam remembered that you needed to wait on a roadside that led in the direction you wanted to go, preferably before highway access. She went to the small park to ask someone and found a young couple. „Excuse me, to get to Bonn in Germany by car, which way do I need to go?" she asked.

„Oh, this is actually not too difficult. You just need to get to Avenue de Cortenbergh and exit at roundabout Robert Schuman. Just pass the big park over there and take Rue Belliard. Once you are on Cortenbergh, you just stay on it until you reach Germany."

Sam thanked them for their advice and was about to walk in that direction when she remembered something else. „One more thing. Do you know where I could buy paper and a pen? And perhaps some food?" She was directed to a sandwich shop and a general store across the street. Listening to her growling stomach, she decided to go to the sandwich shop first and get breakfast. She then went to the general store to buy a large, thick piece of paper and wrote „Bonn" on it, hoping it would be understandable in any language.

Well fed, she made her way across the park towards the direction of the roundabout she was directed to. It took her almost half an hour, longer than expected, but eventually, she reached the large, busy roundabout Robert Schuman. Big enough to have a small park in the middle of it.

At the main square in front of it, there was a large building with EU flags, easily a dozen. It was shaped like a distorted star and seemed to go far back. It radiated importance, the power to decide over the lives of over 400 million people. On the face of the building was a long banner with a young girl smiling into the camera and below a tag line: „Freedom. Equality. Justice. My European Union."

Yeah right, Sam thought. None of this she had experienced in the past two days. She used to be an idealist, believing in these values, but she had lost it all when they abducted and wrongly accused her. This was not the Europe she had believed in, and she did not believe in it anymore.

Sam went along the roundabout until she saw a sign pointing to a highway with „Bonn" written on it. This would be the location she would try her luck to hitch a ride. She stood there with the sign in her hand for about half an hour when a car stopped, right on the roundabout. A young couple was sitting in front, waving for her to get in. They turned out to be students from Spain on a European road trip, and they were more than happy to get some company for a few hours. Sam got along great with them, and they shared stories of their experiences living in different countries. Sam was happy to get distracted from her situation and feel normal again, at least for a few hours. Soon, she would arrive in Bonn and will stay at Erik's place. An ally, who would help her figure everything out.

BRUSSELS
DAY 3
10:00 A.M.

Lina Juska was having a smoke, trying to relax. It was a beautiful February day, and she enjoyed looking at the busy Robert Schuman roundabout below. Every time she came to the Berlaymont building, the headquarters of the European Commission, she tried to get to the terrace to enjoy the view. From up above, the scene looked unreal, like a toy city with toy cars and toy people urgently trying to get places. Watching all the hustle and bustle below brought things into perspective; it reminded her of who they were working for. In all those committees and working groups, it was easy to forget that it was the people of Europe whose lives they were trying to improve.

Last night, she had received news from Gusta that Brussels police had found the suspect and chased her through the city. But after Samanta Di Vincenzo hid inside Sablon church, she never came out again. And when the police entered, she was nowhere to be found. Unless she hid in one of the tombs, she was just not there anymore. To Lina, this incompetence was unfathomable. Losing the same person twice on the same day required a special kind of ineptitude. Now, Samanta Di

Vincenzo could be anywhere out there, even at the busy Robert Schuman roundabout below.

Lina had been summoned by the Vice-President of the European Commission to the HQ. The VP wanted an update on the situation of the European gas supply, and Lina had not a lot of good news to share with her. Yes, the pipes were open again, and Italy slowly got back to something resembling normality, but the question of the vulnerability of the European gas supply remained. Especially in the face of the remaining threat of further attacks on the infrastructure. They just had a little over 24 hours left before the manifesto deadline passed, and more attacks could be expected. The SGS special committee was working around the clock to come up with a range of initiatives, but Lina doubted that any of them would do any good in the next 24 hours.

That reminded Lina that she had gotten lost in her thoughts and had lost track of time. She looked at her watch. She was supposed to meet the Vice-President now. Lina put out her cigarette and went back inside. The Vice-President's secretary was already waiting for her, ushering her in as soon as she arrived.

„Commissioner Juska, good to see you. I trust you are well?" the VP said.

„Very good, Madam Vice-President. And you?"

„As well. So, tell me, where are we with the SGS?"

„We are working on three different pillars at the moment: prevention, mitigation, and resilience. Europol, in collaboration with local police forces, is doubling efforts to apprehend the suspect and find potential collaborators who might work with her. So far, no connection to other persons could be found, but we have to be sure that if we stop Samanta Di Vincenzo, the threat of further attacks will be averted. Further, security is being increased at all major gas facilities across Europe to avert any further attacks," Lina said.

„Good, good. We need to stop the terrorist as soon as possible. But how do we make sure our citizens are not freezing if we can't?"

„This is why we are working on resiliency as well. Plans are being put in place as we speak to limit the disruption to the energy supply in case of further attacks. This includes filling gas reservoirs as much as possible. It's easier said than done since filling them usually occurs during summer when consumption is low. Now in winter, almost all gas coming in is immediately used by households to heat. 40% of gas consumption in Europe is due to the residential sector, which generated especially high demand in winter."

„Yes, yes, spare me the details," the VP said.

„With all due respect, Madam Vice-President, but these details matter. They can make the difference between making it through the winter or freezing in the cold."

„Thank you for the lecture, Commissioner. Sometimes I think politics is like being back in high school. And you are the class nerd. Don't be one of the nerds, Commissioner. They are never the heroes of the story."

This was completely out of line. Technically, the VP was Lina's superior, but that did not give her the right to insult Lina this way. But part of politics was also to choose the battles to fight, and this was not one of them. So she kept her mouth shut.

„Sounds like Moulin is right. We need more pipelines," the VP continued. Now, this was a battle Lina would be willing to fight.

„With all due respect, madam, no. To avoid a similar situation in the future, we are putting a strategy in place to make our infrastructure less vulnerable. We must introduce minimum standards on how much gas can be stored by member states. If Italy hadn't speculated with gas prices and had filled up their reservoirs, the attack's impact would have been minimal. We do not need more gas to improve our resilience. We need to protect our infrastructure and make sure we store enough for emergencies. I respectfully ask you not to believe Moulin when he says we need new pipelines," Lina explained.

„Well, let's see. The sooner we stop our terrorist and prevent any potential new attacks, the better." The lack of agreement with Lina's explanation came as a shock to her. Now even the Vice-President started to listen to Moulin. If he was able to convince enough people and new pipelines were built, there would be less budget for renewable energy. It would destroy Lina's legacy, and she was determined to prevent that.

„Thank you, Commissioner. Please keep me up to date on any progress. You are dismissed."

Outside the office, the secretary was already waiting with the participants of the next meeting. Lina briskly walked away, fuming. How dare the VP insult her on such a personal level? How dare she ignore facts and listen to Moulin? If it wasn't so early in the day, Lina would have gotten a drink. She certainly needed one. But there was enough to be done. She needed to get back to her office and continue pushing SGS policies. They were all on a clock.

After this conversation, she was more determined than ever to close this whole chapter as soon as possible and to prove Moulin and the VP and anybody else who believed in the old ways of doing things wrong. She would call Gusta right after and ask for an update on the case. She needed a win, and she needed it fast.

VIENNA
DAY 3
10:11 A.M.

It was a sunny summer day in The Hague. The birds were chirping, and there was a light breeze, which brought much-needed relief from the hot air and made the leaves of the trees dance against the sun shining through. Zoé was playing with her friends on the kids' playground, not far away, laughing and having a good time. He sat on the bench, holding hands with his wife as they watched their child having a good time. *This is a perfect life*, he thought.

Moved, Arnaud turned his head to give his wife a kiss on her cheek when he opened his eyes and looked into the worn, scarred face of Manfred Huber. Startled, Arnaud winced as he realized he had been dreaming. Slowly, everything returned to him: the case, the flat, the light beam he noticed as he entered. Nothing after.

Manfred Huber removed his hand and began to explain: „When I came in today, I read in the daily report of the night shift that an explosion happened at the address I had given you. I called the hospital and came here. How are you feeling?"

„I feel like I have slept for the first time in years," Arnaud had to admit.

„Good. And you need more rest. There was a gas explosion in the flat that you went to check out. You did not suffer from any internal injuries but sustained many burns all over your body. You were lucky it did not kill you and that the door of a cupboard shielded off the main blast. What the hell were you thinking? You should have called for backup and not break in into a flat of a suspect alone."

„I guess I wasn't thinking," Arnaud answered.

„Look, I get that. But it was stupid in any case. Anyway, I wanted to let you know I was at the crime scene just before. Let me tell you, there was nothing of substance there, a fried computer screen, a keyboard and mouse, and some burned posters on the wall. Looks like the flat was cleaned before the explosion. Someone was expecting you," Huber said.

„Or someone got cold feet and left just in case."

„At least I think we can rule out that this was an accident. Someone booby-trapped the apartment on purpose, and you were unlucky enough to trigger it," Huber said.

„It looks like Karl Herzog's girlfriend is a hot lead. We need to find her." Arnaud tried to muster his strength and lifted his back to a more upright position.

„Easier said than done. We do not have her real name and no phone to track. The number we got from Karl Herzog was anonymous and is not reachable. Probably in a phone in some dumpster. How do you want to find her with no leads to go on?"

„No idea."

„In any case, you need to stay here for now. The doctors want to keep you for at least a week."

„What? That's out of the question. We have just a day left to solve this case. No way I will stay here."

„Well, the doctors will disagree. You are full of painkillers now. You might not feel it, but your body is not okay. Don't worry, we will do all we can to find her. Just rest," Manfred Huber said, and left Arnaud alone in the room.

No way Arnaud would just sit there and wait while the terrorist who did this to him ran around freely. Manfred Huber and his team would never find her. Arnaud checked his phone lying on the cupboard next to his bed. It had burn marks and a broken screen, but it seemed to work. Five missed calls and a message from Gusta asking for an update. A message from Henrick, asking for an urgent call. Apparently, no one back home knew what had happened, and Arnaud planned to keep it that way.

He looked around. He was alone in the room, no nurse to be seen. An intravenous line was attached to his arm with a transparent bag, dripping liquid into his bloodstream. *Probably pain killers.* A small clip was attached to his index finger, connected to a screen showing oxygen levels and his pulse. Arnaud knew that as soon as this stopped measuring something, the nursing station would receive an alarm. It was like he was on a leash. To get away, he had to be careful and quick.

On a chair next to the bed, his clothes were neatly folded, waiting for him. Arnaud removed the intravenous line and used a piece of cloth he found on a small trolley to stop the bleeding from the wound left behind. He slowly got up, careful not to remove the clip from his finger. He had to stretch quite a bit to reach his clothes and not lose the clip attached with too short of a cable to the machine.

Dressing his lower body was not a problem. How he would get his shirt on was another question. He decided to keep the clip on under his shirt, and when the time came, quickly remove the clip and the cable through the shirt. He was ready to go with one final thing to do. He hid the pillows under the blanket and prepared it so that, at first sight, it looked like someone was sleeping. Arnaud felt like a child who thought they could trick the parents with some pillows under the blanket. But it was the best he could think of. It wouldn't help a lot but might buy him a few seconds of time to get away.

Arnaud took a deep breath, removed the clip from his finger, pulled the cable through his shirt, and briskly moved towards the door. The station was busy this morning, with patients and their relatives walking around, talking. Arnaud closed the door behind him and walked towards the station's exit as naturally as he could.

It was about fifteen meters away, but it felt like an eternity to get there. Ten meters. Five meters. He heard a commotion behind him, and as he looked back, he saw nurses rushing towards his room. That's it. He had to move now. Arnaud made two long strides to reach the door and pushed the button next to it. The door opened, and he rushed outside in the hallway.

Several elevators were waiting. He pushed the buttons, but nothing happened, at least not fast enough. Other patients were waiting for the elevator and gave him disturbed looks. Did he look so bad? Arnaud took the stairs, taking two steps at once. With every step, his ribs felt like someone was poking them with a spear. Even the pain killers couldn't hide the fact that he had been seriously hurt. He had to ignore it for now but made a mental note to get painkillers somewhere as soon as he was out of there.

Arnaud reached the ground floor and opened a door that took him to the hospital's main entrance. Some patients were standing around, and a porter in a glass box was just picking up the phone. Arnaud used the moment when he was busy and walked outside the building. Behind him, he heard some hectic commotion, the porter had been informed of a runaway. Arnaud did not run but briskly walked outside into the sunlight and around the corner. He was free. This must be how Samanta Di Vincenzo felt when she escaped Europol. Arnaud didn't approve of it, but he could appreciate now how liberating it felt.

After walking for a few hundred meters, he dared to take a break and took out his phone to check where he was. The app on his phone informed him that he had been at the *Unfallkrankenhaus Meidling* hospital, which was not even a 20-minute walk from the explosion site where he had left the rental car. He felt for the car keys in his pocket and was relieved to find that they were still there.

Taking the car seemed like a good idea and the fastest way to get to the airport, so he went in the direction of Martina Bauer's apartment. It took him longer than 20 minutes, and he had to make frequent breaks because the pain became unbearable, but, eventually, he reached the address of the flat he had visited just twelve hours ago.

His car was nowhere to be seen. Then it dawned on him that he had double-parked because no parking spot was available. He had expected to be leaving after a few minutes, but now, after twelve hours, his car had been towed. *Damn.* The car rental company would make him pay. *Not again.* The same had happened to him in Amsterdam.

Since he was already here, Arnaud decided to look at the flat where the explosion happened. So he started, once again, to climb the five—five!—floors without any elevator. But this time with pain every step of the way.

VIENNA
DAY 3
10:45 A.M.

Arnaud arrived at the third floor. The hallway looked worse than last time if that was even possible. It had been dusty before, but now everything was covered in a thick, light-gray powder, and the previously white walls were turned black by soot. The door was gone. Just pieces of it were dangling from the hinges. Instead of the door, the entrance was blocked by an enormous amount of red and white tape with something written on it, resembling the word „police". Arnaud ignored it and pulled the tape down to enter the apartment.

Inside, all the walls were black. On the right side of the entrance was the kitchen, the oven door open. This was how the explosion happened. She just let the gas vent, which was ignited by the sensor Arnaud triggered by stepping inside the apartment. The kitchen was badly damaged, cup boards ripped apart, broken glass and dishes were everywhere. He did not expect to find anything of interest there. He moved to the main room, which seemed to serve as a living room and bedroom.

Here, the blast did not do as much damage, but everything was more or less burned. What was left of the windows to the street had black burn marks on them, but most of the glass was gone, letting in cold air from the outside. There had never been much there in the first place, just the necessities. A mattress on the floor with black burn marks on it, an ashtray, and an empty pack of cigarettes next to it. Arnaud picked it up and read the label: „Gitanes". *Just like Herzog said*, he thought. Nothing else noteworthy. All of it was damp from the water the firefighters used to put out the fires that surely ensued after the explosion.

There were burned posters on the wall of an NGO. It fit the picture of an eco-terrorist. It didn't prove anything, but it fit. There were no books or other literature anywhere but a car magazine, which didn't fit the picture. Or maybe it did. She could have been researching Karl Herzog's interests to get closer to him, and he was a car nut for sure. To the right of the mattress, Arnaud found a desk with a computer screen—the workplace. This was what Huber had been talking about, but no corresponding computer existed. *She must have taken it with her,* Arnaud thought.

On the wall above the desk, a corkboard had some papers attached to it. Mostly vouchers and other promotional material that was mostly burned. Among the rest, Arnaud noticed a tag of a conference called H4ckThePlanet, which apparently took place two years prior in Barcelona. It was made of hard plastic, which made it resistant to fire, at least to a degree. No name on it, just numbers:

44 65 73 74 72 75 63 74 69 6F 6E 4B 69 74 74 65 6E

Arnaud put the tag into his pocket as his phone rang. It was Henrick.

„Arnaud, where are you? Everyone is trying to reach you!"

„By everyone, you mean Gusta?"

„Yes."

„Don't worry, I'll talk to her when I talk to her."

„Yeah, you do that. Anyway, something else, I have a hot lead for you. The Estonian police finished their analysis of Samanta Di Vincenzo's PC. That she was a gamer was a great tip. There was no additional evidence, but they did manage to find the names of her gamer friends. One of them sticks out since she mostly hangs out with him. Gamer name FeralMayhem. Weird freaks these gamers, am I right? Now, his real name was not in the system, but we checked with the manufacturer of the game, and they gave us his data: Erik zur Brügge, a German citizen."

„This is great. Thank you, Henrick." Arnaud was doubtful that Samanta Di Vincenzo was connected to the explosion, or even the whole case. But she might be able to explain how everything fit together, and it was not unreasonable to think that she would reach out to her online friend. So finding a connection to this zur Brügge was a good lead albeit no breakthrough.

„You don't seem excited. Everything all right? You sound... exhausted," Henrick said.

„Yes, all good. I'm just not sure about Di Vincenzo anymore. I'll explain more when I see you."

„So what about this zur Brügge guy? Do you want to give him a call? I already researched his phone number."

„Do you have his address too? Maybe I want to pay him a personal visit right away."

„Yes, he is living in Bonn, still in his parent's house where he grew up. I'll send the address over now," Henrick said.

„Thanks, Henrick, it's very much appreciated. And thanks for letting me know right away."

„Anything for you, my friend. See you later!"

Arnaud hung up. He finished his inspection of the apartment but couldn't find anything noteworthy. Nothing else on the walls and no computer to be seen, let alone any ID. The Austrian police probably did their job and took anything relevant. And there would be crime scene photos in case he ever wanted to check back.

Arnaud decided to leave the apartment and make his way down the stairs. Going down turned out to be even more painful than up. Who would have thought?

Arnaud had to make frequent breaks, so it took him a while to finally reach the ground level again. He went outside. Since his car was gone, he called a taxi and directed the driver to go straight to the airport. He wanted to check out this Erik zur Brügge in person and get on the first plane to Bonn. It was the only lead he had.

BONN
DAY 3
02:10 P.M.

„No way!" Erik could not believe Sam's story of how she was first captured by the police, abducted across the continent, and interrogated by Europol. No, actually, this was the most believable part of her story. Escaping from the police, fleeing across country borders, hiding in a church, and escaping through a secret medieval tunnel was completely wild. It sounded like a story out of a computer game, and not a very realistic one.

Sam and Erik were sitting on the couch in Erik's living room—his parents' living room, to be exact. Erik was living in the place he grew up in, occupying the upper floor of a detached house close to the Rhine river in central Bonn. It was a quiet spot to live. Like most of Bonn, this area was mainly frequented by nearby university students riding on their bikes through the city. Being close to the river was great growing up and served as a peaceful retirement location for Erik's parents. Now, Erik enjoyed being able to get on his bike and ride along the river to clear his mind.

Sam and Erik were eating pizza, which they had ordered just after Sam arrived, not even half an hour ago, and she brought him up to speed on everything that had happened.

„Yes way. Now that I talk about it out loud, it sounds unreal to me too. But it actually happened, just yesterday. It's one of those experiences where afterwards you are not sure if your mind made it all up, like a weird nightmare, or if your memories are actual reality."

„Wow. When all this is over, it will be a cool story to tell your friends. Well, if it ends well..."

„Of course it will end well! I am innocent, and innocent people should not go to prison under the rule of law."

„Yeah, right, rule of law," Erik said.

„Call me naive, but I still refuse to believe that our system is broken. Though first doubts are creeping in," Sam said.

„So you think you were set up?"

„That's the only reasonable explanation I can think of."

„Why would anyone do that? And who?"

„I have no idea. That's what I have been trying to figure out, but I cannot think of anyone who would want to harm me."

„We need to answer this question. The only way you will ever be free again is if we can prove your innocence. Let's start at the beginning: what do you know about the attack?" Erik took another bite from his slice of pizza.

„Nothing more than what was on the news. A terrorist attack on a gas facility caused a state of emergency in Italy. There was a manifesto with an ultimatum that more attacks would happen. So it looks like a well-planned operation, executed by professionals."

„And why do the police think it was you?"

„In the metadata of the manifesto document, they found my name."

„Okay, that can easily be faked and doesn't mean anything. Any other evidence?"

„I am seen on a video surveillance video as I enter the security room while the attack happened. I have seen the video myself, it is real, but I cannot remember being there, and I am pretty sure I spent my evening in a bar in Tallinn and not in Austria committing eco-terrorism."

„Ouch, that will be hard. Video can be manipulated, but it requires a lot of time, and the police probably have copies of the original recording of the video surveillance system. This is not like some random video clip on social media. Apart from manipulation, any other idea how this could happen?"

„Could someone create a mask of myself and wear it?"

„Possible, but I imagine that's hard to pull off well enough to fool the police. The mask would have to be extremely natural looking."

„I could have been drugged at the bar. But what kind of drug makes you do things you have never thought of doing and then you have no recollection of it at all?"

„I have never heard of a drug that could do that. Roofies can break your will, but you wouldn't be in any state to break into a critical infrastructure facility. Sounds unlikely and hard to prove. Even if we could test your blood somehow, my guess is any trace of a drug would be gone after two days."

„I guess so. And as I already have told the police, it is unlikely that anyone at the bar recognized me. I don't have an alibi, and we also have no way of knowing how long I was at that bar." Sam replayed the night in her mind but could not remember any situation that would indicate that she had been drugged. Her memory did have gaps but not enough to account for flying across Europe.

„Wait, you have a smartwatch, right?" Erik said.

„Yes, I do. Why?"

„Some smartwatches track your location with GPS. We could use that to figure out where you have been!"

„No, I already thought of that. My watch does not have a SIM card. To get online, it needs a Wi-Fi connection. Otherwise I would have thrown it away long ago so the police cannot track me."

„Okay, fair enough, but most of these watches track the location even if they are not online and store it locally on the device. Manufacturers use this data to improve their artificial intelligence applications by training them on real-world data. There have been a lot of debates if this is an illegal invasion of privacy, but nothing has changed. Now it could help us, we should be able to access this file."

Erik rushed to get the equipment they needed to connect to the smartwatch: a laptop connected to a large screen and a specialized cable to connect the watch. It took him some time to get everything connected and download the right software.

„Okay, I mounted the watch as an external storage device and have access to all local files." Erik had access to the internal files of the smartwatch now. This was not meant to be used by regular users but was a way for software developers to fix things. Erik didn't have to break any password to get in, but he did have to know what he was doing.

„Here is a text file with the GPS coordinates, one location per minute, so we have a lot of data in front of us. To have fewer locations to check, we will pick one location every half an hour on the night of the attack and search for it in a mapping application. That should give us a good idea of where you have been." Erik took one GPS location after another and copied it into the mapping application, adding each location as an additional stop on a longer trip, slowly reconstructing Sam's movements on the night in question. After he was done copying about fifteen different locations, Sam and Erik looked at the result. It was a map of Tallinn that showed Sam's movement with blue lines connecting the different locations.

"Well, we can rule out the drugging theory," Erik said. On the screen, they saw Sam had never left the city. She had gone from her home to Valli bar, spent one and a half hours there, and then went home again. She did not leave her home until the next morning.

"The police won't take this as an alibi in the face of all the other evidence. After all, any person could have worn your watch. But I think, between us, we can be certain that you didn't leave the city," Erik said.

"We have ruled out one theory, but this doesn't get us any further in finding out what happened."

"At least we know now for certain that I am getting framed. But by who?" Sam asked.

"Let's concentrate on the motive first. That might take us closer to a person. What did the manifesto say?" Erik said.

"The manifesto is freely available on the web, we can just download it. Essentially, they want the European Union to switch to renewable energy."

"Not a bad idea per se but resorting to violence for this is extreme. So the motive seems to be climate change. Where was this manifesto posted? Maybe we can trace it?"

„Give me your laptop. Let's see." Sam opened a browser on the computer, searching for the manifesto posted the day before. Many copies were already available on various forums and social media channels, and she had to search for a few minutes before finding the original one. Eventually, she found it in a post on BirdSong, a social media forum site that allowed users to post on different kinds of topics. The post just stated „Manifesto of the citizens of Europe" with a download link. The download contained the PDF, which, sure enough, had Sam's name as the author in it. But anyone could have written her name there. It was located on an anonymous download site and gave no hints as to who uploaded it there. The user who posted the manifesto was new and had not posted anything before. Clearly, it was created just for this purpose. Both Sam and Erik sat in silence for some minutes, thinking. It felt like they had hit a dead-end and were no closer to finding the person who did this to her.

This was when the doorbell rang. „I'll get it," Sam said. She got another slice of pizza, took a bite, and went to the front door. She opened it. With her slice of pizza in hand and her mouth open, Sam was staring at the face of Arnaud Navarro.

„Hello, Samanta."

BONN

DAY 3

03:05 P.M.

Sam felt her head turn red, neck first, ears second, and then all the rest. She considered running but knew it would be hopeless. If they wanted to catch her, they would have the house surrounded before ringing the bell. They would arrest her and probably Erik too for conspiring with her. She was just standing there, mouth open, head red, unable to move. With Sam not doing anything, Arnaud took the opportunity to speak first.

„Samanta, let me set one thing straight from the beginning. I know you didn't do it. I cannot prove it yet, but you might be able to help me solve this case."

„What?" Sam couldn't believe what she was hearing.

„I am here because I need your help, Samanta. I will explain everything. Can I come in? It's cold outside."

Sam opened the door and let Arnaud in. She introduced Arnaud to Erik, who was as stunned as she was. They offered Arnaud a spot on the couch and a glass of water to drink. Both of them were staring at Arnaud, still shocked that the enemy was in their house. And what's more, he claimed that he was not the enemy anymore. Arnaud explained.

„Listen, except for the video and the manifesto, no evidence connects you to this crime. I know you had nothing to do with this, but to prove it, we need to work together. My superiors do not know I am here, and they are still searching for you in Brussels. They won't start searching for you here for another day or so, so this buys us some time."

Sam was suspicious. Could this be a trap to collect more evidence against her? The last time she saw this inspector, he was interrogating her in a tiny room in The Hague after abducting her. Why the sudden change of heart?

"Why don't you think it was me? How do I know this is not a trick? Prove to me that you are not lying."

Arnaud lifted his shirt to reveal his bruised upper body, filled with stitches and tape. "I just survived a bomb attack in a flat in Vienna. This flat was registered to a dummy name of a person that does not fit your description at all. So either you two are working together, or this girl is trying to frame you somehow. I had a bad feeling about this case from the beginning. Everything looked too obvious, too easy. And in my experience, if evidence looks too good to be true, it usually isn't. So I'm following my gut here and choose to think you are not responsible for the crime. But you might be connected somehow without you realizing," Arnaud said.

He did seem sincere, and what he said made sense. She would stay alert but decided to give him a chance for now.

"Alright, first, please call me Sam. Second, how can we even help? We just spent the last hour trying to find a clue as to who could have done this, but found nothing," Sam said.

"It is obvious someone is trying to pin this on you. You are the scapegoat of this terrorist. We need to find out why." Arnaud grabbed a large piece of pizza and took a bite without asking.

„No idea. I have no enemies and certainly do not know anyone capable of this. We were trying to trace where the manifesto came from, but got nowhere," Sam said.

„At the flat I was investigating in Vienna, I found this conference badge. Do you know this conference?" Arnaud showed the badge he took from the crime scene in Vienna.

„Uhm, H4ckThePlanet, never heard of it. I'm more into software dev than hacking," Sam said.

„What do those numbers mean?" Arnaud asked, pointing to the row of numbers:

44 65 73 74 72 75 63 74 69 6F 6E 4B 69 74 74 65 6E

„Those are Hex numbers," Erik interjected.

„Hex what?" Arnaud asked.

„Okay, I'll try to explain. In mathematics and programming, numbers can be encoded in different numeral systems. The most common way is the decimal system, also called base-10, which represents all numbers in sets of ten. For example, we count from zero to nine in single digits. Starting from ten, we need another digit to represent the number ten. It is the most human-friendly way of representing numbers and the way we count in our everyday lives. Some speculate that the origins of this system go back to the fact that we have five fingers on each of our hands, so ten in total.

But you can also represent numbers in other ways that are more efficient in some cases, such as binary. Binary uses base-2 because it only uses ones and zeros. For example, the number one is represented as 0001, the number two as 0010, the number three as 0011, and so on. Besides base-10, binary is probably the most well-known way of encoding because it is used as the basis for all computer operations. But there are many other types, such as Hexadecimal, which encodes with base-16, instead of base-10 or base-2. And these are obviously numbers or letters encoded in the Hexadecimal system," Erik explained.

„I literally stopped following after the word computer. Can you decode it?"

„Of course. We could do it the fun way and do it manually with pen and paper or do it the fast, boring way by typing it into numerous websites that transcode between different formats."

„Let's do the boring way," Arnaud said.

Erik opened another browser window on his laptop and searched for a website that could convert between Hex and decimals or text. He typed the numbers into the text field of the website. Anxiously, all three of them stared at the screen as Erik hit „convert". In the results field, they saw the converted text appear:

DestructionKitten

Disappointed, Arnaud said: „What is that supposed to mean?"

„Looks to me like a username or alias. Given the sensitive type of the conference, they likely didn't use real names but their hacker names. And for a certain nerd-factor, they encoded their names using Hex. Kinda defeats the purpose of names, though, if you cannot read them. Still cool," Sam said.

This was when Arnaud's phone rang. He picked it up and listened. After a while, he said: „Thanks. On it."

„What is it?" Sam wanted to know.

„There has been another attack. I must go to Croatia right away."

„Okay. Meanwhile, we will search for this DestructionKitten and dig up what we can find."

They exchanged phone numbers and email addresses and agreed to connect later as Arnaud got up to go straight to the airport.

VRATA ISLAND
DAY 3
10:05 P.M.

Vrata Airport was a small airport with one landing strip and a single-story building that served as check-in, duty-free, and baggage pick-up spot all in one. In summer, planes full of tourists would land here, who vacationed all around the island of Vrata or on Croatia's mainland, which was just a short trip over a bridge away. But now, on a cold February night, the airport looked abandoned. A single security guard was leaning against the wall, bored, smoking a cigarette.

The plane had been almost empty, with just ten other passengers besides Arnaud. He was surprised there was a flight at all during this time of year and felt lucky he managed to get one from Bonn. Then again, Vrata was not just home to numerous hotels and beaches but also to one of the few liquefied natural gas, or LNG, terminals in Europe and was the largest employer in the area. It was opened a few years back as part of an initiative to diversify Europe's gas supply. So far, only a few LNG terminals had been built because of the high cost associated with LNG.

With nothing else to do, Arnaud had read an article about this technology in the flight magazine and now better understood what LNG was. Essentially, if gas could not be transported via pipelines, for example, because the sources are too far away or overseas, it needed to be transported on ships. But storing gas took up a lot of space and was not safe due to the high pressure required for transport. So for a long time, it was impossible to utilize gas that was extracted too far away from the consumer. You needed pipelines to transport it. Liquefied gas had changed all that. By cooling down natural gas, it became liquid and did not need to be stored under pressure anymore. This made it safe for transport and furthermore reduced its volume by an incredible factor of 600. The process revolutionized the gas market as it brought more stability and predictability. But it was expensive. Liquefaction, transportation, and regasification, the process of turning the liquid into gas again, required time and energy.

The Vrata LNG terminal served as a landing spot for ships carrying liquefied gas and featured facilities, which regasified it to feed it into Europe's gas pipeline network. It supplied mainly the Croatian market but carried significance for Italy, Slovenia, and Hungary, to which a pipeline was built from Croatia just for this purpose. Initially, the pipeline was supposed to be extended from Hungary to Austria and the rest of central Europe, but Hungary had blocked the effort on political grounds.

And now there had been an attack. At the moment, the terminal was significantly less important than the Oberberg gas distribution facility, but it had greater significance for the future of Europe's gas market as Europe tried to diversify its suppliers.

Arnaud called a taxi to take him to the LNG terminal. They drove through the small town of Šije, which lay between the airport and the terminal. It was a typical Adriatic town, with small streets and stone houses with orange-red roofs. *It must look beautiful in summer*, Arnaud thought, as he imagined bushes with violet blossoms lining the busy streets, between tourists and sellers offering their wares. Maybe some kids would be playing with dogs in the middle of it all. Of course, now, late at night in winter, all the streets were empty. Still, it was easy to see the beauty of this town.

From there, they drove along an empty road, sporadic bushes left and right, and after five minutes arrived at a parking space where they stopped. The operations manager Tomislav Matić was already waiting in front of a small building, which served as a reception. Arnaud had called him before taking the plane from Bonn. He was a short man with short, dark-black hair. He looked matter-of-fact, like he had been doing this job for a long time.

„Hello, I'm Tomislav. Good to meet you."

„I'm Arnaud. Thank you for taking the time to meet with me at this hour. I'm sure you heard on the news what happened in Oberberg and that we are under immense pressure here. We haven't expected another attack before the deadline of the manifesto. Maybe the terrorist wants to drive the point home. Or maybe this is completely unrelated, though that seems unlikely. But that's why I am here, to establish what happened."

„Maybe. It is a catastrophe for us for sure," Tomislav said.

„I understand. We need to get to the bottom of this as quickly as possible. Let's take a look right away at what we are dealing with."

„Certainly, come along. We will take my car and drive there now."

Arnaud was glad to see that he didn't have to go through the same extensive security check and safety video he had to endure in Oberberg. Tomislav guided Arnaud to his car, and they drove through the wide-spread facility, which was connected by a network of roads. During the drive, Tomislav provided some background.

„Our LNG terminal uses a so-called FSRU, or floating storage and regasification unit, which is the modern way to build LNG terminals. Instead of building a regasification facility on land, we re-use a ship that was used for LNG transport and permanently dock it at our terminal. We re-purposed it to store LNG and regasify it again. Using such a floating facility makes us more flexible to extend in the future, and to be quite frank, it is much cheaper than building one at land."

They approached the coast, and Arnaud could see the large ship, permanently attached to the dock with various thick steel ropes bound to concrete blocks. When they approached the ship, they made a right turn and took the bridge that connected the ship to the land.

„When we receive an LNG shipment, the arriving ship docks at our FSRU, and the liquefied gas is unloaded and stored directly onboard. In a separate process, it is being regasified and pumped into the pipeline over here." Tomislav pointed at a pipeline to the left that went along the road they were just taking to drive onboard the ship. „Right now, no ship is docked, but the regasification process is running using the liquefied gas in our storage tanks. Or the process would be running if it hadn't been disrupted."

„I don't see any cameras anywhere?" Arnaud had noticed the lack of security before when they arrived with the taxi at the parking spot.

„Yes, that's correct. The terminal was finished not long ago, and towards the end of the project, there were unforeseen budgetary issues involving a corruption scandal, so some investments couldn't be made, including the security system, which is usually one of the last systems to be installed. We are trying to get more funds to eventually procure the security system, but for now, we have to rely on guards for our security. Frankly, we didn't think that this terminal could even be a target since it isn't running at full capacity yet. But that didn't stop the terrorist," Tomislav explained.

He parked the car on a platform attached to the ship and they got out. Tomislav directed Arnaud to stairs at the side of the ship that led to the main deck. Up until here, all surroundings were dark but onboard the ship Arnaud could hardly tell if it was day or night. Floodlights all around covered the deck in bright white light so that Arnaud saw multiple shadows of himself around him, one for each floodlight. They looked like ghosts of various degrees of intensity, following him as he went across the main deck.

They went to a small building not far from where they boarded the ship. Arnaud noticed that the pipeline they saw on the bridge led there and vanished in the floor shortly before the building.

„After we regasify the liquefied gas we pump it into the pipeline. But gas does not move by itself..."

„...which is why you need to compress it," Arnaud interjected.

„I'm impressed, you did your research!" Tomislav said.

„No, this just sounds all too familiar. Let me guess, the terrorist attacked the compressor station?"

„Yes, that's correct."

„By pouring acid over the electronics?"

„Exactly! This has happened before?"

„The attack on Oberberg was identical." There was no doubt anymore that they were dealing with the same terrorist. None of these details were released to the public so it was highly unlikely that they were dealing with a copycat.

„But you do not have any video recordings of the incident because the cameras were never installed?" Arnaud asked.

„No."

„Any witnesses then?"

„No one. We noticed it for the first time when the next compressor station reported that gas had stopped flowing. We only have a skeleton security crew, and they didn't see anything," Tomislav said.

„That's unfortunate. We will send the broken equipment to the lab to get any residual acid analyzed, but I am sure it will turn out the same as in Oberberg."

„Yes, the local police already picked it up," Tomislav said. „Oh wait, I almost forgot. After the police left, we found this close by." Tomislav handed Arnaud what looked like a student ID. An Italian student ID with the photo and name of Samanta Di Vincenzo. *So they want to pin this attack on Sam, too.*

Of course, the terrorist couldn't have known that Sam was with Arnaud at the time of the attack, providing her with the perfect alibi. This was their mistake. Maybe leaving the ID was not even part of the plan, not plan A at least. Maybe they wanted to follow the same modus operandi as in Oberberg and when they came here, they were surprised that there was no video system. Maybe they had to come up with a plan B fast. *Sam might be able to provide more background on the student ID*, Arnaud thought.

Arnaud made some photos of the crime scene and thanked Tomislav for all his efforts. There was nothing else to see here, he got what he came for. Tomislav drove him back to the entrance, where Arnaud took a taxi back to Šije. On the way back to town, Arnaud called Gusta to give her an update. There was not much to share, especially since he left out the student ID. It would further implicate Samanta Di Vincenzo, who was just the scapegoat. He also left out the explosion in Vienna and his little interlude at the hospital. No need for her to know that he was badly hurt after illegally entering a suspect's apartment. And that he continued to investigate afterwards. So, as usual, Gusta was not happy with his progress. Next up was a call to Henrick.

„Hoi," Henrick answered.

„Salut, this is Arnaud. I just had a look at the crime scene on Vrata. Did you get any new information from the local authorities? Any kind of evidence who might have done it?"

„No, I asked for video material, but they didn't have any. They did give me a general update but not much news. The chem lab is not done with their analysis yet. But I just got off the phone with them, and preliminary results do indicate that the substance used to fry the compressor on Vrata was the same as in Oberberg. So it is safe to assume that we are dealing with Samanta Di Vincenzo here, too."

„If she is responsible for Oberberg."

„I don't see how it couldn't have been her. All evidence points in her direction."

„I have my doubts. It all looks too easy, too clean. And she didn't strike me as the person who could do it."

„Uhm, interesting thought. Your gut feeling is usually right, but I just don't see how it fits together with our evidence. Anyway, I'll let you know once we have more info on the Vrata attack."

„Thanks Henrick, see you later!"

„Zie je later."

At this hour, it was too late for any plane to take off from Vrata Airport, so Arnaud decided to stay in Šije overnight and head to The Hague the next day. He was lucky to find a pension that was still open, a small house that looked like it once served as a spacious home to a family but was converted into a hotel once tourism took over the town. The owner, an old woman, had a room for him and brought him to the first floor. His room had a view over the Adriatic Sea—no doubt the hotel's best accommodation. Arnaud was offered a glass of white wine, which he gladly took. It was Malvasia, typical for the neighboring Istria region, and a particularly fine wine. He sat on his small balcony and marveled at the calm sea that reflected the receding moon while pondering over the events of the day.

He had started the day in a hospital bed in Vienna and was ending it on an island in Croatia while having been in Germany in between. After all this, one thing was clear: Samanta Di Vincenzo was not the perpetrator. On the contrary, she tried to solve this case as much as Arnaud did. Together with Erik, they would be a good team.

And then there was this new terror attack, which sparked more questions rather than providing answers. Why now? The deadline was not over yet. They had another full day. Was it to drive the point home? Or did something go wrong? Maybe without realizing, Arnaud closed in on the terrorist, and they made the rash decision to change the plan? And what did the student ID of Sam mean? Whoever left it at the LNG terminal must have met Sam at one point or had to have been close to her somehow.

Sam knew the terrorist; she just didn't realize it yet. The perpetrator was lurking in the dark of Sam's past. They needed to dig around to bring light to her memories and connect the dots. Maybe the ID will help her remember. Tomorrow morning, Arnaud would see how he could send Sam a copy of it. For now, Arnaud would get a good night's sleep to heal his wounds. The wine would certainly help.

PRIVATE GROUP CHAT
DAY 3
22:45 P.M.

FightForTheFuture entered the room

FightForTheFuture: „WTF!? Who did this? Who sabotaged Vrata?"

....

FightForTheFuture: „No one?? Well, let me tell you that this was a big mistake. We did not stick to our own deadline. How can they take us seriously now? And when you make rash decisions, mistakes are being made. Now I will have to fix what you screwed up."

FightForTheFuture left the room

EN ROUTE
DAY 3
10:45 P.M.

Mia Bernert was looking out of the window, trying to make out details of the landscape passing by as the train moved through the country-side at high speed. She was sitting alone in the train compartment, which was not luxurious but good enough. She was used to much worse. Mia could not afford a night train ticket with proper beds, but being alone allowed her to relax on the worn red cushions that Croatian Railways hadn't cleaned in a while. Traveling by train had so many advantages over planes. The comfort. The scenery. The much lower carbon footprint. And most importantly: no one was asking for your passport.

Her phone was lying on the small table next to the window when it vibrated. A BirdSong message; it had to be important. Mia smirked when she read it. FightForTheFuture was upset about Vrata, but who cared? This was the real fight for all their futures. All that was important was the cause. After reading that Oberberg had been repaired and Italy was not in a state of emergency anymore, Mia decided this was not good enough. She could make her own decisions. She did not need the approval of FightForTheFuture. It had to hurt for real change to happen. And slowing down Vrata was a way of showing them that LNG was not a viable option, either. They needed to switch to alternative energy sources.

It was much easier than expected. Mia had thought she would have to overcome similar security systems as in Oberberg, just more difficult because she had no time to prepare. But she had been flabbergasted when she found a complete lack of security. No cameras, no sensors, and hardly any security guards. It was almost too easy. But it also meant that she could not pin the attack on Samanta like in Oberberg, so she needed to find another way to create a trail of breadcrumbs that led to Samanta. A low-tech way to frame her. This was when Mia remembered the student ID. *How fitting*, she had thought. Everything started with the student ID, and everything would end with it. This would put Samanta behind bars for a long time. *She will pay for her betrayal. Revenge at last.*

BRUSSELS
DAY 3
11:50 P.M.

The phone next to her bed was ringing relentlessly, and it just wouldn't stop. Lina Juska had been glad to get into bed before midnight for once, a chance to make up for some sleepless nights. But it was just not meant to be. After the seventh ring, she finally gathered enough strength to roll over and see who it was. Her assistant John.

„What is it?" Lina was not in the mood for pleasantries.

„Sorry to wake you at this hour, but you should really check your emails," John said.

„Why?"

„Jean-Baptiste Moulin just sent out a draft proposal that is meant to be brought before Parliament and the Council tomorrow morning." The same Jean-Baptiste Moulin she had to work with in the SGS special committee.

„What kind of proposal? What does it say?"

„Well, that's why I called you at this hour. It states that 40% of the funds earmarked for green energy should be re-designated to build new gas pipelines in Europe, starting with the Trans Carpathian Pipeline. My sources tell me that this has been coordinated with the Vice-President, and the Council is on board as well."

„Are you frickin kidding me?" Lina was furious. This was clearly her area of responsibility. Proposals for changes to the energy budget should come from the Energy Commissioner, not from Counter Terrorism. Sending such a draft at midnight before this was being discussed in the general session in Parliament was clearly an attempt to pass her over. They knew she would veto it, so they sent it at a time she could not read or object to it.

„This is treason, and I will not accept it. This is far from over. Are you in the office?" Lina asked.

„Me? No, I was just having dinner with my girlfriend."

„Meet me there in half an hour. We will read this and respond. This is the time to act." Lina could hear a soft sigh on the other end of the phone line. The sigh of someone regretting he had woken up his boss.

John and Lina met in the office shortly after. They were not the only ones in the building; light was coming from the odd room here and there. It was not unusual for assistants and other employees of high-ranking officials to prepare documents late at night. They sat down in one of the small conference rooms and printed two copies of the document, which piled up next to them. It had 92 pages.

Before going into politics, Lina had never understood why these kinds of documents needed to be so long. But once she got an inside view, she understood. Each possible scenario and conflict with other legislation needed to be addressed. If you passed directives or regulations that were not done properly, there was a good chance they would be thrown over afterwards, and all the work would be for nothing. This was also why legislation took so long to pass. Not only did every scenario have to be considered, but each page added additional points to discuss and negotiate over. But she learned that it was better to do it properly right away. Right now, she wished this one was shorter, though.

After reading for an hour, they were contemplating if they should get their fourth coffee or if caffeine had lost all its effect by now. There was nothing unexpected in the document. Essentially, John had summarized it well. But they needed to read through it all to respond. They decided against another coffee and instead pulled through. After another half an hour, they were finally done.

„Okay, it's well written," Lina had to admit. Writing legislation, which did not leave any wiggle room, was an art form by itself.

„Yes, it is. Actually hard to believe that they wrote it in just three days," John said.

„You mean in the three days since the terror attack?"

„Yes."

„Yeah, I was wondering about that too. Hard to believe indeed... But that's the least of our worries now. We need to write a response arguing that rash policy changes based on single events are never a good idea. And that we cannot jeopardize our long-term energy strategy for short-term fixes. We need to show them that Moulin has no right to bypass me like that, for Christ's sake!"

It took them another half an hour to write a lengthy response that Lina emailed to the other commissioners. It was made clear that this draft was not agreed upon with Lina as the responsible commissioner. That it did not reflect the official energy policies of the Commission. And that there was no way this proposal could go into the general session in the morning. If they wanted to proceed with it, it would need serious reworking. Unfortunately, there was nothing else she could do now. There was no formal veto process in the Commission. She could just voice her strongest opposition; that was it. Exhausted, Lina decided they had done all they could for the day and let John get back to his dinner, which probably was cold, and his girlfriend asleep by now. It was 2:30 a.m.

Sitting in the taxi on her way home, Lina thought it over once more. This was personal. If the Vice-President of the European Commission was in on this, it meant that she didn't respect Lina, maybe never had. This fit together with their hostile exchange the last time they met. The VP was just not on her side. The VP was supporting Moulin for whatever reason.

Lina needed to increase the pressure if she wanted to stop this. So she decided to write another email, this time a personal note just to the Vice-President. It was a short message where she wrote: „If this goes through, I'll resign." *This will show her how serious this betrayal is*, Lina thought. If that did not turn things around, nothing would. She was looking outside the window of her taxi and thought about the consequences of all of this when, after a few minutes, Lina's phone vibrated again, signaling the arrival of an email. It was already a reply to the one she had just sent. She opened it and stared at the content: „OK."

DAY FOUR

ŠIJE
07:35 A.M.

Coo, coo. Coo, coo. Arnaud opened his eyes and looked around the room. It did not resemble his small bedroom in The Hague, with its old furniture whose sole purpose was serving as a rack for worn clothes. Arnaud remembered that he spent the night in a pension on Vrata island. It was a small but cozy room, looking traditional, with a lot of wood paneling. A large king-size bed, a small table, a TV. Drapes with a red and white tile pattern at the window where light rays shone through. A door led to a small balcony. Outside the window, a dove was looking at Arnaud. *Coo, coo.*

Croatia was a wintering spot for a lot of birds who migrated south during the cold season to return to the north in summer. Maybe this dove was one of them. Maybe she remembered Arnaud from The Hague, Arnaud thought, but he immediately dismissed the thought as a result of him not being fully awake yet. Looking out the window, the day seemed to be promising a lot of sunshine and a clear sky.

Arnaud took a shower and got dressed to go downstairs. Next to the entrance of the pension was a small breakfast room, and, being the only guest, Arnaud had the whole buffet to himself. The room smelled of freshly brewed coffee. He gladly took a cup and ate some toast with Croatian ajvar, a spread made out of peppers and eggplant. Having had a good night's sleep and a proper breakfast did wonders for his mood; he felt great. His wounds didn't even hurt so much anymore.

Arnaud's first mission of the day was to send Sam a copy of the student ID. So, after breakfast, he went to the front desk and asked the young man behind it if they had a fax machine. Arnaud just received a blank look in return. „A scanner, maybe? I need to scan and send this ID to someone." Without saying a word, the young man took the student ID, unlocked his phone, and took a photo. „Where do you want to send it to?" Arnaud gave him Sam's email and felt really stupid. Even he, with his technological inaptitude, knew you could take photos with your phone. But it never occurred to him to use it to send copies of documents via email. Of course, if it did, he could have sent it already last night and saved some time.

Now that this was settled, Arnaud checked out of the hotel and took a taxi to the airport. He wanted to take the first plane out to The Hague to show his face there and find out if they uncovered new evidence. Besides, there was no point in staying on Vrata. On the way to the airport, he looked out the window as the town of Šije passed by. They drove by the sea, and the water had a beautiful, deep-blue color as the sun reflected on the small waves. It reminded Arnaud of a family vacation on the islands of Greece. It reminded him of better times.

On the other side of the street, he noticed a souvenir shop and asked the driver to stop. Arnaud entered the small shop, which was empty except for the owner sitting behind a counter, reading a newspaper. Once he realized that an actual customer had entered, the owner looked up and became interested in the prospect of selling something. There was a lot of cheap tourist stuff like football jerseys, caps, T-shirts, and the like. Arnaud had been looking for the right thing for quite a while when he finally found something that would fit his purpose—a small turtle made out of clay that moved its head and legs when you moved it. It was perfect for his daughter, and she would love it for sure.

Arnaud was glad he took the time to get something for Zoé. He knew he did not spend enough time with her. Her mother had made that abundantly clear. And it annoyed Arnaud as well. After all, Zoé was the sole reason he stayed in The Hague in the first place. He needed to change the priorities in his life, to put her first and work second. Once again, he promised himself to do so once this case was closed. Plus, he would call her from the airport.

When Arnaud came to the airport, it looked as abandoned as the night before. One check-in desk was open, where he inquired about a ticket for the next plane to Amsterdam. Arnaud was lucky, apparently, they had introduced a direct flight to Amsterdam only recently to account for the number of workers for the LNG terminal from there. The plane would leave in one hour. Arnaud used the time to make some calls. First to Sam.

„Hi Sam, I just sent you a copy of a student ID. Did you get it?"

„Yes, sure."

„So? Do you recognize it? Is it yours?"

„Yes, of course it is. I actually lost it during my Erasmus semester in Munich. How did you get it?"

„It was found at a crime scene. There has been an attack on an LNG terminal, and next to the broken components, they found this ID."

„Well, obviously it wasn't me. I was in Bonn. Someone tries to frame me again. Why would anyone do that?"

„Good question. Do you have any idea who could have your ID? Did you give it to someone during your Erasmus, and could you just have forgotten about it later?"

„No, it was just lost. And that was actually a real problem for me because I needed to get it re-issued at my home University and needed to travel back to Italy to get it. Super annoying. That's why I remember this episode vividly."

„Okay, try to think about it. Maybe it will come to you. It is obvious that our terrorist is somehow connected to your past. This is about you. This is personal."

He hung up.

Arnaud was just about to call his ex-wife to speak to his daughter when his phone rang.

„Hi, Henrick."

„Hoi, Arnaud. I need to speak to you right now." He sounded agitated, restless, pumped with adrenaline. And excited, the way he always was when he had made a discovery and had important news to share.

„Sure, what is it?" Arnaud answered.

„Last night, after you called me and mentioned that you didn't think Samanta Di Vincenzo was our perpetrator, I couldn't sleep. I kept thinking about the video recording of her breaking into Oberberg. If she didn't do it, how could the video be explained? So I went back to the office to check it out. It took me all night, but I finally figured it out," Henrick said.

„You figured what out?"

„How the video was faked. How they put the face of Samanta Di Vincenzo in the video instead of another person!"

„Yes! I told you she didn't do it! How could it be fake? It looked very real to me."

„Are you familiar with Deep Fakes?"

„Did you expect me to be? Never heard of it."

„Okay, so Deep Fakes are types of manipulated videos that use artificial intelligence to make people act and say things they never did. It is somehow like creating a video animation, just that it looks completely real. Pretty spooky. With artificial intelligence becoming so advanced in recent years, we reached a level of perfection that was unconceivable just a few years ago. Deep Fakes got famous on the Internet when people created video clips of politicians saying controversial or funny things. They are also used a lot in disinformation campaigns for propaganda reasons. Pretty dangerous stuff, actually. Just imagine what would happen if a president declared nuclear war in a faked video. The consequences are unimaginable.

Anyway, the way it works is that you take any picture of a person, and then the program will make it move the way you want. It is tricky and not easy to do, but this way, you can create a moving animation of a face and overlay it on another video to make it look real," Henrick explained.

„You know I don't know anything about this computer stuff. Can you just cut it short without the technical details?" Arnaud said.

„Okay, so I tried to figure out if this was what happened here, if someone added the face of Samanta Di Vincenzo into the video. Since it looks absolutely real on the video, it was not easy to figure out. I already did a forensic analysis on it when we first got it and couldn't find anything wrong. But if you start with the assumption that it was doctored, you can take a different approach. What if I wouldn't try to find a clue in the video itself but tried to find the picture of Samanta Di Vincenzo that was used to create the fake?"

„I guess you will answer that question for me?"

„I went back into Hawksight and ran a search for pictures from her social media profiles, the ones we looked at when we first ran her through the system. Remember that photo of her on a hiking trip, in the Alps somewhere? In that photo, there is some mud on her left cheek. And guess what? In the recordings of Oberberg, she has mud with the exact same pattern on the same cheek. I think it is too big of a coincidence that on both occasions, she had the same mud pattern on her face. This photo was the source file that was used to fake the video. This is proof that we do not see Samanta Di Vincenzo in this video but someone else," Henrick explained.

„Henrick, you are a genius!"

„Don't forget to mention that to Gusta! What I do not know is how it was done. This recording was taken directly from the security system. Even if a video clip could be replaced in the security system, meaning you need access to it, creating a Deep Fake takes time. Faking the face and rendering the video, even if short, like in our case, takes an hour, at least. So after the attack, they must have somehow got a copy of the recording, doctored it, and put it back into the system. With remote access to the system, which is hard to get. And all of that before the police came on site. I don't see how they could pull that off."

„Or it was done before the attack even happened. This explains the gap in the timeline. After the break-in, the terrorist spent two hours in the control room before going out and actually disrupting the pipeline. Now we know why, and it makes complete sense. They were not getting cold feet, collecting themselves for two hours. They were manipulating the video of when they entered the control room to pin the whole attack on someone else. This gave them all the time in the world to manipulate the video because the attack hadn't happened yet, and the security guard was sedated. The sole reason why they entered the control room was to get a good shot of their face at the entrance and then manipulate the video. To take us down the wrong track! It was all a setup!" Arnaud said.

„Wow, pretty sophisticated, genius even. I have never seen anyone pull something like that off. But I agree, it is the most reasonable explanation."

„Now, can you reverse the fake and reveal the original face of the person?" Arnaud asked.

„Unfortunately, no, the original face is gone forever. I cannot even prove to you that the video was doctored besides the fact that I found the source picture."

„Okay, that's unfortunate. But anyway, thanks for the info. Well done, Henrick. I'll pay one round once I'm back."

„Thanks. Have a good trip home."

Arnaud hung up. He couldn't help himself but let a smirk escape his otherwise serious face. Finally, some progress! As much as he usually detested calling Gusta, he was happy to do it now and deliver the good news. To his surprise, she was less enthusiastic than expected and pointed out that he was not closer to stopping the terrorist than two days ago. In a way, he was further behind now. Two days ago, he had the supposed terrorist detained. Now he didn't even know anymore who he was searching for. And she reminded him, correctly, that the deadline of the manifesto was approaching fast. When they talked last night, they had 24 hours left. They now had just over 13 hours until the deadline, and then they could expect more major attacks on the European gas infrastructure. Arnaud had to hurry to get answers.

STRASBOURG
DAY 4
09:00 A.M.

Lina was occupying her seat in the European Parliament when the session opened, 09:00 a.m. sharp. The main hall of the Parliament was shaped like a semi-circle, with MPs sitting in spots assigned to their respective party. They were all facing the central podium where they could listen to whoever was given the floor at the moment. Above the semi-circle was one large balcony with an area designated for TV crews and visitors listening in.

All debates were public, and European citizens had the right to hear what their representatives had to say. The TV crews broadcast the speeches live, and any visitor coming by could watch them as well. However, in reality, politics was not made on the Parliament floor but long before proposals were presented, and, of course, this process was not public. But at least the public had some insights into how their lives were being shaped.

In the middle of the semi-circle, the President of the Parliament was located. The right-most side of the semi-circle was assigned to the European Commission, facing the Council of the European Union, which occupied the left-most side of the semi-circle. The seating order reflected the internal political hierarchy, and, as one of the less powerful commissioners, Lina had a seat a little further back. Her assistant John sat behind her. He was leaning forward and whispered: „Full house! Haven't seen that in a while. Feels like in a soccer stadium."

„I guess they all want to know what this is about. Just like me." Lina tried to project confidence but had the feeling that she did a bad job faking it. In reality, she was very anxious. She hadn't slept at all. After Lina received the reply to her email, essentially daring her to resign, she couldn't find the peace to get some rest. And then she had to leave early to catch the plane down to Strasbourg, where the parliament was gathering. The circus of traveling between Brussels and Strasbourg annoyed everyone, ecologists and economists alike. And MPs and commissioners too. But it was a highly political topic, with Brussels being located in Belgium and Strasbourg in France at the German border. And rather than starting a fight with the two most powerful nations in the European Union, the issue of settling for Brussels as the sole headquarter of the Union was not debated, at least publicly.

Lina did not get any reply to her other late-night email, arguing that the proposal to re-designate funds earmarked for renewable energy was not ready to be brought in front of the MPs. But no reply was also a reply. It meant they didn't care that she was opposed and that it would be brought up today, as reflected by the agenda of the plenary session. And if it was, Lina had to follow through on her threat to resign. Otherwise, her standing in the Commission would be tarnished forever, and her relationship with the Vice-President as well.

During her sleepless night, she had started to prepare a short letter of resignation that she would hand to the Vice-President should the need arise. But then she had thought of something better. She would make it public for all the world to hear. Any member of the Parliament had the right to speak time if requested, which was exactly what she did. When she had seen the order of the debates, and she had found the proposal for the re-designation of the funds on it, she had asked to be placed on the agenda right after. And then she had plotted her revenge.

It was 09:20 a.m. when the proposal came up for debate. Jean-Baptiste Moulin was the one presenting. *That spineless worm*, Lina thought. He was making the case that the attack on the gas infrastructure showed the weakness of the system. Not only was the attack on Oberberg proof that Europe's critical infrastructure relied on too few critical pipelines that could easily be attacked, the second attack on Vrata confirmed that not even the LNG terminals were safe. Europe needed to build new pipelines to be more resilient towards such disruptions. Each pipeline would need a „backup" pipeline, and each LNG terminal would need a „backup" terminal. And security would need to be strengthened massively to protect this infrastructure.

To achieve that, no new funds would be needed. They could just delay a few other projects that were long-term anyway and wouldn't show results for many years to come. This crisis required fast action, and the time to act was now. The proposal sounded straightforward enough, and few would realize the massive impact this would have.

Without saying it, he was attacking Lina's pet project. It was just not true that renewable energy wouldn't deliver results fast. They just needed to invest in new wind parks, distribution networks, and storage facilities to make Europe less dependent on fossil fuels. Investing this money into fossils was exactly the wrong thing. Jean-Baptiste Moulin had it upside down. It would make Europe more dependent on this highly politicized, finite energy resource. It wasn't making Europe energy independent but dependent on third countries supplying gas. Lina was fuming. She would give her resignation speech as planned.

The debate ended at 11:30 a.m. There were some critical words by the opposition, including the Green party that Linda belonged to, but that, of course, didn't change the outcome. The vote was clear. The proposal had passed. The European Commission would re-designate funds from renewable energy to building gas pipelines. Now it was Lina's turn to speak.

,,Mr. President, Mrs. Vice-President, Members of Parliament, citizens of Europe. The charade we just witnessed exposed everything wrong with the European Parliament. What you saw was a carefully planned rubber-stamping of a piece of legislation that will shape our future for many years to come. It shifts billions of Euros away from renewable energy towards fossil fuels, making it impossible for Europe to reach its carbon emission goals and pushing more money toward special interest groups. This legislation was worked on without involving the responsible Commissioner for Energy because they knew I would oppose. It was well prepared in advance, just waiting until the next crisis happened to push this through. Attacks on our energy infrastructure are ruthlessly exploited to push a political agenda that no doubt is being driven by special interest groups and their lobbyists.

And make no mistake. No politician would put on such an act for free; this has a price. I urge you to forever remember the names of those who pushed this legislation, Jean-Baptiste Moulin first and foremost, and watch them in the years to come. Watch their self-righteous faces as they screw you, each of you, all of us, for their personal benefit. Watch them as they silently retire from their political roles to reap the rewards of years of working for dirty multi-nationals. Watch them as they become board members in oil and gas conglomerates, shareholders in pipeline projects, and consultants to shady dictatorships in exchange for billions of Euros from European citizens.

Does that sound like a good deal for special interests? Absolutely, corrupt politicians are cheap. Is it a bad deal for everyone else? Of course. And this is why we need to expose them, prosecute them, and remove them. We need to make it as expensive as possible to get paid by special interest groups and to make it unfeasible for those groups to pay off corrupt politicians. And if we cannot make them pay financially or with prison time, we need to make their shady doings public and make them pay in reputation, try them in the court of public opinion, at a minimum. So, next time a corrupt politician is considering being paid off for a harmful piece of legislation, they will think twice if it is worth it.

I, for one, will have no part to play anymore in this political circus. This is why, as of today, I am resigning as the Commissioner for Energy. I cannot reconcile working in this corrupt administration with my conscience. Instead, I will dedicate my life to exposing cases of political corruption. And I'm starting with this one. Today. "And with this, she walked off stage.

BONN
DAY 4
11:30 A.M.

Sam sat in the living room and looked at the cold pizza—leftovers from the night before, which they had spent searching for more information on the case. They were both still wearing their pajamas, and while Sam was trying to decide if cold pizza was appropriate for breakfast, Erik was brewing much-needed fresh coffee. The smell of it filled the air and gave the room a cozy feeling.

They had spent all night scrutinizing the Internet in the hopes of finding traces of DestructionKitten, and they did uncover some activity. It turned out that DestructionKitten posted quite a bit of messages on BirdSong, all concerning some kind of environmental issues. Whoever DestructionKitten was, it was clear that they were environmental activists willing to go to extremes to make their voice heard:

r/climateaction . Posted by u/DestructionKitten
„*This planet belongs to all of nature, and it is not to be exploited by humans.*"

r/friendsofearth . Posted by u/DestructionKitten
„Nature was in balance before humans arrived on Earth. They are a plague to this planet!"

r/friendsofearth . Posted by u/DestructionKitten
„This is the final hour of Earth. Somebody needs to do something to avert all-out catastrophe!"

r/globalwarming . Posted by u/DestructionKitten
„In five years, we could all be dead if we continue to let our politicians decide our fate..."

This fit into the picture, both of the attacks, on Oberberg and Vrata, and the manifesto. You could certainly imagine someone like that getting radicalized and channeling their anger into acts of real-world aggression. After sifting through all the posts in different individual groups dedicated to specific topics, Sam and Erik continued to search for comments DestructionKitten had made on posts from other people. And this was when they stumbled upon a post that stuck out from the rest:

r/climateaction . Posted by u/FightForTheFuture
„Europe is on the brink of collapse. Summers are getting hotter, winters are getting wetter. In the south, forest fires and droughts wreak havoc. Farmers do not have enough water to feed their animals. Food stock is drying out. Spain and Portugal are becoming deserts.

Northern Europe is becoming significantly rainier, with winter floods becoming more common. Animals and plants that used to thrive in the northern climate are dying out while they get replaced by new species coming from the south.

The poorer the country, the more dramatic the situation. There has been a drastic increase in heat-related deaths in some regions and cold-related deaths in others. And the wetness of the north brings new disease vectors for water-borne illnesses.

And what do politicians do? Nothing. They are ignoring the problem because special interests and profit are more important to them than the citizens of Europe. The only way for a turnaround is decisive action. Europe must stop using fossil fuels and change to renewable energy immediately. It must reduce energy consumption dramatically. No fuzzy 30-year goals anymore that will not be met. This must happen now. It is the only way we and our children can survive.

We, the people, need to fight back and show Brussels, and all the fossil fuel industry they feed off of, that we will not tolerate this inaction any longer. Radical change cannot come without radical action. Sometimes you need to burn down the old before something new can rise from the ashes.

Join me in our fight for the future."

DestructionKitten

„I'm in."

This had been the first significant lead they had found. It looked like someone with the alias FightForTheFuture was searching for users on BirdSong for „radical action" in the name of the environment. Without any context, this post could easily be read as another outburst by a frustrated environmentalist. But with the benefit of hindsight, after the attacks in Oberberg and Vrata and together with the connection to DestructionKitten, this was clearly a message to recruit like-minded people, especially the likes of DestructionKitten. To radicalize them to commit terror attacks on European energy infrastructure.

Finding this clue had given both Sam and Erik the energy boost necessary to stay up late and search further but unfortunately the lead had ended there, it had been a dead-end. Private messages between users could not be read publicly, so they had no idea how the conversation between DestructionKitten and FightForTheFuture continued after. FightForTheFuture had not posted anything else, this was the only message they could find. And the user did not exist anywhere else on the Internet. So while it looked like a hot lead, it didn't get them anywhere. They had had to give up for the night and without any further leads, they, reluctantly, had gone to bed.

At least they had learned that there was more than one person involved. Which made the fact that they had less than 12 hours left before the deadline of the manifesto even more chilling. Even if they could stop the actual terrorist, it didn't mean that there weren't more. Right now it was 11:30 a.m., and at 11:00 p.m. more attacks could be expected if they did not stop the terrorists. All of them.

Sam decided that eating cold pizza was not an appropriate breakfast and focused on fresh coffee instead. She sat on the soft sofa in the living room, and with her cup warming her hand, she kept thinking about the student ID that Arnaud had sent her. During her studies, as part of the Erasmus student exchange program, she had spent a semester at the University of Technology Munich, one of the top universities in Europe. It had been the best time in her life, and the lost student ID had really been the only blemish on otherwise perfect five months where she had made many friends and spent time with the international student community.

She remembered that she couldn't find her ID one day after spending a long night at an Erasmus party, a night she only had fond memories of, especially of a boy named Ricardo from Spain, who she went home with. Could she have left the ID at his place? But he would have given it to her afterwards if he had found it, since they spent a lot of time together in the weeks after. Unless he had planned something all along, and he was the terrorist? No, that didn't make any sense.

Back then, she had searched everywhere she could think of, eventually giving up and conceding that her ID was gone. She had to apply for a new one at her university at home, which meant that she had to drive from Munich back to Napoli, an 11-hour trip she hitchhiked to save the money of a plane ticket. An adventure for sure, but not a pleasant one.

She had no clue who could have taken her ID. Whoever had found it and knew her would have given it back; unless they had disliked her somehow. But Sam could not think of anyone. If she had a photo, she might remember the person out of the many students she met during this time. Yes, a picture would help them further in this case. This could be the lead they were looking for. Sam had an idea of how they could get ahead in this case.

„Erik, remember that we looked at the website of this hacker conference yesterday, was it H4ckThePlanet? The one where DestructionKitten attended?"

„Yeah, sure. Why do you ask? There was nothing of interest there. Just a run-of-the-mill academic conference website. Another dead-end."

„There was a section on photos from the conference that was password protected."

„So?"

„How about we try to hack it?"

„Do you seriously think that the website of a conference about *hacking* would be so badly secured that we could just waltz in there? I mean, that's basic stuff to make it hard for people to get in."

„Well, worth a try, I'd say."

„Whatever you say, we can try. There is nothing else to do anyway."

Erik opened his laptop again and typed in the address of the conference website. A green page opened, with a navigation bar in the center and a large white banner on top with an ugly font that simply read, „Welcome to the 9th annual H4ckThePlanet conference. August 17-19, Budapest". *Hackers and nice graphic design are simply not compatible*, Sam thought. As a passionate video game player, she had an eye for aesthetics, and badly designed websites left her with an uneasy feeling in her stomach. But she was used to bad conference websites, the nerdier the conference, the uglier the website.

Erik clicked on the section of the conference photos, and a page opened that asked users to provide an email address and a password to enter. Now came the interesting part. To break into this page and circumvent the login, some magic needed to happen. If, in fact, they were careless when developing the website. In his browser, Erik right-clicked on the page to reveal its source code.

„Okay, we have two text fields for the email address and the password, and once the user submits this form, the information is sent to a page called photos.php," Erik said. „What do you think?"

„SQL injection?" Sam said.

„Yes, I thought the same. If that works, great. If not, it will be difficult. But again, I have a hard time believing that they did not sanitize the text field input."

SQL injection was a common way to gain unauthorized access to a website. SQL was the name of a database used to store user data, such as email addresses and passwords. Normally, when a user entered their email address and password into the fields and clicked submit, the application would check in the database if a user with this password existed and would provide access or not by returning TRUE or FALSE.

However, a hacker could, instead of just writing in their email address, add commands for the database in the email address text field, which would overwrite the original commands that checked for the correct user and password. They could add a command that was always true, no matter which email address or password was entered, and thus let anyone who entered these commands in the email text field in. Instead of providing a valid email address and password, the hacker would just change the rules to let anyone in who knew how. It was like instead of forging the correct key to open a door, they would ignore the key and change the lock to accept any key instead and let anyone with any key in. They changed the rules of the game.

To protect against these kinds of attacks, any experienced developer would sanitize the input text, which meant making sure that any database command entered by the user wouldn't have any effect.

Erik tried the SQL injection by entering the following values into the email address field:

„123@123.xxx' OR 1 = 1 LIMIT 1 — ']"

And in the password field:
„1234"

„Okay, 1 = 1 is always true, of course. So what this command does is let you in *either* if your email address and password are correct *or* if 1 = 1 is true, which of course is always the case. So no matter which email or password you provide, the code would always return TRUE and let you in?" Sam said, explaining that the rules of the game had changed. If this worked, any key would open this door and let them into the website.

„Yes, exactly. Now let's see if our hacker colleagues have been sloppy when coding this." Erik hit Enter, and they both waited while the website was loading. Even with high-speed Internet, it felt like it took forever. Finally, it was done.

A page opened, which listed the conference photos they were looking for. To both of their surprise, it worked, and they were in the internal photo section. It showed three links to click, one for each conference day: August 17th, August 18th,

August 19th. Erik clicked on the first day, and the page filled with small thumbnails of photos, hundreds of them. Sam and Erik would have to open each photo individually to check if they found anything interesting. Hopefully, they would spot the woman they were looking for, the one pretending to be Martina Bauer. Someone with a badge that read:

44 65 73 74 72 75 63 74 69 6F 6E 4B 69 74 74 65 6E

which they now knew translated to „DestructionKitten". If they found that badge, they might get a shot of the woman's face. And with that, they would likely have the owner of the flat that exploded in Vienna, who likely was the girlfriend of the security guard in Oberberg, and who likely was connected to the attack on the facility, maybe even the terrorist itself. This would be the breakthrough they needed. It was a long shot finding the right badge on any of the photos. But it was the only shot they got. Hopeful, they began their search.

After half an hour, they finished with the first day—nothing. Just many photos of coffee breaks and presentations with heads from the back but no readable badges and certainly no DestructionKitten. They switched to August 18th, the second day. Just more of the same. Coffee breaks and presentations. Many people but no badges. No luck with the second day, either.

They switched to the third day, August 19th. There were less pictures. Probably the conference program was shorter on the final day. They clicked through the photos again, but it seemed hopeless. Most of the people were standing too far away from the camera for the badges to be read. You would have to be very lucky to find a picture where a readable badge would flash right into the camera. But they weren't lucky. There was no photo in the gallery that showed a badge with the code they were looking for. Even worse, they couldn't even read any code on any of the badges. When Erik arrived at the last photo, he sighed. He knew it was unlikely they would find something to begin with, but he had had hope. Not anymore. Also, just like the all the others, the final photo showed no badge either. Searching for it in the conference photos had been a good idea, but it went nowhere. So, back to square one.

But then Sam said: „Wait. Go back a few photos." Erik clicked back a few times until Sam stopped him. „This one, zoom in here. In the back, next to the coffee machine." After zooming in, you could make out a woman with white, mid-long punk hair in the middle of her head and clean-shaven sides waiting to get a coffee. She was wearing a black leather jacket, black jeans, and black Dr. Martens shoes. She looked isolated from the rest, maybe a bit anxious, playing with an un-lit cigarette in her hand. Sam stared at the photo, shocked.

„Oh mio dio, I know her."

BONN

DAY 4

12:05 P.M.

„You know this girl? How?" Erik said. He was sitting next to Sam on the living room couch, and they were looking at the photos of the hacking conference.

„I met her during my semester abroad, at Erasmus in Munich. It must be five years ago by now. Her name is Mia, and I never knew her last name. Smart girl, studying computer science in Vienna. I liked her; we became friends. We had shared interests in nerdy stuff and were mostly in the same courses. We spent some time together outside of class, going on bike trips and hiking and such. Otherwise, she was pretty private though, never really interacted with the others, and kept to herself..." Sam paused for a few seconds, recollecting her memories from back in the day. „Actually, that's not true. She used to be together with Ricardo from Spain..." Pieces of the puzzle started to slowly assemble in her mind, and they formed a bigger picture, one that made everything clear.

„Oh, no, no, no!" Sam said.

„What is it?"

„Ricardo was my Erasmus boyfriend, too."

„What? You dated the boyfriend of your friend?"

„No, it wasn't like that. He told me that he had broken up with Mia, so I didn't see anything wrong with it. But I wouldn't put it past Ricardo that he hadn't broken up with her at all. He might have just said it to get together with me and wanted to keep his options open."

„Such an idiot. And you think she found out?"

„Maybe. This was when I lost my student ID. I must have left it at his place, and maybe she found it, probably lying next to his bed. Maybe she came to his place to pick something up or just wanted to drop by. She must have been furious. Probably she even took it with her, and that's how it got lost. I never saw Mia again, but to be honest, I haven't thought much of it. I was just sad that I didn't see my friend for the final two months of our Erasmus. She must have thought that I betrayed her and wanted me out of her life. And that is why she left Erasmus."

„And now, five years later, she found a way of getting her revenge: framing the terrorist attacks on you."

„Exactly."

„Sounds a bit extreme your theory if you ask me. All of this just for stealing her Erasmus boyfriend, who doesn't even sound like such a great catch? There must have been better opportunities to vent her anger. Usually, people just block each other on social media over something like this," Erik said.

„But then again, if she was planning to commit the terror attacks anyway, by framing me, she kills two birds with one stone: finding a scapegoat and getting revenge," Sam said.

„First, she gets radicalized on BirdSong and convinced that she needs to commit a terrorist act, and when planning on how to do it, she gets the idea of framing you. It fits."

„Yes, it all makes sense. This is what ties me to all this mess. It's a personal vendetta. Oh mio dio, I would have never thought that I would hear from Mia again. I didn't do anything to her, not on purpose. I don't deserve this! All of this because of a misunderstanding?" In Sam's mind, the events of recent days flashed by as she imagined how Mia orchestrated all of it to put Sam behind bars.

„No, you don't deserve it. And I promise you, I will do everything to help stop her!" Erik said.

Sam gathered her thoughts. „But finally, we are getting somewhere. I think we have found our terrorist. Mia sabotaged Oberberg, crippled Vrata, and booby-trapped her flat in Vienna that almost killed Arnaud. Her only mistake was that she left the conference badge in the flat and that she made it personal. If I wouldn't know what she looked like, we would have never found out who she was. She might be planning her next attack as we speak. I need to call Arnaud right away," Sam said. She dialed Arnaud's number. After a few rings, he picked up.

„Arnaud? It's Sam."

„Hi, Sam. I just landed in Amsterdam. I'm still in the plane, so it might be a bit loud, and I cannot talk about any sensitive information in such a public space."

„Okay. Listen, we found our terrorist. It is a girl who I met during my Erasmus. Her name is Mia. She is framing me because she thought I stole her boyfriend."

„Are you serious? This is amazing news! Finally, the break in the case that we have been waiting for. Well done!"

„Amazing is not what goes through my mind right now, but I know what you mean. It was just a lucky shot. I cannot believe our luck myself. We need to find and stop her as soon as possible!"

„Good work in any case. Send me her full name, and we can run a Europe-wide search."

„That's the thing. I just have her first name, unfortunately."

„Oh. Well, that's a different story, then. Just a first name does not help us at all."

„I do have a picture of her, though. The picture on which I identified her. Does that help?"

„That helps. Send it to my email. As soon as I arrive in The Hague, I will let forensics run it through our facial recognition system."

„Okay, I'll send it right away. I will also search through my old photos to see if I find one of her from back in the day."

„Thanks. Oh, and by the way, Sam. We found out that the surveillance video was faked. Europol now knows it was not you. You walk around freely again. Your search warrant was withdrawn. Congratulations!"

Sam let out a long sigh. It was indeed good news that she wouldn't be public enemy number one anymore. She would be able to leave the house without being afraid of getting apprehended.

„Thank you, Arnaud, this is very good to hear. It feels good not to be a fugitive again. And I know Erik will be very interested to hear how it was faked. He had a sleepless night pondering over it."

„Take care, Sam."

„Thanks, Arnaud. See you later".

Now it all depended on Arnaud, if he could find out Mia's full name and get her current location.

STRASBOURG
DAY 4
12:42 P.M.

Lina Juska had just finished her resignation speech at the European Parliament when she was approached by Annika Björklund. Annika was the only one among all the commissioners that Lina had built up some kind of relationship with since they had first met at the start of the current Commission cycle. She was the Commissioner for Cohesion and Reforms, a less important department inside of the Commission, but one that touched many different areas and that required her above-average communication skills. To say she was well-connected wouldn't do her justice. She knew every piece of gossip that was to be known, and she wasn't shy about sharing it. Annika had congratulated Lina for doing the right thing and had asked her out for lunch.

They were now sitting at Le Männele, a traditional, down-to-earth restaurant not far from the Parliament building on the outskirts of Strasbourg. The food there was predictably heavy, but it had a homey atmosphere with wood paneling on the walls and wooden furniture. It was packed full with many other people working at the Parliament who were using this restaurant as a good excuse for a change of scenery over lunch.

The house itself was built in the traditional timber framing style found all over Strasbourg, with wooden beams cutting through the otherwise white walls. It was a welcome break from the modern glass construction that made up for the round shape of the Parliament building.

„Lina, I can only commend you again on your speech. Integrity is becoming rare in the political circus, and it takes courage to take such a step," Annika said. She was wearing a pink, two-piece dress suit, which was complemented by her signature over-the-top makeup and blonde hair. She was observing Lina through her blue eyes.

„Thank you. I am a very accommodating person, but I will not let myself get pushed around like this." Lina meant it. Her ex-husband was always surprised when she exploded out of nowhere. He couldn't figure out where it was coming from since she never complained about anything. She was the type of person that would tolerate a lot, but when a certain level was reached, she would completely lash out, which was also how their relationship ended. You could argue that this didn't give her husband any warning, but she really had to put up with too much over the years to feel bad for him. He deserved what he got.

„I am also impressed by your commitment to uncovering corruption. I do believe that someone needs to step up against it in our day and age. Someone needs to take a stand, be the poster child for anti-corruption and say that it couldn't go on like this," Annika said. Lina read between the lines that Annika would not be this person, because it was obviously political suicide. When people say that someone needs to do something, they rarely refer to themselves.

„Listen, I heard a lot of talk today behind closed doors. I can tell you that most people had no idea this was coming. This was prepared by a small group that worked for months on it, in secret," Annika said, and Lina believed her. This made it worse. If not even Annika had heard about it, then it was a carefully planned and well-protected political attack against Lina that was kept as a closely guarded secret.

„Well, obviously Moulin is one of them. And the Vice-President seems to be on board too," Lina finally responded.

„Yes, Moulin was sponsoring it, and it's no secret that he is not very fond of you. But this goes beyond him. I heard there were outside forces involved that were pushing this."

„Who?"

„No idea. But I did hear that Moulin's wife recently bought a house in St. Tropez. And that self-righteous woman is not embarrassed to talk about it all day. I think we cannot complain about our commissioner salary, but even that is not enough to buy a house in St. Tropez, especially if it's your third. Moulin's wife is a schoolteacher, so I do not believe it was paid for by her Christmas bonus," Annika said.

„It is obvious that Moulin is dirty, but I need to find out more to do something about it."

„If I were you, I would dig around the assistants to the commissioners. They are a source of rumors like you wouldn't believe. I had an affair with one of them once and couldn't believe what he told me. I learned more about what's going on in the Parliament than during all my years there. Try it out yourself, it's fun!" Annika said with a smile on her face.

„Well, I don't have time for that now. But thanks, this was very helpful. And thanks for being a friend," Lina said.

„Any time. Women in politics need to stick together," Annika said while Lina thought, *or they stab each other in the back*. But she had no reason to suspect that this was the case here. Getting more intel from the assistants was a good tip, and Lina would try it. They finished their lunch with small talk, and after they were done, they headed back to the Parliament building.

After they said their goodbyes, Lina called her assistant, John.

„John, I need you to do something for me."

„You do know that as of one hour ago, I don't work for you anymore? Technically, I'm unemployed, thank you very much."

„I know, and I'm sorry that this affected you, too. But this is bigger than both of us. If not us, who else will expose this as the scandal that it is?"

„What do you need, Lina?"

„We need to find out who plotted this and why. Who is behind it all? Moulin is in there deep, but he didn't act alone. Can you listen around among the assistants of the other commissioners and find out more?"

„You have come to the right person. I know exactly who to ask. Give me an hour."

„Thank you very much, John. I'll buy you a drink."

„And I'll happily take it. See you later," John said and hung up.

Lina wasn't sure if she sensed a flirtatious tone in his last statement and wondered what it meant. Maybe she would indeed follow Annika's idea.

THE HAGUE
DAY 4
01:15 P.M.

Arnaud was standing in the run-down elevator of the ESOC. He had just arrived from Amsterdam airport and was on his way to give a status report to Gusta Jansen, his boss. On the fifth floor, the door opened, and Arnaud went to Gusta's office, a glass box in the corner of an otherwise open office space where inspectors of Europol were working. He went through the rows of colleagues sitting in front of their computer screens. Some looked up and gave a mumbled greeting, but he was mostly ignored. Arnaud was glad about the lack of interest, still sore from his wounds and eager to get on with the case. The clock was ticking, after all.

Gusta was on the phone when Arnaud entered her office and hung up when she saw him.

„My god, Arnaud, you look terrible. Did you join a fight club or what?"

„I fell down the stairs," Arnaud said.

„Right. Well, that's your business. But stopping this terrorist is mine. What the heck is going on? Do you realize we have less than 12 hours before the deadline runs out?"

„Nine hours and 45 minutes, to be exact," Arnaud said.

„Don't get all wise with me, like suddenly you care about detail. I have the energy and interior ministers of virtually every member state on my back, in addition to the Commissioner for Counter Terrorism and the Commission Vice-President. Did you hear that Lina Juska, the Commissioner for Energy, just resigned over this?"

„I was rather focusing on catching our terrorist than reading about politics."

„Good that you had some progress this morning in finding out about the Deep Fake, but it doesn't get us any closer, does it? Anything new yet?" Gusta asked.

„In fact, yes. We seem to have found the real terrorist. Her name is Mia."

„Mia, who?"

„We don't have a second name yet, but we do have a photo of her. I'm going to see Henrick right after to run it through Hawksight."

„How did you find her?"

„I was working with Samanta Di Vincenzo."

„My God Arnaud, do you know how many regulations you violated by working with a fugitive suspect? What if she didn't turn out to be innocent? You could have ended up in jail."

„But she is innocent."

„Yes, very inconvenient for me. But good to hear that you have a new lead. Now what are you waiting for? See Henrick!"

„Already on my way, boss."

Arnaud left Gusta's office and made his way back to the elevator. He went down to the third floor to forensics and found Henrick sitting at his workstation.

„Hi, Henrick, good to see you!"

„Hoi. Good to see you too, my friend. You look terrible. But you know me, no questions asked," Henrick said.

„Henrick, I have something for you. A photo of our terrorist, the real one this time. I'll forward you an email."

„Nice! I'll start up Hawksight right away."

Henrick opened Hawksight. Just as last time, Henrick loaded the image that they wanted the program to search for. But this time, it was not the recording from the video camera in Oberberg but the cropped photo of Mia at the hacker conference. Henrick started the search, and the progress bar was loading slowly.

„The search will take about fifteen minutes to complete. Let's get a coffee while we wait." They walked over to the coffee machine to get a cup of coffee made from instant powder. Normally, Arnaud would not drink it. He called it sweet motor oil that did not deserve to call itself coffee, but this time he was glad for some sugar to keep him awake.

„So tell me, how is your daughter, Arnaud?" Henrick asked.

„I wish I knew. I am so caught up in this case that I did not have time to even call her."

„Jobs change, but family doesn't. She won't be five forever, you know."

„Thanks for the advice, I know. I even brought her a present from Croatia. I will go see her tonight."

„You do that. Don't make the job the most important thing in your life. It should be your family," Henrick said.

Arnaud did not reply because there was no point in it. Of course, he knew that family was important. Of course, he wanted to make his daughter a priority. But all too often, work prevented him from doing just that. Or that was what he was telling himself. Deep down, he knew that he used work as an excuse to blame some external force for the fact that he was simply a bad father—just another divorced husband who did not take care of their kid after the divorce. But Arnaud was too embarrassed to admit that to himself.

Family was a weak point for Arnaud, and he preferred not to think of his private life. It was one of the reasons why he turned into a workaholic. Work distracted him from admitting the truth. Eventually, he would have to face it and bring his private life back into order, he thought. Once this case was done, he would get started with it.

They stood there in silence for a while, sipping their coffee, unsure what to say, until finally, Arnaud broke the silence. „Shouldn't the search be done by now?"

Glad to get out of the uncomfortable situation, Henrick said, „Yeah, it should. Let's check it out."

They headed back to Henrick's workstation to see if Hawksight turned up any search results for the picture they provided. When Henrick opened the program, it indicated that the search had indeed finished. Just like before, when they had searched for the photo of Sam, the picture they provided was listed on the left side of the window. The search results were displayed on the right. Only now, there were not multiple pictures but a single photo with a name: Mia Bernert. The photo looked like it was taken from a passport or a driver's license.

„Are you searching through the passport databases, too?" Arnaud asked.

„For some countries, yes. It depends if a state agreed to connect their passport database to Hawksight. In this case, we were lucky because this woman does not seem to have any social media profile we could search through. But here you have it. Her name is Mia Bernert, Austrian citizen, age 28, height 160 cm.“

„Do you see when this passport was used last?“

„Yes, two years ago, she used it at the airport of Vienna to exit the Schengen zone.“

„Okay, that means she has not traveled outside of Schengen since then, but it doesn't help us find her now. Can you access other local databases from here? Criminal records, living address, phone tracking, and so on?“

„No, those are different systems, and we need assistance from local authorities to get this info. You need to check with the Austrian colleagues.“

„Alright. How about we run a search if she was seen on any public cameras recently?“

„Sure, that we can do. I just have to run a separate live search.“ Henrick right-clicked on the photo they uploaded and chose the functionality live search. Again, they were looking at a loading bar, waiting for the search results. When it was done, they could just see a single pop-up window on the screen displaying, „No results.“

„This woman is a ghost,“ Henrick said. „We always get something. Nowadays, it is almost impossible to avoid public cameras and be seen.“

„Unless you do not want to be seen. If I wanted to, could I hide from the cameras?“

„Almost impossible. Many places are covered by multiple cameras from different angles. If you turned away from one camera, you would look into the next. We can always catch you."

„What if I am wearing a cap or cover my face with sunglasses and a scarf? The cameras would see me, but can the system still track me?" Arnaud said.

„Well, if you completely cover your face, the system will have no way of knowing it was you. Don't expect the system to do magic."

„So far I have the feeling that Europol does think it can do magic. Seems to me like it is like any other tool with flaws of its own, and it won't replace good old police work. Covering my face is exactly what I would do if I wanted to hide from the police. No wonder we do not find her. And given that she seems to be highly skilled technically, I am not surprised she made sure we wouldn't find anything on social media."

„So what do we do?"

„Keep the system running. If she does turn up on one of the cameras, I want to know right away. Meanwhile, I will talk to our Austrian colleagues and see if they have any more luck finding this woman."

Arnaud left Henrick's desk and went to his own on the fourth floor. His cubicle looked the way he had left it a few days ago: a landline phone and an old PC with a mouse and keyboard on top of an otherwise largely empty desk. The wall behind his computer screen featured a single photo of Zoé when she was three years old, riding a tricycle. Other than that, there was nothing in this cubicle that would suggest it belonged to Arnaud. He liked it that way; he did not want to have details of his private life at his workplace, for all the world to see.

He picked up the phone and dialed the number of Manfred Huber, the Austrian inspector, and waited for him to pick up.

„Hello, this is Arnaud of Europol. I need your help with the Oberberg case."

„You have some nerve calling me, and the first thing you ask is a favor. Do you know what kind of hoops I had to jump through to rectify your escape from the hospital? I had to lie and say that I asked you on official police business to avoid them filing a police report. What got into you to just run away with all the injuries?"

„Listen, I don't have time for that. We have a case to solve, urgently. Which, by the way, was the reason I did not want to spend useless hours in a hospital bed. But if it makes you feel any better, I apologize that I caused you any trouble."

„Thank you, that's all I needed to hear."

„I need your help finding our terrorist. We have a name now: Mia Bernert. Can you help me find everything there is to know about her? Where she lives, who she meets, and most importantly, where she is right now?"

„Sure, I see what I can do. By when do you need it?"

„Yesterday." And with that, Arnaud hung up the phone.

BONN
DAY 4
01:35 P.M.

Sam and Erik were just finishing their lunch, pizza again. After dismissing the cold one from the day before, they decided that pizza was never the wrong choice and ordered some more from a new hip place. Sam got a pizza called „Inspiring Istanbul" with honey-glazed pears, and Erik a „Saucy Sevilla" with vegan chorizo. They were both drinking a basil seeds drink with raspberry flavor and were sitting in the living room of Erik's place, wondering how to find Mia.

„Let's recap what we know," Sam said. „The terrorist attack in Oberberg was likely committed by someone going by the alias DestructionKitten, a radical climate activist who is active on BirdSong and who was recruited there by a user with the alias FightForTheFuture for what we believe to be the attacks on both Oberberg and Vrata. Based on the photos we found on the conference website, we are quite certain that DestructionKitten is a girl named Mia, who I met during my Erasmus semester abroad in Munich. She apparently holds a grudge against me for taking away her boyfriend, and she wants to get me into jail for it. In seven and a half hours, the deadline set in the manifesto runs out, which is when we can expect more attacks. Now the question is: How do we find and stop Mia in the next seven and a half hours?" Sam summarized.

"Good question indeed. Obviously, now that we found a photo, the police will search for her, but I would not trust that they will come up with anything. And unfortunately, we have no means of finding or tracking Mia, either. She is not stupid and will avoid leaving any trace that will allow the police to follow her: no credit cards, no travel outside Schengen countries, disposable phones, avoiding public cameras, and so on," Erik said.

"Did we look at the timing of all these BirdSong posts? If some were recent, we might be able to find out where she posted them from."

"I doubt it will help us. You can see the IP address for each post, but she likely routes her Internet traffic over some other servers to hide her location." IP addresses were the addresses attached to each machine on the Internet, like a phone number. Certain ranges of them were assigned to certain providers in different regions. While not providing an exact location like a street address, an IP address could tell in which city a machine was located based on where the provider to which this address was assigned to was located. Like one can use the area code of a landline phone number to know the approximate location of the owner.

Erik opened his laptop again and navigated to the BirdSong posts they had looked at before, most about climate action. They found five posts that were not older than a week.

"Okay, checking the IP of the first one." Erik copied the IP address in a search field on a website that provided locations for such addresses. "Just as I suspected, Hongkong. Let's try the next one." Again, the IP address he typed in was located in Hongkong. Erik tried another one—same result. „Each IP address of the posts of DestructionKitten points me to a server in Hongkong. If she is who we think she is, we can be certain that she was not actually in Hongkong at the time. She just masked her address to pretend she was there," Erik said.

„What about the last one? We haven't seen that one before. It was just posted one hour ago."

r/climateaction . Posted by u/DestructionKitten

„*The Commissioner for Energy just resigned over corruption charges and special interest influence in Brussels. The disruptions in Oberberg and Vrata of the toxic blood that powers European infrastructure have made a difference already. I told you that decisive action is needed to bring change, and I was right.*"

„Huh, that's curious. This IP is different, I can see that right away. Let me check the location." Just like before, Erik entered the IP address on the website to reveal its location. „You got to be kidding me," Erik said. „Munich."

„Wow. This cannot be a coincidence. She returned to Munich where we did our Erasmus semester. The place where it all began," Sam said.

„This address is not masked anymore. She must be getting sloppy. Or she is on the road with no proper setup to mask her IP."

„Good for us. We have to go to Munich, now," Sam said.

„Wait, what? We cannot go out and chase an international terrorist just like that. This is what the police is for. We need to tell them."

„No way. You have seen what they have achieved so far. Apart from arresting an innocent person, they did nothing. We have to do it on our own," Sam said.

„Sam, listen to me. You know that we team up online all the time, and I support you in the quests in our games no matter what. But nothing can drag me out of these four walls to go face a terrorist in real life. Computer games are one thing. This is reality. And you know what? I fear for your safety, too," Erik said.

„Fine, stay here, but I am going. If it makes you feel any better, I will take your phone and let you track it, so you always know where I am. Happy?"

„No, but I know I cannot stop you from going. This is crazy!" Erik said.

„You know who's crazy? Mia. She needs to be stopped. What is the best way to get to Munich?" Sam said.

„Munich is a five-hour drive but a one-hour flight from here. If you hurry to the airport now, you can be down there in two and a half hours. I'll drive you there."

„Ugh, I hate taking the plane. The lack of comfort is one thing. But the environmental footprint is another. It's terrible. It's crazy that I need to take a plane to travel inside Europe," Sam said.

„Well, if you do not want to lose any time now, there is no choice. Unfortunately, a European high-speed rail network is nothing but a dream at the moment."

Erik bought a plane ticket for Sam and gave her some money and his phone—she hadn't gotten her things back from Europol—while she packed her things. With the car of Erik's parents, they drove off to Cologne-Bonn airport in the north. Erik walked with Sam through the airport until she had to go to the boarding gate.

„I guess this is goodbye," Erik said.

„Don't be so melodramatic, I'll be back tomorrow. I will find Mia, talk to her, and convince her to give up. It will be fine, don't worry."

Erik was not convinced. The undertaking sounded extremely dangerous to him, but at the same time, he knew that once Sam decided on something, there was no way of stopping her. He just took a long look and then hugged her before she went off to the gate to face Mia Bernert, her friend turned foe.

MUNICH
DAY 4
03:30 P.M.

Sam landed at Munich International Airport after a short flight from Bonn. During her flight, she had been thinking about Mia and what might go on in her head. It wasn't unheard of that someone would hold a grudge for many years, but this was the first time she heard of someone going to such extreme lengths to get revenge. The events during Erasmus must have shaken her to the core and pushed her off the rails.

Some people got stuck at things like this and could not move on with their lives unless it gets resolved. And this was Mia's way of resolving it. To Sam, Erasmus was a part of her life that was long gone and that she didn't think of at all. So much had happened since then that, while being a source of fond memories, Erasmus was a distant part of her life that did not bear any relation to today's reality. Until now.

Sam was walking from the plane towards the main arrival hall, a curious mixture between indoors and outdoors. It looked like a large open square surrounded by shops. If there wasn't a roof high on top, one could easily believe it to be a central town square. It even featured an ice rink in the middle where children were skating.

When she entered the hall, she saw a large banner promoting the airport's commitment to sustainability and fighting climate change: „The first airport in Europe. Carbon neutrality within 10 years.“ Sam thought about all of those ambitious goals of energy diversification, carbon neutrality, and energy preservation. *Nice goals, but, in reality, just baby steps*, she thought. Things needed to change much faster in order to make an impact. All the climate NGO's and climate scientists were saying that for years, but the political reality looked different. The fact that she had to fly here instead of taking the train just proved that point. *This should not be necessary in the 21st century, we should have high-speed rail running on renewable energy sources, and not planes spraying kerosene over the face of the earth.* In a way, she felt sympathy for Mia. Her intentions were good, just her actions were wrong. She had gone down the wrong path.

Sam took one of the many taxis waiting in front of the airport and asked to be driven to the University. It was a half-hour drive since the airport was located in the north of Munich in the outskirts, and the University was as central as it gets in the city. Sam was looking out the window while they were driving, reveling in old memories. She had forgotten how beautiful this town was with its many green areas, like the large English Garden, which ran from north to south through the city and was as large as a forest, surrounding a river and its many arms, which were used for recreational purposes of the city's residents.

Sam remembered that she and her friends often went there for a swim, as did many other students in the city who filled the streets with bicycles on the way to the English Garden. Bavaria was known to be very conservative, and it certainly was, but that stood in stark contrast to its vibrant student community in Bavaria's capital. Munich had won prizes as the best student town, and Sam could just confirm this fact. Innovation and academia living in unity with conservative values. Going forward while protecting what was. Sam liked the sentiment.

The taxi arrived at the University's main building, and Sam got off there. She didn't really have much of a plan. Her reasoning was that if Mia was indeed in Munich, it was quite likely that she would stay close to the places that they frequented during Erasmus. Sam would just go there and try to find her. And once she succeeded, she would reason with Mia to at least not cause more damage than what she had caused already. Sam remembered Mia as passionate but reasonable. It could work.

There was no way of locating Mia exactly, so Sam would just walk around and try her luck. First, she checked out the main campus of the University. Sam entered the University through the main entrance, a plain building opening up to a large courtyard with many trees and pathways that led to the entrances of different departments and lecture halls. A feeling of homeliness overcame her, mixed with a bit of confusion that one sometimes feels when reality does not fully match one's memories, which were idealized in one's head over many years. Things looked familiar but not as she remembered. Some distances were larger than she remembered, and some things were much closer together than she thought.

Sam was walking through the courtyard but hardly saw anyone. First, it was winter, and second, it was February, which was a free month for students. So only people who were working for the University and who were brave enough to spend extended time in the cold outdoors would be seen. But most importantly, no Mia. Of course, that wasn't really a surprise. The campus was vast and seeing her here would have been an unimaginably unlikely coincidence, if she was even close to the University. But Sam had to try. She decided to make another round and then head out again.

Sam remembered a cafeteria that she and Mia liked to frequent: Cafè Glyptothek. It was located in a park next to the University, inside the sculpture museum Glyptothek, which housed the large collection of sculptures of king Ludwig I. He was a great patron of the arts but was mostly known for starting the famous Oktoberfest with his wedding in 1810. The cafeteria was located in the museum courtyard, but now the guests were sitting inside. Sam was sitting down at one of the small coffee tables to drink an espresso. There were not many guests today, and Sam could see that Mia was not here. But she would take a few minutes to enjoy her coffee and see if Mia would turn up by chance. She didn't.

Sam was thinking of where to go next. She had put a lot of hope into finding Mia here. It was probably the place they had spent most of their time at, besides the University building. The only other place she could think of was their student dorm. There was not really a reason for Mia to be there since only students could rent a room, but it was worth a shot. Sam paid for her coffee and made her way to the Studentenwohnheim Geschwister Scholl.

The dormitory was named after two famous siblings from Munich who fought against the Nazi regime. It had been founded in the 1950s to instill democratic values into the students. The dormitory was located close to the other end of the University, so Sam had to make her way around the main campus before arriving at the student dorm. It was hidden inside a large courtyard formed by a row of residential buildings. There was no doorkeeper, and Sam could just walk in. She decided to go and see her old room first. Sam knew she wouldn't be able to enter, but since she had no better idea of where to go, she might go there just as well. Staircase 1, second floor, door 12 used to be her home for five months. She took the stairs to walk up to the second floor.

An empty hallway opened up before her. No one to be seen. Probably most of the students went home for the holidays. If you had a dorm room, you were not from here. And there was no point in staying in the city when you could be home with your family or at a more exciting place over the holidays. Sam was walking down the empty, windowless hallway. Neon lights at the ceiling were illuminating everything, except one or two of them, which kept flickering. The flickering, together with the emptiness and silence of the hallway, created an eerie feeling reminiscent of a 19th-century sanatorium at night.

A shiver ran down her spine, but she kept going, her shadow moving with her on the floor. Once before her and then moving to the back of her as she moved from one neon light to the next. Door 9, door 10, door 11. Finally, she arrived at door 12, located on the right side. It looked as it had always had, with messages of love and hate carved into the wood of the door frame and a name tag next to the bell. Just that it was not her name anymore but someone else's.

Sam was considering if she should try to ring to get a chance of a look inside her old room. Would it be embarrassing asking a stranger to enter their space? It was not her room anymore, after all. Then again, would someone even be home? Probably not. But before Sam could make up her mind, she heard steps behind her, and just as she was about to turn, something hard and heavy hit the back of her head.

MUNICH
DAY 4
05:10 P.M.

Sam slowly opened her eyes. She felt dizzy, like she had just woken up from long, deep sleep. Her head hurt, the back of it felt swollen, and she could feel every pump of blood as it was going into her brain and back again. Every once in a while, there was an intense sting in her brain that lasted for a few seconds. Sam was about to raise her hand to check for injuries when she realized she couldn't move.

Her hands were tied behind her back, and her legs were fixed against the legs of the stool she was sitting on. Sam looked around. She was in what looked like a cheap hotel room, hardly lit, with heavy drapes covering the windows and blocking whatever little light would have come in from the outside. She noticed a suitcase on the floor, a small table, and a bed. And in front of her, the silhouette of a woman, watching her. There was no doubt who it was: Mia.

„Hello, Samanta. Did you sleep well?" Mia said.

„What have you done? Let me go!" Sam said through her dizziness. It took all her strength to focus.

„I must say, I am impressed you found me. I expected you to rot away in a jail cell somewhere, but I guess our police is not what it used to be. Then again, who, if not you, would figure out that I am in Munich, the location of the original sin, of the big betrayal."

„Mia, I know you are not a bad person, just misguided. Yes, humanity needs to change to tackle the climate crisis, but this is not the right way. There are many possibilities to influence policy: start a grassroots movement, demonstrate, vote, go into politics yourself. But terrorism will always trigger the opposite reaction of what you want!" Sam said.

„Oh, that's cute. They just call it terrorism when they don't agree with you. Otherwise, it would be a fight for freedom, rebellion, or resistance. If you don't agree with the actions of those in power, they label you a terrorist. Little, naive Samanta. Just like during Erasmus, wandering about in the world, never realizing what actually happens around you."

„Look, I'm sorry you were upset that I dated Ricardo. I didn't want to steal him from you. He told me you guys broke up!" Sam said.

„Are you fricking kidding me? You think this is about Ricardo? He was nothing but a distraction. I couldn't care less about this numbnut! This guy thought Lambda is a camel from the Andes."

„Then why are you so mad at me? Why do you pin all of this on me?"

„You still don't get it, do you? After so many years. But then again, it was probably hopeless from the start. I was fooling myself that there could ever be more. I was in love with you, Sam! I broke up with Ricardo because of you! And what do you do in return? You choose this idiot over me. You betrayed me! How could you?"

"I thought my life was over. It completely destroyed me. That's why I returned home early, because I couldn't bear the thought of seeing you every day, the love of my life! Or so I thought. You broke my heart, Sam." Mia was close to tears, her cheeks red and her voice breaking. „But I'm over you now. I outgrew you. And you are finally paying for what you did. This is the closure I was searching for, for so many years. Finally, I can move on."

Sam was staring at Mia in disbelief, shocked. Not in her wildest dreams did it occur to her that Mia could have wanted more. Mia was a friend, nothing more. Sam hadn't had a clue. „Mia, I... I don't know what to say. I am so, so sorry, I had no idea. If I would have known..."

„Well, now it is too late. You should have realized it years ago, but it won't save you now. Don't worry, I won't hurt you. I just cannot let you interfere in the final act of my effort to save all of our future. This will show everyone that no part of the gas infrastructure is safe. There is no way around it. We have to move away from fossil fuel towards renewable energy. When a gas storage facility is attacked at the end of the deadline, the politicians in Brussels will see that they have to act."

„Mia, please don't do it. These attacks will have no effect at all. If anything, they will embolden anyone who wants to build more gas infrastructure. Violence is never the answer."

„Sometimes, it is," Mia said. She took a final look at Sam, turned around, and left the room. Sam could hear how the keys were turning in the lock, trapping her inside the room, strapped to the chair.

Sam wondered what to do. She had to break free somehow and stop Mia, but she had no idea how to untie herself, let alone get out of the locked room. Sam tried to wiggle around in the chair, loosening the rope she was tied with. No luck. She tried twisting and turning her hands that were tied behind her back to somehow free up one of them. That always worked in the movies.

Nothing gave way, the rope was tight, and the knot did not loosen. Somehow, in movies, the bad guys always tied bad knots that the hero was able to open easily. But this did not work in the real world. Sam screamed, cried for help. To no avail. She was twisting around until the chair tipped over, and Sam fell on the floor. Now, she was lying there on her side, still strapped to the chair, and tried to wiggle herself free, but she was not getting any closer to escaping. She did not want to give up and tried everything she could to break free until her strength slowly vanished, and she ran out of energy. Exhausted, she fell asleep.

MUNICH
DAY 4
10:05 P.M.

Sam woke up with a wince and a feeling of panic. There was a loud *thump* coming from the door, which had woken her up. It sounded like hitting a hard pillow with a wooden stick. Another *thump*. And another. Finally, the door to the room gave way, and Arnaud stumbled into the room. His curly black hair was all messed up, hanging over his sweaty face. He was breathing heavily, staring straight at Sam. She could not remember when she was ever happier to see someone than she was now. Arnaud rushed to untie her from the chair she was bound to and lifted her up.

„Are you all right?" he asked.

„Yes, I am. A bit dizzy still, but otherwise okay. I must have fallen asleep while I was trying to break free."

„I am so glad you are okay. I feared the worst!"

„And I am so glad to see you! I don't know how I could ever have gotten free if you wouldn't have rescued me."

„All part of the job."

„How did you even find me? I didn't tell you where I was."

„Erik tried to reach you, and when you didn't answer, he checked the location of his phone. When he realized you are not moving, he got worried and called me to let me know where you are. I came as fast as I could, but it is quite a long way here from The Hague."

„The deadline! What time is it?"

„10:05 p.m."

„10:05! I slept for 5 hours! That means we only have 55 minutes to stop Mia from committing the final attack," Sam said.

„How do you know she will commit an attack?"

„Long story, I'll tell you later. She said that her final attack would be on a gas storage facility."

„Well, if she was in Munich, her target would be close as well. Can you search for gas storage facilities in this area?"

„I can try, let me see." Sam unlocked the phone and typed in a search for gas facilities close to Munich in the browser, which opened a page with an overview of facilities across Germany.

„There are three facilities in this area. But we don't have enough time to check all of them. Even if we split up, we might easily choose the wrong ones, and all was for nothing," Sam said.

„Then let's think about it a bit. Mia wouldn't choose a facility randomly. She wants an impact that makes for big headlines. The facility she chooses will be an important one. Can you sort them by size?"

„Sure, let's see." Sam was ordering the list by volume of gas storage.

„Well, look at that," she said. „Germany's largest gas storage facility happens to be in the south of Munich."

„That's the one," Arnaud said.

„It's a 30-minute drive. We need to leave right away," Sam said.

Arnaud led Sam out of the small three-star hotel and across the street where he had parked the rental car. He immediately stopped, baffled.

„You got to be kidding me!" Arnaud said.

„What is it?"

„I parked the car right here, and now it's gone!"

„You mean to say that you parked right next to this ‚No parking allowed' sign here and are surprised that it got towed?"

„Well, I didn't exactly have time to search for a proper spot. I hate parking enforcement officers. They always sabotage the work of the real police! Two times in two days, that must be a new record. Gusta will be furious when she finds out," Arnaud said.

„We don't have time for that. I will order us a ride." Sam used a ride-sharing app on the phone to order a car to take them to the gas storage facility. After just a few minutes of wait, a car arrived.

They had 30 minutes to pass before reaching their destination, and Sam wanted to make use of it. She was opening up a satellite image of the facility to get familiar with the surroundings. From above, it looked like any other industrial complex. It was located in the middle of a forest and had just a few buildings on the premises and some pipes. Nothing noteworthy. Sam was expecting big, round gas tanks, but there was nothing of that sort, no tanks whatsoever. There were just a few buildings, which looked like any other administration building. Sam mentioned this to Arnaud.

„Yes, I know, it's weird. The people at Oberberg told me about gas storage facilities. Artificial gas tanks are seldomly used anymore, and if they are, then only for temporary, short-term storage. Long-term gas storage is done in underground natural rock formations, most commonly in former gas fields used for storage once most natural gas has been extracted. It actually makes sense. If an underground cavern is leakproof enough to hold gas naturally, it will also hold any new gas you pump down there. Plus, you save on the cost of building an artificial storage facility," Arnaud said.

„Well, at least the area we have to search is small then. The facility also seems easily accessible. There is a wall but no other visible protection. Looks like they are not prepared for a break-in," Sam said.

„An easy target for an attack. No wonder Mia chose it. And the proximity to Munich and your Erasmus story is almost poetic. It must have looked like destiny to Mia. But we won't let her get away with it. We will stop her," Arnaud said.

„This ends tonight," Sam responded.

MUNICH
DAY 4
10:40 P.M.

They were driving on a small road through thick forest and fields covered by white snow, reflecting the light of the full moon. The facility appeared on their left side, and the car stopped in front of the main entrance. They got out and inspected the premises. Lights were illuminating the entrance and parts of the wall, but it was otherwise dark, no person in sight.

„Where is everyone?" Sam asked.

„See those cameras around here? Often these kinds of facilities are run without any personnel on-site. They are just monitored remotely. This way, they save on staff. Probably all three storage facilities in this area are monitored by the same guards in some control room somewhere. Once they see anything out of the ordinary, they drive by. The problem is that it is much easier to miss something if you have to look at three locations simultaneously. Plus, you lose the input from your other senses that help me in my everyday police work. Just another way how technocrats make us less safe, all in the name of efficiency."

„So that means that there is no one else here? No security guards we could ask for help?"

„Likely not. Let me alert the local police, just in case. But by the time they get here, it will be too late."

Sam looked at the watch on her phone: 10:45 p.m. Only fifteen minutes until the deadline ran out.

„Okay, let's use this tree on the right to climb over the wall. It's not too high. The worst that could happen is that the security guards see us and come here too," she said.

„You realize I am not the youngest anymore? And according to my brother, neither the fittest," Arnaud said, but Sam was already at the top of the wall, offering her hand.

„Less whining, more climbing. I'll help you up." With a lot of cursing and Sam's help, Arnaud made it up the wall. *If my brother could see my pathetic performance right now, he would hold a speech about the necessity of more sports*, Arnaud thought. They carefully jumped down on the other side, conscious of the thin ice layer covering the ground.

They were standing in front of a large building. Apart from some light from the entrance, the surroundings were only lit by the moonlight. Everything was quiet, except the crushing of the ice beneath their shoes whenever they took a step.

„Okay, you go left, and I go right," Sam said.

„No, we should not split up. That's the first thing they teach you in the police academy," Arnaud interjected.

„By now, we have only ten minutes left to stop her, less if we continue discussing this. There is no way we find her in time if we don't split up. We have to risk it. Besides, you will be fine with your gun!" Sam said, and before Arnaud could complain, she went along the right side of the wall, moving counter-clockwise around the facility. He cursed under his breath. She had run away even before Arnaud could explain that no Europol

252

officer carried a gun. He was as defense-less as Sam was. He sighed and went to the left, the north side of the premises, crossing the entrance towards other, smaller buildings on the other side.

There was an open area, a small square, that opened up after the entrance, space reserved for parking, except that there were no cars here. On the other side, where Sam was going, there seemed to be the main location for pumps and other machinery for pumping down and retrieving the gas. But Arnaud kept moving on his side as they agreed.

Carefully, he approached the first of the two small buildings, towards a window, and looked in. Complete darkness. He tried a few other windows but found nothing. He continued to the second building and did the same. No lights inside, and certainly no flashlights. He continued along the north side of the wall and went by a container that seemed to be sealed shut. Unlikely that Mia would be in there either. Arnaud was wondering if Sam had more luck. If he continued like that, time would run out, and they would be too late to stop Mia.

***

Sam had taken the right side of the facility, the southern wall, and moved between the wall and the large building. She had a hard time making out details, with only the moonlight illuminating the surroundings. For a moment, she considered using the built-in torch on the phone but decided it would do more harm than good and would alert Mia of their presence. So she continued in the dark. More than once, she was startled by a shadow that she saw in the corner of her eyes and that she thought might be Mia. But it wasn't. Sam continued along the building and soon realized that she was at the back of it and would have to find an entrance on the other side. She went around and peeked in one of the windows. Nothing but darkness, no one to be seen. But she continued to do the same with other windows until she finally reached a door ajar. Someone clearly had opened it and left it open. *She must be inside*, Sam thought, her pulse increasing rapidly.

Sam quietly went through the door, which led into a small room. She could make out some hangers on the wall with helmets and vests and some lockers. *This must be the locker room for the workers*, she thought. There was another door on the other side of the room, which she slowly opened. It led to a large space with heavy machinery standing here and there and pipes crisscrossing through the room. From here, she had a good overview and was looking for light from a flashlight that someone who broke in would use.

But she was facing darkness again. Sam slowly moved into the center of the room, going from one machine to next. After the third machine, she thought she saw something move to the right. It could have been just another shadow, but she turned, nonetheless. Hiding behind a machine, she saw someone fiddling about at a console at the wall. The figure was wearing dark clothes and a backpack and was moving deliberately and fast. *It's her.* But how could she work without the light? Then Sam saw something covering Mia's eyes. Night goggles! No wonder it was so hard to find her.

Sam looked at her watch: 10:58 p.m. Only two minutes left. She had to act now. It was too late to inform Arnaud. She looked around for something that could act as a weapon and found a heap of spare pipes close to the wall. They were about one meter long each, ideal to be used as a stick to hit someone over the head. Sam picked one of them up and moved slowly towards Mia, who was standing with her back to her, but Sam did not want to take any risks and stayed close to the machines. She walked along the side of them, switching from one to the next until she was only two meters away from Mia. Sam took a deep breath before moving closer to hit her over the head with the pipe. She lifted her weapon over her head, but, just as she was about to strike down, Mia turned around and caught the pipe. Clearly, Mia had some kind of combat training that prepared her for this. For a moment, they were fighting over control of the weapon, but Sam had to realize that Mia was stronger, and she had to give it up quickly. Sam turned around and ran, Mia racing behind her.

Sam quickly moved towards the heap of pipes and took another one to fight her opponent. What followed resembled more a sword fight than anything else, but it was over soon. Mia hit so hard that the pipe flew out of the grasp of Sam, who stumbled backward and turned around to run again. She managed to throw down the heap of pipes between Mia and herself, blocking her opponent for a moment and giving Sam a head start. But it didn't stop Mia for long, who was already chasing after her again. Sam could hardly see in the darkness and could just make out the silhouettes of the machines as she was running. Mia had a clear advantage with her night goggles and moved swiftly as she was chasing Sam.

This was when Sam saw her escape: a metal ladder leading up to a gangway running around the room. Sam rushed towards it and climbed up. When she reached the gangway, she pushed the ladder down, preventing Mia from going up. Mia was startled by this and did not know what to do. She looked like a hyena, waiting for her prey at the bottom of a tree that it had escaped to.

Finally, Mia spoke. „Well, well, well, looks like it is harder to get rid of you than I thought. Why can't you let me finish this one thing? After that, it'll all be over."

„I'm sorry, Mia, but I can't let you do this. Do you even know how you affect the lives of people with your attacks? My Nonna was freezing without any heating!"

„This is a small price to pay when saving our planet for generations to come. Besides, it looks like you trapped yourself up there and won't be able to do anything for a while. I will have all the time in the world to finish what I started."

She is right, Sam thought. Sam was so focused on preventing Mia from coming up that she forgot that she couldn't get down again. She looked along the path of the gangway, trying to find another way down, but there wasn't any. It was one path, running around the room in a circle, starting and ending with this one ladder that Sam had just thrown down.

In retrospect, she should have pulled it up instead of thrown it down, but hindsight was always 20/20. Now she needed to find another way. From above, she followed Mia as she moved back to the console she was working on before. Apparently, Mia was confident that Sam couldn't do anything from up there and was not bothered by her walking along the gangway above. When Mia arrived at the console, Sam was standing almost above her, but she couldn't do anything other than watch. This was when she noticed another shadow slowly moving through the room. *Arnaud!* He had finished his side of the premises and was searching for her, maybe led by the commotion of the fight with Mia.

He had not seen Sam but was focusing on Mia while trying to stay unnoticed. Sam had to get his attention somehow. She couldn't call him on the phone, that would just alert Mia to Arnaud's location, and she could also not make any suspicious noise. So she started to small talk with Mia.

"Do you remember where we always went for coffee during Erasmus? Glyptothek. I went there today; it hasn't changed a bit. Still the same courtyard in the statue museum. Remember what a great time we had?"

Mia ignored her, focusing on whatever she was doing. But it had worked, Arnaud had noticed Sam, and their eyes met, trying to communicate how to overpower Mia. Where he was standing now, he could not sneak up to her unnoticed, especially with her night goggles on. Sam made a hand gesture in the form of a gun, asking Arnaud to use his. But Arnaud just shook his head, no gun. That was unfortunate. So Sam had to distract Mia somehow. She continued to speak, and Arnaud nodded in agreement.

"Well, I didn't expect you to remember anyway. You weren't such a good friend, after all. I always thought you were quite self-absorbed, rather thinking about yourself than others." Sam noticed how Mia's head moved slightly. It disturbed her what Sam was saying, and she wanted to turn around to stop it but felt compelled to continue with her work. It had provoked Mia, but not enough to distract her.

Sam had to bring out the big guns. "Now that I think about it, I never really liked you, anyway. You were just a means for me to get to Ricardo." That was not true, but it was a white lie to stop Mia. She had to trigger an emotional response, and Sam knew this was the best chance she had to upset Mia. And it worked. Mia turned around, forcefully ripped off her night goggles, and stared Sam straight in the eyes.

„This is a lie! You are lying!" Mia yelled, her voice echoing from all parts of the large room. After the echoes died down, silence again. Just the sound of heavy breathing. „Deep in your heart, you know it's true, Mia," Sam said.

„It's not, it's not!" Mia yelled louder this time, her voice breaking.

Meanwhile, Sam observed Arnaud as he was moving in a small semi-circle around Mia while she was turned towards Sam. He had just two meters to go. He raised his arms, on tip-toes moving closer behind Mia. Suddenly, Mia pulled a weapon out of her pocket and pointed it towards Sam. „Stop talking before you regret it!" Mia shouted towards Sam. Just when Sam was about to duck and cover, shocked by the pulled-out weapon, Arnaud struck Mia with a powerful blow on her neck, which forced her to the ground, collapsing. Arnaud fixed her arms behind her back and pushed the weapon away from Mia.

It was over, they had caught Mia, the terrorist responsible for two attacks and almost a third. Exhausted, Arnaud sat down on the floor next to the unconscious Mia and breathed heavily. His eyes met Sam's, who sat on the gangway above. Both were glad they had stopped Mia and the final attack was averted. They had to smile. It was the first time both could relax in four days. They just sat there in silence, smiling, and reflecting on what had just happened. They couldn't really believe it was over.

Arnaud and Sam waited for the police to arrive, who came ten minutes later, put up the ladder for Sam to get down, and secured the crime scene. Finally, the inspector in charge came to Arnaud and Sam to thank them.

„Thank you for your fast action, even if it was unwise to go in there without backup. A colleague like you should know, Mr. Navarro. But it was the right decision to alert us. You might be interested to know that the gun was not loaded," the inspector said.

„It wasn't? So she wouldn't have hurt me after all," Sam said, facing Arnaud.

„Well, you never know. We did the right thing," he said. „Inspector, I am in charge of the Europol investigation. I would like to interrogate the suspect as soon as possible."

„Yes, of course. But not today. We will take her to a secure facility in Munich. You can talk to her tomorrow morning. I will give you the address, come there at nine. Need a ride to the city?"

Arnaud and Sam accepted gladly. During the drive, Sam thought about what had just happened.

„You know, I feel bad for lying to Mia. Yes, of course I had to do it, so you had a chance to bring her down, but the fact is that I always enjoyed her company. I was actually pretty sad when I never saw her again. I liked her."

„Don't get too sentimental about this. Let an old veteran tell you: Criminals remain criminals, no matter how bad you feel for them. It doesn't matter if you liked her when you two met years ago, she still committed these terror acts. And even worse, she tried to pin them on you!" Arnaud said.

„I know I should be mad at her but I'm not. I don't really understand it either. I guess my rational mind is saying one thing and my heart another."

„Well, I suggest sleeping it over. Let's find a hotel and meet for breakfast tomorrow morning before interrogating Mia." They were dropped off in the center of Munich and Sam booked two rooms using the phone. After this day, both of them were glad to get into a cozy bed as soon as possible and sleep, with the comfort of a case closed.

DAY FIVE

MUNICH
08:05 A.M.

Arnaud and Sam were sitting in the cafeteria Glyptothek and were having breakfast. They had managed to convince the owner to be allowed to sit outside, even though it was the middle of winter, and to enjoy the bright sun that was illuminating the courtyard. They were talking about this and that, about the necessity to do more sports (both agreed), how technology was improving everyone's lives (Arnaud disagreed), and how computer games made the youth violent (Sam disagreed ferociously).

Arnaud told her about his daughter and how he would finally be able to spend some time with her now that the case was over, and Sam shared how she loved living in Tallinn—except for the snow. They discovered they both had international backgrounds, and they thought that they were better people because of it. Both were glad to be thinking of something other than the terrorist attacks for a change and let loose a bit.

But eventually, the conversation turned to the case again. „It won't be easy for me to face Mia today, after all that happened," Sam said.

„You choose how much you want to see her. You are in charge. If you don't want to, you don't have to speak to her."

„But I do. Don't worry, I will handle it. I'm just glad it is over."

„It is. This will just be about wrapping it up. If we are lucky, we get a confession, but even without one, we will have enough evidence to lock her away. We will be able to tie her to the explosion at her flat, and both of us are witnesses to the last attack."

„And who knows, maybe she can tell us who FightForTheFuture is. I would have really liked to know before we close this chapter."

„Who?" Arnaud asked, confused.

„FightForTheFuture. The BirdSong user."

„Never heard of it."

„Oh, right, I guess through all the commotion, there was not enough time to tell you about it. This is a user who seemed to be the trigger for why Mia committed the attacks. Erik and I found it before we discovered that Mia was in Munich. She was in contact with that user."

„Are you telling me that there might be another person we should be searching for, a person that might be behind Mia's attacks?"

„If you say it like that, yeah, I guess this person could be the one organizing the whole thing."

„Oh, my god. Seems like our case is not closed after all. We will have to find this person too. Otherwise, all of this might continue, even if we have Mia locked up. You need to tell me everything you found."

After they finished breakfast and went through everything Sam knew, they took a taxi to the headquarters of the *Kriminalkommissariate* Munich, where the major crimes unit of the police was located. Situated on the city's west side, it was a large, gray, square-shaped building with little indication that it housed over a thousand police officers focused on investigating crimes all over Bavaria and numerous jail cells to apprehend suspects until they were transferred to more permanent facilities. Built at the beginning of the 20th century, the building came to fame when Nazi Germany used it to produce the uniforms of the party, and it became to be known as *Reichszeugmeisterei*. After the war, the United States used it as barracks before the Munich police got to occupy it.

They went through the inconspicuous main entrance and passed the security check where their bags were being searched. After they walked through a metal detector, they were greeted by the inspector who they had met the day before.

"Good to see you again. Follow me."

They were led through long, dark hallways on the ground floor. The signs on the doors indicated that offices and interrogation rooms were located here. They finally arrived at room 1.14A. A screen was mounted above the door outside the room, showing a live view from the inside. Mia was sitting on a table, hand-cuffed, waiting. She was still wearing the same clothes as the day before: black jeans and a leather jacket. And white-blonde, punky hair. They were watching her for a few seconds.

„She hasn't spoken a word since yesterday. Maybe you can get something out of her," the inspector said. „I will watch from the outside. If you need anything, just say the word."

He opened the door for them, and Arnaud and Sam went inside. Mia looked at them with a smile. „Look who we have here. Have you joined the police now, Sam?" she said. Arnaud and Sam sat down opposite her.

„You two do look cute together. Are you dating for long?" Mia said.

„Mia Bernert. Or should I say Martina Bauer?" Arnaud started the inquiry.

„Martina Bauer only existed for this security guard idiot at Oberberg. You can call me Mia."

„Mia Bernert, then. So you admit that you tricked the security guard in Oberberg to get access to the facility and sabotage the gas pump?"

„Sure, why not? I'm proud of it. Getting in there required some good old social engineering, but with this security guard, it was almost too easy."

„Such an effort just to get revenge! So crazy!" Sam said.

„Not everything is about you, Sam. Pinning it on you was just a small side-project. A hobby if you will."

„How did you do it? How did you make it look like Sam broke in, in a way that even fooled our forensics experts?"

„Creating deep fakes is not that difficult nowadays. You can buy ready-made apps on the dark web. The problem is that it takes time, so I tried to keep the video clip as short as possible. It still took a couple of hours to complete, though. I found it a nice touch, must have misled you quite a while."

„Tell us about your handler."

„My handler?"

„FightForTheFuture."

„Oh, this guy. He isn't ‚my handler'. We just had some conversations online."

„What did you talk about?"

„This and that. Mainly about climate activism, and how to get politicians to take action. We agree on a lot of things."

„How did you get to know FightForTheFuture?"

„I responded to one of his posts. We were getting in closer contact after."

„Who is this person? In real life."

„No idea. We only ever wrote online, and I never found out his real name. I don't even know if it is a ‚he'. I was just assuming that it was."

„Did ‚he' encourage you to commit these acts of terror?"

„Sure, it was his idea originally, but I am still proud of what I did. We all have our role to play in this fight, and I did my part. It worked."

„It worked? Do you forget that they just passed new legislation to build more pipelines, not less?" Sam said.

„That's just collateral damage. The Energy Commissioner stepped down. That's a first step. It shows that change is possible."

„Are there others like you that FightForTheFuture worked with?" Arnaud asked.

„I don't know."

„Are there other attacks planned?"

„I don't know."

Arnaud was getting impatient. He had to focus on not starting a fight with the suspect. He tried one last time.

„How do we find FightForTheFuture?"

„Look, I have no idea. And even if I did, why should I help you? He and I are fighting on the same side. I won't help you get anyone else in jail who fights for our environment."

„Because it will help you get your sentence reduced. But it is up to you. Anything else you can tell us?" Mia just looked at both of them and smiled. She didn't say anything. She didn't have to, to make her point that there was nothing else to be gained here.

„I think we are done," Arnaud said. They got up, and Arnaud waved toward the camera in the corner of the room. The door did not have any handle or lock on the inside and needed to be opened from the outside.

„Well, at least she talked," the inspector said after closing the door again.

„Yes, but nothing useful. We already knew all of that."

They thanked the inspector and were led outside the building again. Without any new lead, they decided to go back to the hotel. Just when they were about to step into the taxi, Arnaud's phone rang.

„Yes?"

„Hello, my name is Lina Juska. I used to be responsible for energy in the European Commission."

„I know who you are. How may I help you, Commissioner?"

„Gusta told me you are the person at Europol investigating the attacks on our energy infrastructure?"

„I am."

„Then I might have information that could help you solve the case."

„We just arrested the terrorist yesterday. The case is solved."

„Is it?"

Arnaud paused and took a few seconds to process this new turn of events. They haven't told anyone that they had a loose end. Not even Gusta knew about FightForTheFuture. Could this politician really have information that might help them find that person? Why, where did that come from? In any case, they couldn't afford not to follow any possible lead. Especially since they did not have any other.

„Okay, what do you have?" Arnaud finally said.

„This is too sensitive to discuss over the phone. We need to meet in person. Can you come to Brussels? We can meet in the afternoon."

„Okay, we'll be there by three o'clock."

BRUSSELS
DAY 5
02:40 P.M.

Arnaud and Sam had landed at Brussels airport. Their plane had been half empty; the afternoon flight was not the most popular one, not like Monday morning or Thursday evening when all the politicians and diplomats flew to and from their workplace in Brussels and their respective homes.

If you wanted to meet important people, you just took the 07:00 a.m. flight on Monday from any EU country towards Brussels, and you would be sure to find someone worthwhile to talk to. The afternoon flight they had taken now was rather reserved for occasional tourists and businesspeople on their way to meetings.

Arnaud and Sam navigated between the chocolate shops towards the exit of the airport. Arnaud had made a small detour and bought some chocolate for his daughter that he would bring her the next time they met: small, assorted nougat pralines with cocoa powder on top. She loved chocolate, and she would love those pralines too. When they came outside, Sam suggested taking a rental car, but Arnaud refused: „Never again, I'm done with rentals. They are just getting towed. Let's take a taxi."

They got into a taxi and gave the driver the address Lina Juska had provided. Lina had promised a cozy coffee place that she liked to frequent when she did not want to be disturbed by her colleagues. After a 30-minute ride, they arrived at their destination, a cafeteria in central Brussels. Located at a corner, it looked small and not the first place you would notice when you went down the street.

They went inside and looked for Lina Juska. The place had a modern layout, with wood paneling and high ceilings. In the back, a glass roof provided sunlight and a winter garden feeling, with plants hanging down the walls. Students were sitting at the tables, staring into their laptops, and sipping coffee. They found Lina in the back, under the glass roof. She was wearing a green costume, complemented by a red scarf that, together with her blonde hair, framed her friendly and open face. She was waving at them to come over.

„Hello, Mr. Navarro. Good to meet you." Lina stood up to greet them.

„Good to meet you too, Ms. Juska," Arnaud said and shook Lina's hand.

„And you are… ?" Lina asked, looking at Sam. Arnaud and Sam took a seat opposite Lina.

„This is Samanta Di Vincenzo. She is helping me with the investigation," Arnaud answered.

„Oh, how interesting. Our former suspect, who had been wrongfully accused. I am very sorry for that, Ms. Di Vincenzo. Even Europol sometimes makes mistakes," she said, glancing at Arnaud.

He ignored this stab at him and his colleagues. Especially since he agreed and did not believe in Sam being the perpetrator from the beginning. Europol did jump to conclusions too fast. Sam had the feeling that Lina was actually serious about the apology and was grateful her unfair treatment was being recognized. It didn't make it go away, but the apology of a—former—European Commissioner meant something. Sam might give this institution another chance.

„Thank you. You can call me Sam."

„And you may call me Lina."

Arnaud and Sam were looking at the menu; Arnaud settled for an espresso and Sam for an espresso macchiato, which they ordered from the waitress. Arnaud was curious about what information Lina might have and was anxious not to lose any more time.

„So, Lina, to what do we owe the pleasure of meeting you here in Brussels?"

„You know that I resigned from my post as Energy Commissioner yesterday? Yes? Well, my new mission is to reveal the conspiracy against me, to make it public. So I was researching a bit, poking around, and talking to my colleagues. But after I looked deeper, I uncovered something much bigger than I expected. And it connects to your case." Lina waited for a few seconds to let the gravity of what she was saying sink in.

„So are you saying that the attacks on the gas network are connected to a political conspiracy against you? Care to explain how?" Arnaud deducted, skeptical but also conscious of the potential implications of what she was suggesting. If this was true, the whole case would shine in a different light and would be much more consequential than he suspected so far. It would be the greatest political scandal in Brussels in years. But experience taught Arnaud that it was all too easy to connect things that weren't connected if they made for a good story. The more sensational something sounded, the easier it was for humans to believe it. Deep down, we are all looking to uncover a scandal, a conspiracy, or the next big news story. We feed on sensational news to distract us from our dull lives. Any time a case sounded too sensational, one had to be extra careful to look at the evidence before concluding too soon.

„Let me start from the beginning. I resigned because a proposal for new legislation funding new gas pipeline development was brought before Parliament behind my back. A proposal I would oppose otherwise. That by itself just shows that some colleagues of mine were working behind my back, either to push me out or to get policies passed that I would oppose."

"So far, so good and not unusual. It might be immoral and despicable but not unheard of in the political arena." Lina made a pause while the espresso and the espresso macchiato arrived. After Arnaud and Sam took their cups, Lina continued. „Okay, where were we? What made me suspicious was that the proposal had over 90 pages. I know how much work these things are. It was presented as a reaction to the attacks on the gas infrastructure, but there is just no way you could write a 90-page proposal in three days, let alone get it translated. So this means it was prepared prior."

„That doesn't sound suspicious to me. I guess there are drafts for all kinds of proposals already prepared, waiting for the right time to be taken out of the drawer," Arnaud said, still skeptical.

„Very true, I myself have, ehm, had, a few of those on my desk. So I asked around among the assistants of the other commissioners, especially the one of Jean-Baptiste Moulin, Commissioner for Counter Terrorism, the one who was driving all of this. And guess what?" Lina paused for dramatic effect and watched Arnaud and Sam as they sipped their espressos. When none of them said anything, she continued. „Prior to the terror attacks, no such draft existed, in no drawer, of anyone!" For some time, none of them said anything, pondering the implications of that.

„Uhm, who wrote it then?" Sam asked, confused.

„That's the big question." Lina smiled mischievously, satisfied that she had the answer to the question. But before revealing it, she would explain how she got there. „So I was poking around some more among the staff of Commissioner Moulin and found out that he received a draft proposal from a lobbying group. And when I compared the draft copy with the final version, it turned out that they are a 100% match." Lina took a sip from her own coffee, watching the reaction of the others. „It is not unusual to get such drafts from lobbying groups but taking them over without any changes is highly unusual. If that happened, it meant that someone had a vested interest in not changing anything. Moulin's wife lives quite a luxurious lifestyle, I'm sure an investigation into their finances would reveal that they received funds from lobbying groups. At least that's what the rumors tell me."

„This is worth an investigation for sure, but it is not my investigation. How does all of this connect to the gas attacks?"

„Don't you find it a bit suspicious that right after the attacks, a proposal is passed that diverts massive funding towards new gas infrastructure instead of green energy? A proposal that was written, from beginning to end, beforehand?"

„So what are you saying? That someone committed the attacks just to get the right pre-text for more funding? To create an emergency that would make it easy to pass a controversial piece of legislation and divert funding to the fossil fuel industry?"

„You said it, not me," Lina said. „If this were true, it would be unprecedented and a major crime."

„It would also mean that Mia was misled. That someone used her to push their agenda, which was the opposite of what she intended. It would mean that the goal of all the attacks was to expand fossil fuels in Europe, not to reduce them!" Sam said, her eyes drifting off as she pondered what Mia might say to all of this. Mia had fallen for an evil plot. What she thought were noble goals was just a ruse to make her commit terrorist acts. She was deceived. Not only Sam was a scapegoat, but Mia, too. It did not negate Mia's acts, but it made everything look in a different light. Mia needed to know, and Sam was committed to clearing this up. „So, again, who wrote the proposal?"

„It was sent by a representative of the Trans Carpathian Pipeline Consortium who are planning to build the pipeline that will benefit the most from this new piece of legislation. Essentially, the EU will fund a big portion of the construction cost of their pipeline through Romania into Poland across the Carpathian mountains to transport gas from Turkmenistan into Europe," Lina said.

„And who is this representative?" Sam asked.

„His name is Pal Farkas, a Hungarian lobbyist who is very active in pushing the agenda of his clients here in Brussels. He knows all the tricks and will do anything to get what he wants. He is overly friendly but also ruthless, someone to look out for."

„Could this be FightForTheFuture?" Sam asked, glancing at Arnaud.

„Could be. But we would need to prove it somehow," Arnaud said.

„Who is FightForTheFuture?" Lina asked.

„Someone that was communicating with Mia Bernert, who committed the terror acts," Arnaud said.

„Then, if Ms. Bernert would set up a meeting with Farkas wearing a wire, it might give us the evidence we need to prove that it was him who was behind all this," Lina suggested.

„Good idea. We would just need to convince Bernert to do it," Arnaud said.

„I will talk with Gusta Jansen, your boss. She can make sure the sentence for Ms. Bernert is reduced. Given that she helps us, of course," Lina said.

„Okay, let's talk to Bernert," Arnaud said.

PRIVATE CHAT
DAY 5
05:35 P.M.

DestructionKitten entered the room

FightForTheFuture entered the room

DestructionKitten: „We need to talk."

FightForTheFuture: „Sure, talk."

DestructionKitten: „Not virtually, in person."

FightForTheFuture: „Why?"

DestructionKitten: „I have something that might interest you. Something that might be very uncomfortable for you if the police ever catch me. A document that links you to your real identity, Pal."

FightForTheFuture left the room

...

FightForTheFuture entered the room

DestructionKitten: „You are back. I was afraid I scared you away. You were gone for almost five minutes."

FightForTheFuture: „You called me Pal. How do you know this name?"

DestructionKitten: „Did you really think you could hide something from a hacker? You should have worked with someone less computer savvy, Pal."

FightForTheFuture: „Okay, let's meet. But, in exchange, I get the document, the only copy of the document."

DestructionKitten: „Deal."

FightForTheFuture: „I'll send you a time and a location. Just to be clear: come alone or not at all."

DestructionKitten left the room

FightForTheFuture left the room

CHARLEROI
DAY 5
09:30 P.M.

The soft moss growing on the ground was wet from evening dew. With each step that Mia Bernert took, it would give way, so when she lifted her foot again to take the next step, the imprint of her boots would move up into their original position. Slowly, she was moving forward in the hallways of the old building. Pal Farkas insisted on meeting in an abandoned building in the town of Charleroi, south of Brussels. It used to be a coal power plant, the most important one in the country when it was built at the beginning of the 20th century. In operation for almost a hundred years, it had been abandoned when it was discovered that it was responsible for 10% of Belgium's CO_2 emissions. And it had not been in use ever since, left to nature to slowly claim it back.

Mia was using a flashlight as she moved through the old, dark hallways. Doors left and right, forced open by curious explorers or teenagers in search of a place to sit around a bonfire. The walls, the ceiling, the floor, everything was covered in moss, giving the place a unique look one would otherwise only know from adventure movies. Mia continued to move forward, illuminating every corner of the hallway with her flashlight as she moved along. Farkas told her to meet in the cooling tower of the plant, which would be a little further down the hallway, out in the open.

Having served in the foreign legion, with ample military training, she was not one to get nervous quickly, but this situation stressed her, anxiousness mixed with rage. When they told her that she had been tricked into committing the attacks on the gas infrastructure, she had been furious. All her life, she dedicated herself to a good cause, to protect the environment, but unwittingly she had done the opposite. She could not believe that FightForTheFuture was not who he said he was. She could not believe she got tricked by a gas lobbyist, of all people! So Mia had vowed to help bring him behind bars and make him pay for what he did to her. She knew this would not keep her out of prison, but it didn't matter as long as Farkas was there, too.

She also knew that every word she said was being recorded and listened to, that Sam and Arnaud were hearing everything picked up by the small microphone hidden between the folds of her black winter jacket. As soon as she stepped into the cooling tower, multiple drones would film them from high above; too high to hear them but close enough for the high-resolution cameras to pick up every move. They were placed there an hour before as Special Ops teams scouted the location and prepared everything for the trap.

***

„Shouldn't we see her by now?" Sam asked.

„Give her some time. You don't rush into these kinds of situations. She will be in the cooling tower soon," Arnaud said.

They were sitting in a van parked behind a small building a hundred meters away from the cooling tower, staring at video screens, which showed a live bird-eye view from the top of the cooling tower, looking down. Each of them was wearing large headphones, which allowed them to listen in on Mia. All they heard was heavy breathing and the squishy sound of walking on damp moss. They were surrounded by more members of the police, all from Belgium.

„Do you think she would bail on us and run?" Sam asked.

„She might try. But if she does, we will catch her. Our SWAT teams are standing by, and she has a GPS tracker hidden in the microphone," Arnaud said. Both continued looking at the screen, waiting for Mia to appear.

***

Meanwhile, Mia had walked further down the hallway, following a corner. After turning, she saw the opening leading into the cooling tower. It had begun to lightly snow, snowflakes dancing in the wind in the opening ahead. Slowly, she moved towards it. When she arrived, she realized the vastness of the tower: a large round open space with a giant hole in the middle, leading down to engine rooms where coal used to be burned to be converted into energy using turbines. The excess steam would escape through the hole and be pulled up through the tower into the open sky. The walls ran high, maybe 30 meters, and bent inwards as they got closer to the opening on top, which showed the night's sky.

The wind was howling through the space. The tower looked like a giant cone with the top cut off, and her standing in the middle. She thought she could make out two drones at the edge of the walls on top, but she wasn't sure. Mia looked around, but no one was to be seen. Farkas had been insistent on meeting at this time and at this place. He should be here unless he uncovered their plan and had set a trap for her himself. Maybe he was watching her from a corner, making sure she was alone. Mia walked around the hole in the middle of the tower, keeping a safe distance from it, so as to not risk slipping on the snowy ground and falling in. She was panning her flashlight left and right, covering the walls, in search of Farkas.

When she had made one round around the hole and couldn't find him, her flashlight fell upon the original entrance where she had come from, and that was when she saw a man standing there, motionless. Dressed in a gray hoodie and a dark jacket on top, he looked more like a bank robber than a lobbyist from Brussels.

„Hello DestructionKitten," Farkas said. Mia took a moment to move closer to him and get a better look. Seeing her ally turned enemy for the first time had an unreal feeling to it. She wanted to make sure she got a good look at who she was dealing with.

„Hello, FightForTheFuture. Or should I say Pal Farkas?" Mia said.

„Clever girl, you figured that one out. I thought I covered my tracks well, but I guess there is never a 100% certainty in our digital age." He was moving closer towards her. Mia realized how tall he was, easily surpassing her by 20 centimeters, and he seemed to be in shape too. She could look him in the eyes now, which were so dark brown that it was hard to make out where the pupils ended and the irises began. He looked at her with a cold, emotionless stare. No hesitation, no fear. Just determination.

„Prove to me that you are who you say you are. How do I know you are not from the police?" Farkas said.

„I think you are mistaken about how this works. I have something you want, and I do not need to prove anything to you. You will have to take my word for it that I am DestructionKitten." Mia observed Farkas as he was weighing potential risks to decide if he should continue this conversation or not. For a few seconds, they stood silently, facing each other.

Finally, Farkas spoke. „Alright, what is this document you were talking about?"

„Farkas, you betrayed me. You lied to me. You used me to further your own interests. I could land in jail while you walk free. Before I give you anything, I want to know why. Why did you do it?" Mia tried to make him talk, aware of the recording device under her jacket. There was no document. It was a story they had made up to lure him into this trap. The more she could make him talk without admitting she lied, the better.

„Why? Business is why. It is my job to get things done for my clients, and my job gets harder by the day. Renewable energy gets more and more funds while oil and gas get de-funded. Politicians support what gets them elected, and oil and gas is not exactly considered to be popular at the moment."

***

Merely a hundred meters away, Arnaud and Sam were listening in while watching the two from above. „Something is wrong," Sam said.

„What do you mean? He is giving us all the evidence we need. This is perfect," Arnaud replied.

„Exactly, it is too easy. Why would he so willingly talk about his motivation and plan? Wouldn't you have expected him to negotiate with her first, giving her as little as possible to get to the supposed document?"

„Some people are just not as cautious as others. It happens," Arnaud said.

„No, something is off. I'm going in."

„Wait, no!" Arnaud shouted after her as she opened the door to the van and jumped out. „Damn this woman," he said under his breath as he watched her move towards the cooling tower, disappearing into the dark of the night.

***

„So you came up with a plan that would shift popular opinion in your favor," Mia said. The falling snow was increasing, and she had to protect her eyes with her hand to continue to watch Farkas as he spoke.

„Politicians are cheap. You can buy them with a fraction of the profit of new legislation. It's a win-win situation, and Moulin was the perfect candidate: his wife is on a constant spending spree, racking up debt that needs to be paid. And I am happy to help. But no matter how much you pay, politicians can only push something through if there is wider support for it. Even if I could pay off all of the Commission, it would never get through all the different institutions if there wasn't public support for changing the course of our policy to fund gas pipelines.

"And what the public needs is a simple message, something that makes it obvious what needs to be done next, something that makes the headlines." Farkas became increasingly louder, pride and passion in his voice. Clearly, he had thought long and hard about all of this and was proud it came to fruition.

„And this is where I come in."

„It's not personal. You were just the first fish to bite. So eager to act on behalf of some ice bears 10,000 kilometers away. And I have to admit, it was much easier than expected to make you attack Oberberg. You can blame me all you want, but deep down, you know that you were ready to do it anyway. I was just your excuse to do it. All you needed was a gentle push in the right direction." Farkas made a subtle movement with his arm, imitating a push, to amplify what he was saying.

„Not everyone is a soulless goon, Farkas!"

„You should have cared more about yourself and stayed away from all of this. Now it is done. New legislation has been passed to divert funds to our new pipeline, and everything turned out just as expected. Moulin got some pocket money, my clients are happy, and I will be rich. All thanks to you." Farkas let a smirk form on his face before getting serious again.

„I should have known better than to trust a random person online. I guess we all believe what we want to believe," Mia said.

„Enough chit-chat. Let's get down to business. Give me this document."

„There is no document, Farkas. I made it up to have a reason to meet."

Farkas opened his mouth to speak, then stopped, mouth half open. He seemed confused, shocked, and was weighing the implications of this new development. He had not expected to be lured here under false pretenses. Ten long seconds passed. Finally, Farkas spoke, „I should be furious that you lied to me, that you tricked me into coming here. But in a way, this is even better than expected. Now that I know that there is no document, I don't have to worry about any copies somewhere once I get rid of you."

„Get rid of me?"

„Did you really expect to get out of here alive? After I told you all that? I cannot risk letting anyone know about a connection between the legislation and the terror attacks." Farkas pulled out a gun from his pocket and pointed it at Mia, who stumbled two steps backwards at the sight of it. She was ready for a lot of things, but the gun came as a surprise. Farkas held the gun steady, with experience. He was not holding one for the first time.

„You know, I researched you a bit as well, Mia. I know about your combat training, about your skills. I wouldn't stand a chance in a direct fight against you, so I brought a gun. No shenanigans here. Move closer than two meters to me, and you are dead right away." Farkas started to move around her, at a safe distance, gun pointed straight at her. He clicked the safety of his gun to *off*. His eyes looked even colder now if that was possible. He didn't blink.

„Did you know that last year a teenager fell down this hole? They only found his dead body in the morning. No wonder he did not survive. It is a 15-meter fall before you land on old machinery. It is very easy to miss the hole and slip, with no guardrails or other safety. This wasn't built as a theme park.

You shouldn't walk around here at night, Mia," Farkas said, smiling.

Mia was walking backwards, away from him, but he followed. She knew her only chance was to jump at him in a moment of carelessness on his part, but he did not take his sight off her. They were standing close to the hole in the middle of the opening now. It was to the left of Mia and the right of Farkas. One wrong step and Mia would fall.

„And tonight, we will witness another tragic accident. An Austrian woman fell down the whole while wandering around the old plant alone. Was it an accident? Or a drug deal gone wrong? Who knows?" Farkas asked. He was motioning with his gun that Mia should step closer to the hole when they suddenly heard a noise coming from the hallway that led into the cooling tower.

Farkas turned around, and Mia seized the opportunity, jumping at him. At the last moment, Farkas saw her and fired his gun, which pierced Mia's right shoulder. She felt a sharp pain run through it and then numbness. She knew that the damage would be worse than it felt. Her arm would swell up, making it unusable to her. With her left arm and using whatever movement was left in her right, she tried to wrestle with Farkas.

Mia managed to push the gun out of his grasp, which fell towards the ground. They were both next to the hole, wrestling dangerously close to it. Under normal circumstances, Mia would have an easy time overpowering him, but with her right side virtually useless now, the large man could use all his weight to push her down. Farkas managed to pin her to the ground, his knee pushing on her right shoulder, which caused unbearable pain to rush through her body. It felt like someone pushed a blazing-hot piece of iron into her flesh. Her head was now close to the brink of the hole, she could feel the cold air rush through as it moved from below up through the opening.

„I'm sorry it has to end this way. It's not personal, this is just business," Farkas said, when Mia saw a shadow quickly approaching from the side, running towards them until it pushed Farkas so hard he lost his grip on Mia, slipped on the wet, snowy ground, and fell into the hole.

His surprised scream changed tone as he fell down the 15 meters, eventually vanishing into the dark. Then silence. Only the howl of the air pushing through the hole could be heard, as snowflakes were slowly dancing in the light wind. Surprised, Mia looked at Sam, who was standing above her, both still shocked at what had just happened. Both were panting, slowly realizing that it was over. They looked at each other and didn't say a word. They didn't have to. Finally, they smiled.

***

Soon after, the SWAT team moved in, together with Arnaud. They had started moving towards the tower as soon as they heard Farkas talk about killing Mia, but moving through the premises from the van to the tower took them valuable seconds. Seconds, which would have cost Mia her life, hadn't Sam already started running toward the tower earlier.

„Are you alright? Did he hurt you?" Arnaud asked Sam.

„I'm fine. Everything is fine. Farkas is dead," Sam said, pointing towards the hole.

„Where is Mia?" Instead of answering, Sam just shrugged.

„Sam? Where. Is. Mia?" Arnaud repeated, his voice becoming louder, insistent.

„I don't know. She went into the hallway. I thought you could track her anyway?" Sam said.

„Check her location. Right now!" He said to the policeman standing next to him. The policeman took out a tablet and opened the GPS tracking application.

„According to this, she should be right over there," the policeman said, pointing towards the entrance. Arnaud went over and searched the ground until he found the microphone with the built-in GPS tracker lying there.

„How did she know we would track her?" he asked.

„That's not too hard to guess. She is a hacker, after all," Sam said.

„Damn it!" Arnaud screamed. Gusta would not like this. But he quickly calmed down, settling on this new turn of events. *Forget about Gusta*, Arnaud thought. He would focus on the positive. They had the recording of Farkas' admission. He was dead, and Mia was gone. Arnaud and Sam had solved the case. Together.

EPILOGUE

Brussels. In a surprising turn of events, both the European Commissioner for Counter Terrorism and the Vice-President of the European Commission were arrested today. This comes after an investigation by Europol uncovered the biggest corruption scandal hitting the European Union in years. In connection with this, eight aides to the Commissioner were arrested and are awaiting trial as well. After conducting extensive house searches, Europol found 950,000 Euros in cash at the Vice-President of the European Commission, who tried to move it out of the country. Pending further investigation, it is suspected that these funds were paid to the Vice-President in connection to alleged corruption. The presumption of innocence applies.

Legislation, which was meant to shift funds from renewable energy sources to new gas pipelines in Europe, was reversed by the European Parliament after it was revealed that the terror attacks on gas infrastructure were staged to push said legislation forward. In the wake of this, the Trans Carpathian Pipeline Consortium filed for bankruptcy, bringing plans of building a new pipeline in Europe to an abrupt halt. Lina Juska, former Commissioner for Energy, and head of a newly founded investigative NGO, stated: „In the end, truth prevailed. The public needs to see that our justice system works, that corruption will not be tolerated. This is the only way we can hope to regain the trust of European citizens in our institutions. We will make sure that slowly but surely, we will bring any misconduct to light and put our politics back on the path of the noble principles the European Union was founded upon."

***

Arnaud sat on a bench in a park in central The Hague and was waiting. It was the same bench he had spent so much time sitting and watching Zoé play in the playground when she was younger. In his lap, he had a bag of small gifts he had prepared: Candy from Austria, the toy turtle from Croatia, chocolate from Belgium. He was looking at his watch regularly—Arnaud couldn't wait to see his daughter again. The events of the past days had made him realize how precious life, how important family was. He hadn't spent enough time with Zoé recently, and he regretted every second he missed watching her grow up. This would change now. He arranged to spend the whole weekend with her. There wouldn't be work disturbing him. They would go play in the park, go to amusement parks and the aquarium, and do whatever she wanted.

Finally, he saw her from afar at the end of the park, walking with her mother hand in hand. When Zoé saw him, she started running, screaming happily. Arnaud was overcome with joy and stood up, waiting for her with open arms until she finally reached him, jumped up, and they hugged for what felt like an eternity.

***

„Prego." The waiter placed two Aperol spritz on the table. It was sunny on the terrace, overlooking a grandiose panorama of the seaside on an island in southern Italy. Pine trees lined the coast, making the resin smell so typical of the Mediterranean coast. Seagulls were flying through the air, squealing once in a while to interrupt the constant, calm background noise of waves breaking at the beach. Spring was about to start, and the temperatures finally allowed to comfortably sit outside and enjoy breakfast. Sam took her Aperol and proposed a toast:

„To our first official date," she said.

„And to many more to come," Mia answered as their glasses clinked, and they smiled happily.

NOTES FROM THE AUTHOR

This novel is a work of fiction. None of the characters or events represent anyone or anything in real life. However, everything described could happen just the same way and is based on the experience of more than 15 years in the security industry. Any technology mentioned in this novel exists and works exactly as described. Nothing is exaggerated, everything could happen. All locations mentioned are real, even if in some cases the names are changed for security reasons. The description of the security operation center in Oberberg as well as the location in Vrata is based on numerous visits to similar locations over many years and represents the reality security operators face every day. The reliance on too much technology that at the same time is not utilized as intended creates real problems for operators every day, who are tasked to protect property and people. Too often, the security industry has too great of a focus on the next technological advancement without looking at the reality on the ground.

While today no Europe-wide facial recognition system exists, it is far from unrealistic, and plans exist to build it. Just like with any technology that has potentially adverse uses, we as a society need to decide how we want it to be used. Whether we like it or not, facial recognition exists and will continue to exist. But it is up to us to regulate how it can be used. Do we want to use it to go faster through passport control at the airport? And to unlock our phones? Or do we want to use it to allow tracking of any citizen throughout Europe? These are questions we and our representatives need to ask themselves. Any technology brings benefits and risks. And just like with any other technology, we have to make sure we know the limits of facial recognition and know where we can rely on it and where we cannot.

ABOUT THE AUTHOR

Florian Matusek co-founded a company specialized in automatically detecting threats and providing insights using AI and security cameras. As a global first, it provided technology that protected people's privacy in video surveillance while maintaining security. Today, this technology is being utilized all around the world to keep people safe while minding their privacy.

Florian Matusek holds an MSc in Computer Vision, a PhD in information processing science, is the inventor of numerous patents in the security industry and regularly appears as contributor in mainstream publications. He serves as an executive at a global security software manufacturer.

In his first novel he combines his deep knowledge of the security industry and its vulnerability with a visionary outlook of the world to come.

ACKNOWLEDGEMENTS

This booked wouldn't have been possible without the help of a number of people.

First and foremost, my parents Fleur and Paul, being authors all their lives, have not only been the main source of inspiration to write but were a tremendous help throughout the writing process. From helping with the story to getting closer to publishing. Their help cannot be overstated.

Further, Lucija Dupliak did an outstanding job in copyediting the book and helped write my cover letters, synopsis, and book blurb.

Praise goes out to Samantha Vanderhyden who created an amazing cover in her free time after sitting through numerous feedback sessions with me.

Finally, thanks go out to Jean-Michel Désiré who, being a successful author himself, showed me the ropes of navigating the jungle that is novel publishing.

To all the above: Thank you!

I couldn't have done it without you.

Manufactured by Amazon.ca
Bolton, ON